D1237913

LAURELS ARE POISON

Mrs Beatrice Lestrange Bradley, psychologist and detective, has become the warden of a house in a college so that she can investigate the disappearance of a previous warden. As soon as the term starts, strange things begin to happen: a bath is left to overflow, girls' clothes are torn to shreds, snakes appear, and a girl's hair is cut off as she sleeps.

Can Mrs Bradley solve the mysteries of the college?

LAURELS ARE POISON

Gladys Mitchell

First published 1942
by
Michael Joseph

This edition 2001 by Chivers Press
published by arrangement with
the author's estate

ISBN 0 7540 8584 8

British Library Cataloguing in Publication Data available

Printed and bound in Great Britain by
Redwood Books, Trowbridge, Wiltshire

CONTENTS

CHAPTER 1

OPEN, SESAME

DEBORAH, who had that true sense of humour – if connoisseurs of it are to be believed – the ability to laugh at herself, felt that she must look rather like Will Hay in *The Ghost of St Michael's*. Up the hill and over the moor she was toiling, suitcase in hand, and although she had been informed at the station that the distance to College was approximately two miles, she already felt as though she had walked at least ten.

The suitcase, which had seemed light enough at starting, now weighed, she thought, not less than three-quarters of a hundredweight, and she was further handicapped against rough country walking by her handbag and a large bunch of chrysanthemums which her landlady had thrust upon her at parting and which she had not liked to leave in the train. In addition to these other discomforts she was wearing a tiresome hat.

Fortunately the College buildings, once she was clear of the town, formed the dominating feature of an almost treeless landscape, and made at once a landmark there was no escaping and a goal towards which, without fear of error, her steps could be directed.

The moorland road was narrow and stony, and it bore out the description given by people apt at simile that it was ribbon-like. Deborah walked along in the middle of it, and was so much occupied by her physical discomforts and mental fears that she did not hear the car until a respectful sounding of the horn caused her to move aside and glance round.

The car stopped purposefully, Deborah politely, although she knew that it would be of little use for anyone to demand of her any knowledge of the country-side. The chauffeur got out and saluted. He was a stocky, grave-faced, irresistibly respectable man, and he spoke quietly, with firmness.

'Madam would be honoured if you would accept a lift, miss, if perhaps you were bound for the College.'

'A lift? To the College? Oh, thank you so much. It's awfully kind. I'd be very glad indeed,' she responded truthfully and with alacrity.

Still grave, the chauffeur relieved her of her suitcase, and led her to the car. He opened the door at the back and observed :

'The young lady, madam, *is* bound for the College.' He then assisted her in, closed the door, deposited her suitcase in front, took his seat and drove on.

'So we meet slightly before Philippi,' said a rich, remarkable voice, completing the statement with an unnerving cackle of laughter.

'Oh? Are you going to the College, too? It was awfully silly of me, but I missed the bus,' said Deborah. Could this be the Principal, she asked herself, terrified at the idea of making her first entry in such dreadful and distinguished company.

'I am *going* to the College,' replied the singular old lady, who, at Deborah's second glance, proved to be black-eyed, small and incredibly costumed in sage-green, purple and yellow, 'but whether I shall stay there is another matter entirely. And to which branch of knowledge do you propose that *your* particular students shall be taught to cling?' she concluded, grinning at Deborah's startled and guilty expression.

'I'm supposed to do a bit of lecturing in English, I believe,' answered the girl. 'But I'm really going to help run one of the College Halls.'

'My talents also appear to show a tendency towards the domestic,' said the little old woman, with a ferocious leer which gave the impression of assessing these talents at their true worth and then of discarding them. 'My name is Bradley.'

'Mine is Cloud – Deborah Cloud.'

So astonishingly different was the speed of the car compared with the progress that she had been able to make on foot that she had time to say no more, for she perceived that they were on the point of arrival at the College. This first intimation that they had reached journey's end took the form of wide-open double gates giving on to a gravel drive. The legend, in large letters, *Cartaret Training College*, on a white board, served the double purpose of introduction and reassurance.

'I think we're here,' she observed unnecessarily. Another disquieting cackle was the only reply.

The chauffeur drove in carefully, and drew up in front of a large, modern building flanked, fronted and generally compassed about by lawns, flower-beds, shrubs and green-turfed banks.

'Delightful,' said the owner of the car. The chauffeur came round and opened the door.

'The main College building, madam.'

He handed his employer out, and Deborah followed.

'George will see to your baggage and find out where to put it,' said the old lady.

'Oh, thank you very much, but perhaps I'd better take it,' said Deborah nervously. 'And thank you very much for the lift, Miss Bradley. It was awfully kind.'

'Mrs,' said the philanthropist; adding, with another hoot of laughter: 'strange to say.'

'Mrs Bradley?' thought Deborah, racking her brain and, at the same time, walking up the first flight of steps she came to in anguished haste to be rid of her uncomfortable benefactor. 'Where have I . . . ? Goodness gracious me!'

For enlightenment came as she passed in through the open doorway of a dim, wide corridor. She stood still, upon the realization that she had been accepting a lift in the car of one of the most famous of modern women. She breathed deeply, thought – for she was only twenty-six, in spite of a formidable degree and three years' teaching experience – 'Something to write home about at last!' – and then glanced uncertainly at the various doors which flanked and confronted her, whichever way she turned.

Making up her mind, she selected the first door on her left, set down her suitcase, and knocked.

Within there was the clatter of tea-cups and the impatient clacking of a typewriter. Feeling – partly as a result of her encounter with Mrs Bradley – rather like a particularly bewildered Alice, she knocked again, this time a good deal more peremptorily.

'Come in,' said a voice, and the clacking of the typewriter ceased as though someone had switched off the wireless. Committing her soul to the angel of the diffident and nervous, she picked up the suitcase, turned the handle of the door, and went in.

'Deborah Cloud,' she said. There were four other people in the room. The one behind the typewriter, a dark-haired, horn-rimmed woman of about thirty-five, smiled slightly and flicked over the lists that lay beside her on the desk.

'Miss Cloud? I don't remember ... Oh!' She looked up. 'Miss Cloud! Are you the new Sub-Warden at Athelstan? Miss du Mugne ...' so it was pronounced 'dew Moon' Deborah gratefully noted. She had been dreading the first time she would have to use the Principal's name. One fence crossed, at any rate ... 'will be glad to know you've arrived. Do have some tea, won't you? My name is Rosewell. I'm the College secretary. This is Miss Crossley, the bursar, and this is Mrs Stone, the librarian. Oh, and this is Miss Topas, who came last term to do history.'

Thankfully Deborah abandoned her suitcase, flowers and hat, placed her handbag on the floor beside her chair, and accepted tea and her first introduction to the College.

The librarian, who wore a grey tweed costume and a shirt blouse, was one of those lanky, overgrown, easy-going, 'helping-hand' sort of women who are found chiefly in vicarages, Girl Guide camps, mixed schools, some country houses and, as in this case, training colleges.

The bursar was also tall; she was a little older than the secretary, Deborah decided; possibly as old as forty, and might have made a nun; never a Mother Superior, but possibly a Mistress of Discipline. Discipline, in fact, was her strong suit, Deborah concluded, listening to the confident masculine tones and noting the short upper lip and obstinate full chin.

The lecturer in history, Miss Topas, was a fair-haired, round-faced, grey-eyed person rather older than Deborah. (It turned out, later, that she was just thirty.) She had the youthful, triumphant, slightly devilish and ineffably raffish appearance of the extraordinarily gifted. Deborah took to her at sight, and greeted her nervously.

'Hullo.' said Miss Topas. 'Welcome to the morgue.' Following her recent encounter with Mrs Bradley, this choice of metaphor gave Deborah a shock.

'I suppose,' she said, after she had drunk two cups of tea and had accepted a couple of biscuits, 'I ought to see Miss du Mugne?'

'Don't dream of it,' said Miss Topas, earnestly. 'It isn't necessary. Tessa can ring through and announce the glad news of your arrival, can't you, Tess? Miss du Mugne will only hate the sight of you if you go and disturb her now, and, after all, that can come later. You cut over to Athelstan and make yourself known to the Warden.'

'There's really no need to beard Miss du Mugne this afternoon unless you like,' said the secretary, with unexpected gentleness. 'I shall have to go in to her as soon as the College list is checked, and I'll let her know then that you're here. If she wants to see you, I'll ring Athelstan. You can't miss it, by the way. The Halls are all in a line here.'

'You'll soon be wishing you *could* miss it,' said Miss Topas cheerfully.

Upon these encouraging notes, Deborah, picking up her suitcase and the flowers, found herself again in the passage. Following the directions she had received, she turned left upon leaving the main College building, discovered an off-shoot of the drive, passed a pleasant grassy bank at the top of playing fields, crossed more lawns and an asphalt tennis court, and mounted a flight of wooden steps to another impressive sweep of gravel.

A maid answered the door.

'Beowulf Hall, miss?' she said.

'Oh, no! I'm supposed to go to Athelstan,' said Deborah blushing.

'Next Hall but one on the right, miss. You can't mistake it. Next door to the bakehouse.'

'Oh, thank you. I'm sorry. I . . .'

'No trouble at all, miss. It's always a bit strange at first.'

Deborah walked past two large rockeries and a building similar to Beowulf, and at last found herself on the threshold of Athelstan. Except for the fact that it was indeed flanked by the bakehouse, she could discern no difference in its outward appearance from that of the two Halls she had already passed. There were five Halls, the two she had not passed being on the further, or east, side of Beowulf. As she stood at the front door of Athelstan she looked back along the gravel walk to get a glimpse of them. There was, in any case, no time for more. A maid answered the door, and, on this occasion, there was no mistake.

'Miss Cloud, miss? Come in, miss, please. The Warden will see you in a minute, miss, if you'll kindly take a seat.'

Deborah was aware of highly polished linoleum on which it would be disastrously easy to slip, and a row of chairs, three of which were occupied. The whole atmosphere seemed to her to breathe the tension of a dentist's waiting-room. She took the end chair, and placed her suitcase in front of her and her flowers and handbag on top of it. Then she picked up the handbag and rested it on her knee.

'Hullo,' said her neighbour. 'You weren't on the bus, were you?'

'No,' replied Deborah, glancing round to make certain that she was the person addressed. 'No, it had gone, so I walked.'

'Heroine!' said her neighbour devoutly. 'I say, Kitty, she *walked*.'

'Golly!' said the second occupant of the row. 'Wanted exercise, I should think. I say, isn't this going to be an ice-house in the winter? Has it struck you?'

'Bound to be a lazar-house, anyway,' returned her friend. Before the conversation could develop, another student came from an adjacent doorway. She was carrying a typewritten list.

'Your turn next,' she said, 'if you're Miss Menzies. Are you?'

'Pray for me,' observed Deborah's neighbour, *sotto voce*, getting up. 'What's the Head's name again, Kitty?'

'Murchan,' hissed Kitty. 'And call her the Warden.'

'Right.'

She was gone. Deborah felt as though she had lost a friend. Kitty, however, moved up one place, and took the vacant chair.

'I say,' she observed confidentially, 'you're not, by any chance, Welsh, are you?'

Before Deborah could reply to this question, the student with the list appeared again and said: 'Are you Miss Davis?'

'No,' said Deborah, and was about to announce who and what she was when the student made a microscopic mark on the paper, and then smiled and looked inquiringly at Kitty.

'Who are *you*?' she asked.

'Trevelyan. I've come on the off-chance, really. Not sure whether there's room. They told me to turn up in case. Same like old Dog.'

'Trevelyan,' said the student, writing it at the bottom of the list. 'It isn't down, but I know one or two aren't coming, so I expect it will be all right. Anyway, I'll ask.'

'Thanks,' said Kitty, adding, as soon as they were alone again: 'I don't think.'

'Didn't you want to come here, then?' asked Deborah, who, for her own part, would as soon have confessed, on her first day at her own College, that she didn't want to go to heaven; not that she had any strong or positive inclination either towards College or heaven, but she now realized that she had always seen them as parts of the same dim future.

'I want to be a hairdresser,' said Kitty.

'But that's...I mean, there's a good bit of difference, isn't there?'

'Well, you don't have to pass Higher or even Matric., that I know of, for hairdressing,' responded Kitty. 'But then, I'm still all right, you see, because I haven't passed either.'

'Oh? Then...?'

'General Schools, my love, by the skin of my teeth, with the result that, goaded thereto by my family, I have written to every training college in the country, without result until now. These places are choosy. I shouldn't wonder if it isn't easier to get to Oxford or Cambridge than into one of these professional death-traps.'

Deborah sat and digested a new point of view, but not for long.

'Miss Boorman?' said the student, emerging once more, list in hand, and smiling kindly upon the hitherto silent member of the community.

'I say,' observed Kitty confidentially to the student, jerking her head in the direction of the door, a bourne from which, it seemed to her, no traveller returned. 'What have they done with the corpses?'

'The corpses?' said the student, who appeared to have a literal mind.

'Yes. The girl friends. They come, they go into that room, and that appears to be the writing on the wall, so far as they're concerned.'

The student smiled, as though at the naïve question of a small boy, and when Kitty had gone in, turned to Deborah.

'My name is Cloud,' said Deborah. 'I suppose you are the senior student. Do you mind telling the Warden?'

The senior student's pose of good-natured efficiency vanished with ludicrous effect.

'Oh, I say! Oh, I *am* sorry, Miss Cloud! I ought to have known! Mary *might* have said! Lulu's usually on the door, so I suppose Mary didn't ask your name.'

'Oh, no, it's all right,' said Deborah. 'I'll go in when they've done with Miss Boorman.'

'A bit under the weather, that specimen,' had said Kitty, who had a very kind heart. The senior student begged Deborah to accompany her. Deborah regarded the Warden's door with mixed feelings. The senior student tapped, listened, opened the door and announced:

'Miss Cloud, the Sub-Warden, Warden.'

Deborah entered, to be confronted, to her immense surprise and confusion, by Mrs Bradley, who was seated in a swivel chair behind a handsome, imposing desk, blandly established in office.

'So we *do* meet at Philippi,' she observed, getting up and giving Deborah her hand. 'Those poor children,' she continued, withdrawing her skinny claw from Deborah's grasp, and waving it towards the three students, who, looking scared and uncomfortable, were occupying chairs about the room, 'have come up today instead of tomorrow, to see whether the College has room for them. What they're to do with themselves for twenty-four hours I can't think, and neither can they. At least...'

With what seemed devilish omniscience she intercepted a wink which passed between Miss Trevelyan and Miss Menzies... 'At least, that was our first impression. Have you met them?'

'Yes,' said Deborah, smiling shyly at the students. 'Yes, we – we met under false pretences. I hope they won't hold it against me.'

'We thought Miss Cloud was a student, Warden,' observed

Miss Menzies. 'Instead of the Second Grave-Digger,' she added, *sotto voce.*

'Of course you did, child,' agreed Mrs Bradley, grinning at the subject of this remark. 'And now, what about tea?'

 Deborah, who had had nothing but the couple of biscuits dispensed under the hospitality of the College secretary, assented with pleasure to this suggestion. She could not have told how she knew it, but the realization came to her, with the inevitability of prophecy, that Mrs Bradley's idea of tea would be something substantial on north-country lines. She was right, for the little party sat down to toast, ham, boiled eggs, sardines, new bread, butter, honey and jam with zest, goodwill and (apart from a spasm of hiccups on the part of the unfortunate Miss Boorman for whom Deborah, herself a prey to nervousness, felt overwhelming sympathy) unalloyed pleasure.

The meal over, Mrs Bradley took Deborah off for what she called (leering hideously at Kitty, who had developed a fit of giggling) a review of the situation, and the three students went over to College, under the escort of the senior student, who had had tea with the rest of the party, and who continued to show herself, to Deborah's relief, to be a sensible homely girl, likely to prove helpful and non-critical. Deborah already felt that the more help and the less criticism her initial efforts evoked, the better everything would be.

At the entrance to College the senior student left the others pleading that she had a list of their study-bedrooms and bath-times to make out.

'But you don't know whether any of us will want a study-bedroom or a bath-time until we've seen the Principal,' objected Laura Menzies. 'I say, what price the Old Trout?' she added to her comrades.

CHAPTER 2

THE THREE MUSKETEERS

In Athelstan the Old Trout aforesaid closed the sitting-room door.

'And now,' she said, giving Deborah a cigarette, 'you and I, dear child, must come to an understanding. You expected to come here as assistant to Miss Murchan. You find me. Have you been notified of the change?'

'Oh, but I didn't know Miss Murchan,' protested Deborah. 'I mean, it's all the same to me, whoever it is. That's to say ...' she floundered, watched by the keen black eyes and appraised by the beaky little mouth, pursed now in kindly but, she sensed, unerring judgement upon her.

'Never mind. The point is that I've been told I must report upon your courage.'

'My courage? But ...' A desire came upon Deborah to retort that she had not any courage; that she had obtained her present post because she possessed good testimonials and a ladylike style of handwriting. She yielded to it. Mrs Bradley cackled. Then, taking from a capacious skirt pocket a notebook and a fountain-pen, she turned over a few pages, scribbled some hieroglyphics in tiny script, and, putting the impedimenta away, said briskly: 'I am here to make mountains out of molehills, child ... or, possibly, molehills out of mountains.'

Deborah searched the witch-like countenance. The black eyes looked into hers. It appeared that the opinion had not been facetiously rendered. She straightened up in her chair and said: 'What do you mean, Mrs Bradley?'

'Exactly what I say, child. I've come here, at Miss du Mugne's request, to trace Miss Murchan, who, it seems, disappeared last June at the College End of Term Dance, and has not been heard of since. The students were told that she had been taken ill – peritonitis – and the Principal herself officiated here in Athelstan Hall for the last two days of the term. That was ten weeks ago. Not the slightest trace of Miss Murchan has come to light. Interesting, is it not? And in the hands of the police, of course, although, so far, at the earnest request of the Principal, not in the newspapers.'

'I see,' said Deborah.

'Well, now, if I'm to have your help I must at least let you know as much about the background of the case as I know myself. That is only fair. It appears that before she came here just two years ago, Miss Murchan had been Biology mistress at the County Secondary School for Girls at a place called Cuddy Bay, and, unfortunately, just before she left, they had a very nasty accident. A child was killed in the school gymnasium.'

'How?'

'She seems to have been lowering the boom, and a rope parted, and the thing came down on her head. It happened after school hours and as it could not be proved that anybody had given the child permission to stay and practise, the verdict was accidental death, with the school authorities completely exonerated from blame.'

'Oh, what a good thing. Children can be disobedient little beasts; don't I know it!'

'Yes. The grandfather of the child, however, wanted further action taken. He persisted in saying that the child *had* had permission to stay; that she had stayed on other occasions, and that one of the mistresses stayed too. He argued that a great deal more was known about the accident than the evidence given in court served to show. He had to be taken to a mental hospital in the end, completely off his head, poor fellow.'

'Beastly sort of affair altogether. But if the evidence was correct – '

'There is some slight indication that it was not,' said Mrs Bradley. 'A month after the inquest the police received an anonymous letter suggesting that Miss Murchan was in a position to offer them definite information if they would assure the writer of police protection if she became involved.'

'She?'

'The handwriting experts thought that the letter had been written by a woman, and thereby hangs a point of peculiar interest. However, when the police interviewed Miss Murchan, not only did she deny all knowledge of the letter, but very soon afterwards she sent in her resignation to the County authority, and, according to Miss Paldred, the headmistress, whom I have interviewed, so far as the school was concerned she soon dropped out. She did not tell anyone where she was going, and it was not until her disappearance from the College was reported that the police here discovered that she had ever been on the staff of that particular school.'

'Oh, you think the grandfather of the child found out where she was, and ... ?'

'That is a possibility, of course.'

'But you don't think it's the truth?'

'Do you?'

'I don't know.'

'And you don't want to ask any questions?'

'Well, I suppose Miss Murchan was going to confess something to the police, and then funked it?'

'Do you really suppose that?'

'I don't know. I don't actually suppose anything, because I haven't enough to go on, so far, have I? You said Miss Murchan was the Biology mistress. That being so, I don't see what she had to do with the gymnasium. Surely she wasn't also the Physical Training mistress?'

'No, but she helped with the games. So did two other mistresses. It is a very large school. Incidentally, the Physical Training mistress resigned immediately after the inquest.'

'Was she on the building when the accident happened?'

'Nobody confessed to having been on the building later than five o'clock that evening, and, according to the medical evidence, the child could not have died before seven.'

'When was she found?'

'When the first physical training class went into the gymnasium on the following morning.'

'But – what about the caretaker? – the cleaners?'

'Thereby hangs a tale which I have tested and found to be correct. The floor of the gymnasium is sacred, being specially made, laid, sprung, and oiled, and so jealous of it was the headmistress that she would not allow people into the gymnasium unless they were wearing the regulation rubber-soled shoes. The Physical Training mistress, a young woman named Paynter-Tree, and, incidentally, Miss Murchan's half-sister, went further. She would not have the caretaker or the cleaners in at all, rubber-soled or not. She tended the gymnasium with her own fair hands, occasionally press-ganging the girls into service. So, you see, there was no reason, if the child *had* gone in there alone, why anybody *should* have found her until the morning.'

'Yes, I see. And I *do* see what you mean now about Miss Murchan. But nothing could be proved, could it? I mean, it would only be one person's word against another's.'

'Yes,' Mrs Bradley agreed. 'One other point comes to my mind. I imagine that the step-sisters may not have agreed very well. It is strongly probable, psychologically, that Miss Paynter-Tree wrote the anonymous letter to the police. It is certainly odd that both of them chose to resign like that, after the inquest. Then, the child lived with grandparents. Of parents I can find no trace at all.'

Deborah shuddered. She was aware that the black eyes were still watching and assessing her. She said, without looking directly at Mrs Bradley:

'Wasn't there an Assistant-Warden here? What happened to her?'

'A young woman called Carr was the Assistant-Warden. But, as it happened, she left to be married at the mid-term, and as Miss Murchan insisted that she could manage until the summer vacation, nobody was appointed. When did you apply for the post?'

'Last Easter.'

'Yes. Miss Carr would have tendered her resignation at the end of the Lent Term, I suppose, and the College advertised immediately. Were many candidates called up for interview?'

'Eight, I think.'

'All of them older than yourself?'

'Yes. A good deal older, some of them. I didn't think I stood an earthly chance.'

'Youth must be served, child. Trite but true, especially nowadays. When was the final selection made?'

'Not until the second week in July. I say!' She looked full at Mrs Bradley. 'Did *you* have anything to do with the appointment?'

'Yes, child. I was an unseen but interested witness at all the interviews.'

'And you decided . . . ?'

'Yes, child.'

'Well, thank you very much, but . . .'

'That is why we are having this very trying conversation,' said Mrs Bradley, cutting short the observation which, from Deborah, was almost inevitable in the circumstances. 'I don't want you to stay if you are at all nervous. I don't know why you *should* be nervous, but, after all, one cannot deny that one has read Mr Montagu Rhodes James's *Story of a Disappearance and of an Appearance*, can one?'

'I'm horribly nervous,' said Deborah, allowing herself to be side-tracked, but perceiving the machinery involved, 'but I did want the job, and I still want it. What am I to do? I mean, why exactly did you decide on me?'

'Because you are young, child, and I can manage you. You don't mind my putting it like that? I must have someone who is young enough to be able to keep her own counsel and my secrets. Older women, even the best of them, sometimes are not good at either. The Sub-Warden here must be my lieutenant not only so far as running this Hall is concerned, but in my other work, the work that I'm really here to do. Do you understand what I mean?'

'Yes, I think so. I – I know who you are, of course.'

'Well, think it over tonight, and let me know first thing in the morning. I might say that your old post is still open to you. I have made certain of that. My son knows the Chairman of the Governors.'

'Can't you tell me any more? About Miss Murchan, I mean.'

'I don't know very much more, child.'

At that moment the telephone rang.

'It's about you,' said Mrs Bradley, answering it. 'Miss du Mugne wants to see you.'

*

Miss du Mugne was a middle-aged, smiling, frosty woman whom Deborah immediately and, so far as she could tell, unreasonably disliked.

There were flowers on the desk and flowers on the piano. There was a copy of a picture by Corot indicating very large, active trees and very small, insignificant people, and there was also a Staff photograph. The picture hung on the wall behind the piano, the other stood in the centre of the mantelpiece.

'Miss Cloud?' said Miss du Mugne. 'I am glad to welcome you to Cartaret. You have met Mrs Bradley, the new Warden of Athelstan?'

'Yes.'

'You understand that – that your appointment is under rather abnormal conditions, don't you, Miss Cloud?'

'I ... Yes.'

'Well, I would not like to have you think that under happier circumstances someone else might have been appointed. I want you to know, Miss Cloud, that yours was my first selection out of the long list of applications received, and that you would have been appointed *in any case* – Mrs Bradley's work here notwithstanding.'

She paused and beamed, apparently anticipating thanks. Deborah nervously gave them.

'Then *that's* all right,' said the Principal. 'I do hope you will be happy and comfortable here. Miss Band, the Assistant-Principal, will let you have a time-table of your lectures. I do hope you will find the work interesting. We get, I am glad to say, a very good type of student. Our standards are high and I am determined to maintain them. Well, good-bye, Miss Cloud, and do come to me if you are in any difficulty. I do rely on you to do all you can to assist Mrs Bradley, especially as regards the *catering* and the *conduct*. I am afraid that ... this in confidence, of course! ... brilliant woman though she is, Mrs Bradley has rather hazy ideas about *food*, and I am not at all convinced that she understands the *deportment* I require from the students.'

Deborah, thinking of the tea Mrs Bradley had provided, could not find herself in complete agreement with the Principal, at any rate upon the first of these points. She made a non-committal noise, and was about to take her leave, as she felt that she had been dismissed, when Miss du Mugne added suddenly:

'By the way, the students know *nothing*.' Upon observing Deborah's expression of surprise, she added hastily: 'I mean, of course, nothing about Miss Murchan's disappearance.'

'Oh, no, of course not,' said Deborah.

'The police have been very discreet, very discreet indeed; but, unless Mrs Bradley can help matters, something must come out soon.'

'Yes, quite. I quite understand. I'll do everything possible to help.'

'I am sure you will. *Good-bye*, Miss Cloud, and don't forget that I am always available in any little difficulties. And do have a periodical inspection of their *hat-boxes*. You'll soon know what I mean.'

Deborah left the Principal's room with mixed feelings. Prevalent among these, however, was the desire – she recognized it with a certain amount of surprise – to return to Mrs Bradley's disquieting, yet, paradoxically, reassuring presence. 'I know; and spit the Principal out of your mouth,' said Miss Topas, who seldom minced her words.

Deborah walked round towards the back of the College this time, and took the path which led directly to Athelstan. On her left was a shrubbery which gave place, when the path joined another, to an orchard. On her right was a lawn with a grass tennis court. The rockery, which fronted Athelstan and beside which steps led up to the main gravel drive which connected all the Halls, was her demarcation line.

'Home,' she thought involuntarily. Suddenly, to her surprise, and, she had to admit, to her pleasure, out from the cover of a bush darted Laura Menzies.

'Hullo,' she said in cheerful tones. She had by the arm the scared and diffident Miss Boorman. 'Come into the Common Room with us. Or are you going into a huddle with the nobs?'

Deborah modestly disclaimed any previous engagement, and Laura thereupon observed that she supposed they had all better hang about to learn the fate of 'old Kitty.' This was settled by the appearance of the heroine herself, who, with a woebegone expression, came out by the front door of Athelstan and informed all and sundry that she was 'for it,' having been enlisted with the rest of the inmates at the end of her first two and a half seconds in the Principal's room.

'What have we here, Dog?' she inquired, gazing kindly upon Miss Boorman.

'A buffer state,' Laura cryptically but intelligibly replied. Kitty favoured Miss Boorman with a long and thoughtful stare.

'Ay, ay,' she pronounced with a satisfied smile. 'Good generalship, Dog.'

'As ever,' replied her friend modestly. 'As for Miss Cloud,' she continued, 'after today, when we are all girls together, she will be ashamed to be seen out with us, so make the most of her company while you can get it and before she knows her way about, and the shades of the prison house begin to close around the growing boy.'

'The thing is,' said Deborah, as all four of them entered Athelstan, 'I can't quite see why there was any question about your being admitted to College, Miss Menzies. I mean, you don't seem to be – '

'A moron like me? Oh, no, she ain't,' said Kitty.

'Bad reputation at school for ragging,' replied Laura, with unwonted modesty. 'In fact, I was given to understand just now by Old Beezer du Mugne – between ourselves, what a pill! – that but for the direct intervention of the First Grave-Digger, I should have been scrapped.'

'Mrs Bradley wanted you?'

'And how!' agreed Laura, squinting down her nose. 'And do you know what I think?' she continued, to Deborah's extreme alarm. 'I think there's dirty work at the cross-roads. Why does the Third Witch come here disguised as a Warden? There is something behind all this. Had it struck you, Comrade Boorman?'

'No,' said Alice Boorman. 'What?'

'What, indeed?' responded Laura cordially. 'Kitty, love, has anything struck *you*?'

'Nope. Nothing ever does. But as soon as Miss du Mugne insisted upon availing herself of my services, I raced back here and secured from that Miss Mathers who deals in lists and things, three perfectly good little dungeons on the second floor, all side by side and hotsy-totsy. I thought we ought to be all three together.'

'Good for you!' said Laura, with enthusiasm. 'Now, young Alice Where Art Thou! Do you, or do you not, become the Third Musketeer?'

'Wilt thou, Alice, take this Thingummy as thy wedded what-do-you-call-it?' demanded Kitty idiotically.

'I will,' said the pale Alice, looking pleased but also slightly apprehensive. 'But I've come here to work, you know.'

'The bleating of the two kids excites the tiger,' observed Laura, linking her arm in that of the third musketeer. Deborah found herself unable to decide whether Alice had chosen wisely or not. The four of them went into the students' Common Room, and at the end of about half an hour Deborah pleaded that she wanted to unpack, and was conducted by one of the maids to her bedroom, and then shown her sitting-room. The Warden and Sub-Warden were similarly accommodated, she had been pleased to see. She had had not more than sufficient time to take a hasty but pleasantly proprietary glance about the large-windowed squarish room when the house-telephone rang, and she discovered that she was connected with Mrs Bradley's sitting-room.

'Let's go to dinner in York,' proposed the head of the house. 'These children can't come to much harm between now and midnight, and I find myself, as Miss Menzies would say, cribbed, cabined and confined in the College atmosphere. Don't loiter. George has the car at the door.'

CHAPTER 3

CLINICAL THERMOMETER

DEBORAH enjoyed her dinner. Neither the College nor her companion's real business there was mentioned until she herself broached both subjects on the way home.

'Oh, dear!' she said. 'I forgot to get the time-table of my lectures from the Assistant-Principal. Do you suppose I shall have to begin tomorrow?'

'I know you will not,' replied Mrs Bradley. 'Tomorrow the rest of the children arrive and are to be received by their various tutors. Apart from that, nothing unpleasant is contemplated. I myself am to lecture during the term, but how, when, where, to whom and on what I have not the faintest idea.'

Deborah giggled.

'I suppose you *do* lecture, though, sometimes, don't you?' she inquired. 'To the outside world, I mean.'

'Yes, child.' Mrs Bradley turned back again to look at the moonlight over the moor. Deborah stared out of her own window for a minute or two; but she was, without being fully conscious of the fact, not very anxious to return to the College. By night the fact of Miss Murchan's disappearance took on a deeper, more sinister significance than by day. It reminded her of her childhood attitude to ghost-stories.

'I would like to know,' she said, speaking very quietly in case Mrs Bradley did not want George (who was, however, separated from them by a glass screen against which his sturdy back looked powerfully reassuring) to hear what she was saying, 'a bit more about Miss Murchan's actual disappearance. You said it was at a College end-of-term dance.'

'Yes; an extraordinary time to choose; and the facts of the disappearance, so far as I have been able to obtain them, do seem a little curious. Have you a mental picture of the situation of the College?'

'Yes, I think so.'

'Well, on the night of the College Dance, Miss Murchan was most certainly present up to the Twilight Waltz.'

'Twilight Waltz?' said Deborah, amused.

'That is what they call it. It seems to be an institution here, and comes almost at the end of the programme. The students are permitted to invite men friends to this one party of the year, and the College Hall was crowded. Now, the senior student of last year at Athelstan – not the girl we have seen today, but her predecessor in office – seems to have thought it incumbent upon her to dance with the Warden at least once during the evening, and the Warden, who appears to have been slightly obtuse, selected this particular dance, although the senior student's young man had already initialled it on the student's programme.'

'And then Miss Murchan disappeared?'

'Well, when the dance ended and the lights were turned up, Miss Murchan discovered that her back hair was coming down. As a matter of fact, the student herself remarked on it. Her story was that the Warden's hair was hanging down and looked very untidy and, to quote the student's exact words, "a bit Bacchanalian," and that she told the Warden of it, but *not* in those exact words, and that Miss Murchan then said: "Yes, I thought I felt someone grasp my hair during the dance. The lights were very low; I must have been mistaken for someone else. There is always horse-play during this dance. I should have sat it out."

'Upon this she excused herself to the student, and went away to tidy herself up. She has not been seen again by any of her friends, or by anyone at the College.'

'That certainly does seem odd. I suppose there is no chance that she committed suicide?'

'If so, where is the body?'

'Yes, where is the body?' Deborah repeated. 'But you would have to ask the same question if you thought she had been murdered, wouldn't you? Oh, but, of course, the murderer would remove it.'

They were silent after that, until they reached the College grounds, which they did at five minutes to eleven. The Halls were in total darkness, and Deborah, stepping out of the car and into the moonlight, felt a chill which was not altogether that of the night air as George drove off towards the garages, which were behind the main College building. Against her inclinations, she found herself filled full of uncomfortable fears engendered by the implications of the conversation she had just concluded.

She followed her companion across the lawn and up the flight of steps between the rockeries. She waited whilst Mrs Bradley produced a latch-key and opened the front door.

'You go and make sure our three little birds are safely in their nests,' said Mrs Bradley, switching on the lights. 'I think we can trust that the senior student has already retired to rest, and time alone will show how far we can trust the servants about bedtimes and everything else.'

Deborah hesitated – and then began to mount the stairs. Mrs Bradley waited in the entrance hall, and then, when she saw the landing light switched on, she herself unlocked the door to the basement and servants' quarters and explored below before she followed her. The study-bedrooms occupied by the three new students were on the second floor, the bedrooms of the Warden and Sub-Warden at opposite ends of the first floor. It had occurred to Mrs Bradley, upon her very first inspection of the premises, that a remarkable field for Hide-and-Seek, whether of an innocent or a criminal nature, existed in a house built on the plan which had been adopted in constructing each of the Halls at Cartaret. The two staircases were replicas one of the other, and were called the 'back' and the 'front' staircase, respectively, merely for reasons of convenience in nomenclature. Actually they were exactly alike, apart from the fact that the 'front' staircase began opposite the Warden's sitting-room and the 'back' staircase mounted from outside the Students' Common-Room. What was called the entrance hall was nothing more than a fairly wide passage which went from side to side of the house.

There was also the basement floor where the servants lived. This, too, had its corridor, the most extraordinary feature of which was that it was carried, by a covered way, completely through all five of the College Halls, beginning, in fact, in the bakehouse, which was used only twice a week to bake bread and pastry for the whole College, and then traversing in turn Athelstan,

Edmund, Beowulf, Bede and Columba. Beyond Columba lay the Infirmary, and the corridor led to that, too, so that it was possible to convey a sick student all the way from Athelstan to the Infirmary without once emerging into the open air, or having to go up and down steps except from the one bedroom to the other.

'Amazing,' Mrs Bradley had observed, when the Principal, who had led her on a personally-conducted tour, pointed out the supreme advantages which this method of joining up the various Halls must confer upon Wardens and students. 'And the same key, I suppose, fits all the doors?'

'Yes, naturally,' the Principal had replied. Then Mrs Bradley's obvious lack of enthusiasm caused her to add with some haste : 'But, of course, whatever has happened to poor Miss Murchan could not possibly have happened to her here.'

To this illogical remark Mrs Bradley had made no reply. As she followed Deborah up the front staircase she was thinking about it, however, and, perhaps for this reason, was sufficiently on the alert to make an irritating but interesting discovery.

Her bedroom doorway was in a small recess. Across this recess, in a business-like manner, a thick piece of string had been stretched. Two U-shaped staples had been driven, the one into a landing cupboard, the other into a wooden partition which formed the bathroom wall, and the string was stretched tightly between them about eight inches from the ground. Anyone going into the room would most likely have failed to see it in time, for it had been painted white to match the bedroom door, and, as a piece of white drugget had been used as a slip-mat, the effect, concluded Mrs Bradley, studying the booby-trap thoughtfully, was that of complete camouflage.

Leaving the string exactly where it was, she stepped along the landing to Deborah's door, to find that the artist, whoever she was, had exactly repeated her effects. She waited there until Deborah came down from the floor above.

'All serene, although not, I am sorry to say, asleep,' Deborah remarked. 'In fact, the little blighters have been smoking. Is it allowed, do you think?'

'It will be,' said Mrs Bradley. 'I must put up a notice about it.

Look, child. The "little blighters" appear to have been doing something other than smoking.'

Deborah looked at the contraption. Then she knelt down and looked at it again. Mrs Bradley noted, approvingly, that she did not attempt to touch it.

'Those three didn't do this,' she said, rising from her knees. Mrs Bradley looked at her with interest and with even more marked approval.

'Are you sure, child?'

'Well, Laura and Kitty – I mean Miss Menzies and Miss Trevelyan – aren't the sort to think a hobbledehoy trick like this a bit funny, and I can't see the senior student doing it.'

'No. Remains the fair Alice,' said Mrs Bradley complacently.

'Or the servants – who may not like us.'

'Speak for yourself,' said Mrs Bradley, grinning. 'Come on; let's go up and bully the witnesses.'

'If any,' said Deborah, following her up the stairs. 'By the way,' she added, as they reached the next landing, 'I do hope we shall remember those beastly strings, and not go tripping over them when we come down again.'

'I shall remember mine, but I think I'll untie yours,' said Mrs Bradley, going down again. The driving-in of the staples, she was particularly interested to notice, had splintered the soft wood, but the splintering had been rendered almost unnoticeable by the application of more of the white paint. Nevertheless (and she had a keen sense of smell) not the slightest odour of paint could be detected.

'Hm!' said Mrs Bradley, switching off her powerful torch and rising from her knees. 'Very painstaking.'

She went up on to the next floor when she had detached Deborah's string, to find the Sub-Warden seated on Alice's hatbox and Alice looking scared and uncomfortable.

CHAPTER 4

A MULTIPLICITY OF PROMISCUOUS
VESSELS

'You know,' said Kitty, sitting up in her narrow bed and yelling over the partition, 'the old girl was up to something last night. What do you suppose was the object of all that third-degree velvet-glove stuff she pulled?'

There was no reply from Laura, but Alice put her head over and observed: 'I didn't know what she meant, and I don't now.'

'But I do,' said Laura, appearing in the doorway of Alice's cubicle. 'On the excuse, if asked, of losing my way to the bathroom – not that you can lose your way anywhere in this geometrically-constructed loose-box – I've been down and had a snoop at those doors. I fig-ew-er that the Duchess of Malfi put on burglar's gloves and undid those knots with a hairpin. The cords still lie *in statu quo*, or very nearly so, my loves, and the staples are still fixed firmly in the doors. Ergo, there is going to be one devil of a fine pow-wow-plus-fight; referee and timekeeper that vicious and unstable Old Maid of the Mountains Principal du Mugne, plaintiffs Old Mutt and Young Jeff, defendants our humble selves. What say you, comrades?'

'Oh, I do hope not,' said Alice, who was now doing her hair. 'I don't want any more questions. It's horrible. It makes you begin to wonder whether perhaps you did do it, after all.'

'Well, did you?' asked Laura. 'Personally, the orange-skin banana-peel jest, ripe though it may be, has never appealed to yours truly. It's unsubtle.'

She went into her own cubicle, and the other two could hear drawers being flung open and thrust in again to the accompaniment of a considerable amount of blasphemous comment.

'What have you lost, Dog?' inquired Kitty, who retained her comfortable attitude in bed.

'Belt,' replied Laura. 'I received a nasty hint yesterday that we're supposed to wear stockings to go over to College, and I've got nothing to hang mine on to.'

'Coming over,' said Kitty obligingly. 'I can wear my evening one.'

'Oh, thanks. Mine's sure to turn up later on. It may be in my trunk. Where *are* our trunks, by the way?'

'Down in the basement,' said Alice, who, they soon discovered, was able to obtain this kind of information, apparently by clair-, voyance. 'We're supposed to unpack them down there, I think, and carry our things up bit by bit. I've got to get a few things out of mine, so if you'd like to give me your keys I'll bring you up anything you want if you can tell me where to lay hands on it without turning everything else upside down.'

'I shouldn't know, love. My mother always does my packing. She says I can't pack properly, and, so far as I can see, if she persists in that view, I never shall. I'll come down with you. As for you, Kitty, you'd better get up, or you'll get no breakfast, if I read the book of words aright.'

On the first-floor landing they met Deborah in her dressing-gown. She was coming out of her bathroom.

'Isn't she *lovely*! said Alice, flushing a little.

'Not bad,' Laura responded. 'But she must be at least twenty-five.'

'Do you think she thinks we did it?'

'Did what? Oh, the screamingly funny string joke? No, I don't. In fact, she knows we didn't. So does Aunt Glegg.'

'The Warden isn't in the least like Aunt Glegg.'

'She is to me.'

'But she can't be. Aunt Glegg – oh, I don't know how to put things, but she definitely isn't and never could be in the very least like Aunt Glegg. You, with your strong literary sense, ought not to talk such rot. You know, you're like most very clever people – you're lazy.'

'Golly!' said Laura, regarding her companion with such intentness that she almost fell down the stairs. 'Are you, by any chance, a dark horse, young Alice?'

'Good heavens, no!' said Alice blushing.

'Well, I've been chewing over a few outstanding points during

the night watches. I'm no sleeper, although you wouldn't guess
it. And I knew I'd placed our Boadicea aright. Her name's Bradley.'

'Yes, I know.'

'Mrs Bradley.'

'Yes. I expect she's a widow or something.'

' "Or something" about whangs the old nail on the clock, snout
or beezer. She is, in short (and in full, see Timothy Shy's special
news-service, copyright in all languages including Sanskrit), Mrs
Beatrice Adela Lestrange Bradley, with degrees from every University except Tokio. And she chooses to come *here*! What I keep
asking myself is – why?'

'But – then she's a detective!' said Alice.

'And *what* a detective,' said Laura. 'Do you know what I suspect, young Alice?'

'No. At least, I hope not.'

This subtlety was lost on Laura, who replied: 'Is it a dagger
that I see before me, its 'andle to my 'and? No, but it is that same
circular saw with which Hawley Harvey carved up his spouse, *et
voici la plume de ma tante.* Goroo! Goroo! (Dickens – or thereabouts.) Stop me if you've heard it before. Young Alice, there
must be a murderer on the premises!'

*

All that day, from about eleven in the morning onwards, students continued to arrive. Every train disgorged them, until by
seven-thirty the whole College was assembled in the various Halls
for dinner. After dinner, on this first day of term, there was a
short meeting of all students in the College Hall, but by half-
past eight students in couples, groups, platoons, or, in a few
cases, singly, were walking across the lawns, through the orchard or upon the gravel paths, back to the various Halls of Residence.

The Athelstan contingent was made up equally of First-Years
and Second-Years. There were no Third-Years. These were housed,
together with the One-Year Students (practising teachers of
some years' experience who had come to College to obtain a
Board of Education Certificate) in Columba, which thus differed

from any other of the Halls, and was referred to by the rest (for no reason that Mrs Bradley ever discovered) as Rule Britannia's.

From their time of arrival until dinner-time most of the students in Athelstan had been occupied in greeting their Warden, meeting their tutor, re-arranging (to the confusion and irritation of Deborah and the senior student) the allotment of study-bedrooms, meeting and greeting one another on the stairs, in passages and even whilst opening and shutting the doors of the W.C.s, and in general creating so much pandemonium that even Deborah, accustomed as she was to the beginning of term at a girls' school, felt, by the time that dinner was over, as though she had added long, heavy years to an already over-burdened existence.

'What you want,' said Mrs Bradley, joining her as she came out of the dining-room, 'is a drink. Come along, child. And let us find out whether Lulu can make coffee. She says she can. Shall we risk it?'

'One thing,' said Deborah twenty minutes later, sipping Lulu's remarkably good black coffee and eyeing with friendly interest Mrs Bradley's old brandy, 'I suppose these wretched kids will go to bed soon? They ought to be completely fagged out.'

'Be yourself, child,' said the Warden, who had learned the expression from Kitty that afternoon. 'I am credibly and respectfully informed by the senior student (whose name, by the way, is Hilda Mathers and whose home is in Middlesex), that the Second-Year Students always rag the rooms of the First-Year Students on the first night of term, and that she hopes I shall not be disturbed by a little extra noise.'

'Heavens! What do we do?'

'Nothing, child. As far as possible the local customs should be respected. That is the first law of government.'

'Tell me,' said Deborah suddenly, 'aren't you bothering much about being Warden? I mean, don't you care particularly what they do? Do you – I mean – well, aren't you – ?'

'You know, you're tired,' said Mrs Bradley kindly. 'You'll feel better than this in the morning.'

She began to cackle. Deborah laughed, and then found that she could not stop. The parlourmaid, Lulu, an American negress, came in to collect the coffee-cups, and finding 'the madams' – a curious traditional name for Hall Wardens and Sub-Wardens – in this silly but helpless condition, she flung back her sooty head and yelped with primitive enthusiasm. This disgraceful scene was interrupted by the senior student.

'I'm sorry, Warden,' she said (looking, as, indeed, well she might, poor girl, said Mrs Bradley afterwards when Deborah canvassed her opinion upon 'what Miss Mathers must have thought,' somewhat startled at the sight of the Warden, the Sub-Warden and the parlourmaid all having hysterics together in the Warden's private sitting-room), 'but there seems to be some water overflowing somewhere, and I think it must be the ball-cocks out of order, as the ragging hasn't really started yet.'

'Dear, dear,' said Mrs Bradley, recovering herself and eyeing the senior student solemnly, 'I had better see about them, then. Is this what usually happens before the Second Years "really" rag the rooms of the First-Year Students?'

'No, indeed, Warden,' said the senior student, as they went out into the passage. Lulu, also restored to gravity, rearranged the tray and went out with it. Deborah, a little hazy as to the precise nature of ball-cocks but having a horrid presentiment that they were something to do with the plumbing, and therefore were hideously unmanageable and important, followed Mrs Bradley and Miss Mathers towards the stairs.

'Oh, Miss Cloud,' said a breathless student, waylaying her before she could catch up with the other two, 'did you know? There's water coming through the Common Room ceiling.'

'Well, you'd better come upstairs and help mop up,' said Deborah, immediately, bundling her up the stairs, where the Warden swung round upon them both.

'Student,' said Mrs Bradley, who had discovered that Athelstan's members answered readily to this optimistic and convenient appellation, 'do you understand the nature and function of the ball-cock?'

'N-no, Warden,' replied the girl, looking thoroughly alarmed.

'Good,' said Mrs Bradley, thoughtfully taking her arm in a firm grip. 'Roll up your sleeves as we go. I will teach you all about them. Don't you bother, Miss Cloud. The student and I will manage.'

*

Word of what was in the wind with regard to the ragging had come to the omniscient Alice.

'I say,' she confided timidly to Kitty and Laura, as they seated themselves on her bed and produced food with which to supplement the dinner they had just eaten in Hall. 'I've heard that the Seniors are going to rag our rooms.'

'When?'

'This evening. We've all got to go to a Common Room meeting called by the senior student, and while she's got us there talking to us about the rules, and that sort of thing, they're going to rag our rooms and make apple-pie beds and things.'

'Lor'! Boarding-school stuff?' said Kitty.

'Not up here they're not,' said Laura, firmly. '"They can't renew their youth at our expense.' She produced a coin. 'Heads or tails, K.?'

'Tails, Dog, but I'm sure to lose, so why toss?'

'You *have* lost. Can you manage?'

'Bob's your uncle,' replied her friend, apparently intelligibly. Laura, satisfied, stuffed a last tomato sandwich into her mouth, cut herself a generous piece of jam sponge and another for Alice, took that shrinking member of the expeditionary force by the arm, and together they went down the stairs to attend the meeting, which was called for nine o'clock.

Left alone, Kitty went into her own room, locked the door, climbed over into Laura's room and locked that, and then did the same for Alice's room. She returned, via the partition, to Laura's room, took off her shoes and her frock, got into Laura's bed, as that room was the middle one of the three, and immediately fell asleep. The sounds of revelry woke her twenty minutes later, and she smiled serenely, listened whilst all the three locked doors were tried in turn, waited whilst a whispered consultation, punctuated by giggles, took place on the landing, and then heard the other four rooms on their side of the landing receiving attention from the wreckers.

She arose when the gang had gone, made her own depositions – the seven study-bedrooms on the opposite side of the corridor had all been allotted to Seniors – and retired to rest again, this time not to sleep but to finish the sponge sandwich and read a detective story.

So absorbed was she that she did not hear the timid voice of Alice until it had called her name for the third time.

'I say,' said Alice, 'the rag's over, but somebody's gone too far, and there's been a lot of water through ceilings and things. The Warden is doing a tour, so I thought I'd let you know.'

'Many thanks. Where's Dog? In the cooler?'

'Oh, no,' said Alice, who apparently understood this reference. 'She's helping the Warden. We've all been helping the Warden.'

'Like hell you have,' replied Kitty, with great appreciation of this jest. 'Lend me a comb. Oh, I forgot. You can't get in. Half a sec.'

She climbed over and unlocked the doors, to confront a flushed and perspiring Alice, whose sleeves were rolled up displaying remarkably sinewy arms, and whose skirt was dripping water on to the polished boards of the floor.

'Here, you'd better stand on a rug or something,' Kitty observed, swiftly and in motherly fashion unfastening Alice's skirt and slipping it down. 'Step out, and I'll go hang it in the bathroom. Stick something else on, or you'll get a cold, with all that perspiration. What on earth have you been doing, to get in such a state?'

'Racing about, trying to check up on the – the – ' She struggled to find a word which should be polite, definite, and, if possible (although she suspected that this was out of the question), belonging equally to her own vocabulary and that of Kitty. Finding the attempt hopeless she abandoned it, and, pulling her dressing-gown round her, stooped to the small cupboard beneath the piece of combination furniture known to Athelstan as a Doris (after the Warden, Miss Murchan's predecessor, who had introduced it into use from what was popularly believed to be her own design); and exclaimed, in a tone of relief which puzzled Kitty: 'Oh, mine isn't there, either!'

'You're what? Oh, the Jerry! Well, you don't want it, do you?'

'Of course not! Only, you see, it's a mystery. See whether you've got yours, would you?'

Kitty investigated.

'No,' she admitted. 'I haven't. And I know it *was* there, before we went over to College, because Dog and I had a bet on whether they would be provided, and we investigated, and she won. Besides we – Let's see whether hers is still there. What's all this about, anyway?'

'You'd better come down and see,' replied Alice. 'And the Warden says that anybody good at mountaineering might be useful.'

'Oh, Martyr's Memorial stuff,' translated Kitty. 'Not for yours truly. Let someone else break their neck.'

There was the sound of hurried footsteps, and Laura appeared. She was even more dishevelled than Alice had been, and her face was wreathed in smiles which gave her, in collaboration with various streaks of grime and the beginnings of a black eye, an appearance as of devil turned chimney-sweep.

'Good Lord, Dog! Your eye!' exclaimed Kitty.

'Ran into the edge of the Common Room door,' explained Laura, dismissing the incident. 'I say, girls, somebody must have collected a bevy of Edgar Allans while we were having dinner and – well, you'd better come. The Duchess wants it all taken down, and someone to volunteer to put the bonfire out. Personally, I've collected a perfectly good watering-can with which we ought to be able to irrigate a few Seniors as well as the fire, if all good men will come to the aid of the party.'

*

The noise inside the house had been so considerable that it was some time before the noise outside had attracted attention. In fact, Mrs Bradley said afterwards, it was doubtful, in her view, whether any mere noise, of itself, would have penetrated to ears already half-deafened by the sounds created by forty students, two officials, half a dozen servants, and the persistent rushing of overflowing water and emptying cisterns. It was the bonfire which had caused notice.

Deborah, having raced up the stairs to trace the origin of the water which was coming through the Common Room ceiling, was aware, on the first-floor landing, of another stream of water which had begun to pour out underneath her bathroom door.

The plug was in the waste-pipe, the bath was full, and the water was steadily overflowing at what seemed to be a geometric rate of progression. She pulled out the plug, turned off the taps, and then, swearing fiercely, went along to Mrs Bradley's bathroom. Here she found the head of the house, with kilted skirts, engaged in mopping up the floor.

'Was your bath full?' she demanded.

'Yes, child. Look in on the students' bathrooms on this floor, too, will you? And I'll mop up this one and yours.'

'The little beasts! The destructive little beasts!' cried Deborah. Mrs Bradley did not reply. Deborah went to the students' bathrooms, but these were all in perfect order, so she went back to her own bathroom and began to mop up the water with towels and a bath-sheet, wringing them into the rapidly-emptying bath until the floor was no more than damp.

Then she went into her bedroom and changed her shoes, stockings and skirt. Not until then did she descend to inspect the Common Room. The damp patch was spreading over one corner of the ceiling. It glistened sweatily, and beads of moisture were ready to drop upon the floor. The meeting, however, was in full swing, being addressed by the senior student.

Deborah rang the bell and it was answered by the obliging Lulu, who, with the instinct of her race for the dramatic, was having a terrifying but satisfactory time, as her wide grin and rolling, frenzied eyes testified without the need of verbal evidence.

'We better use my apron, Mis' Sub,' she announced. 'Sho' we hasn't another dry swab in de house wid all dis water. Never knowed anyt'ing like it since Noah and de Flood.'

So saying, she got to work, removing her apron and using it as a swab with great and mostly superfluous energy, and, the water beginning to drip audibly on to the linoleum, the meeting was adjourned, and Lulu pelted away to wring her apron.

The overflow of water in various parts of the house had fused the electric light, which chose this moment to go out. The Common Room was not dark, however, for a lurid gleam, such as the eruption of Vesuvius may have shed upon the doomed cities of Pompeii and Herculaneum, flickered upon the discoloured ceiling and illumined the clean bare walls.

'Holy smoke, Mis' Sub!' gasped Lulu, returning with the apron.

'I should hardly think so,' said Deborah.

She went to the window, pulled aside the curtain and looked out. Athelstan was proud of its frontage. It scarcely appeared to full advantage, however, as the repository of a pile of chamber pots built up – or so it seemed to Deborah's possibly prejudiced and certainly startled intelligence – into a representation of the *Grave of a Hundred Heads.* Around the pile, but not touching it, a circular bonfire had been made, and dancing like dervishes round the whole erection were about a dozen young men.

'Interesting, amusing and instructive,' said Mrs Bradley's voice in her ear. 'I wonder what the Principal will say? Or is this also one of the local customs?'

Deborah began to reply, but the Warden had gone. Divining Mrs Bradley's intention, Deborah went after her, and was in time to see the end of the affair. Mrs Bradley, standing in the front doorway of Athelstan, scanned the dancing figures for a full minute. Then she darted towards the bonfire, seized one of the dervishes by the seat of the trousers, and hauled him forcibly out of the circle. At the same instant the sound of a police whistle cut short the proceedings, and into the silence was projected a throaty, official voice.

'Now, then, what's all this?' it said. The magic words worked with their usual charm. The trousered figures fled – all of them, Mrs Bradley noticed, in the same direction. She retained a fierce grip on her struggling prisoner, and hauled him inside the doorway.

'For heaven's sake, Warden, don't report me! It was only a rag,' pleaded the victim. 'I shall be sent down for certain if you report me.'

It was a woman's voice, but, in the darkness of the passage, it was impossible to see the victim's face. Students, organized by

Deborah and Miss Mathers, were already stamping out and scattering the bonfire, which had almost burnt itself through.

'Are you an Athelstan student?' Mrs Bradley demanded.

'Yes. My name's Morris.'

'Well, Miss Morris, you had better assist in taking down that monument,' said Mrs Bradley, 'and you must report to me in my study in the morning.'

'Yes, Warden.'

'I shall require a full explanation.'

'Yes, Warden.'

Mrs Bradley released her, and noted that the decontamination squad, as Laura named them afterwards, had been joined by the sturdy figure of her chauffeur George, who was directing operations in the best traditions of an ex-non-commissioned officer.

'What happened to the police?' asked Deborah, when, at midnight, she and Mrs Bradley, having made a last tour of inspection of bathrooms and lavatories, were seated before a small coal fire in Mrs Bradley's sitting-room and were drinking more of Lulu's coffee and were eating biscuits and cheese.

'George was the police. He is a most intelligent man,' responded George's employer. 'And now, I do hope you will be able to get some sleep, dear child.'

'I feel half dead, so I'm sure I shall,' replied Deborah.

'Let us light one another to bed, then,' said Mrs Bradley, picking up one of the candles. Deborah lifted the other and they tiptoed upstairs.

*

The rising bell was rung at seven o'clock. Breakfast, an informal meal spread over about an hour, began at a quarter to eight. The Warden and Sub-Warden breakfasted in their own sitting-rooms at eight, and by about eight-thirty the majority of the students had finished breakfast and had gone up to make their beds.

By ten minutes to nine Miss Morris had not appeared at Mrs Bradley's door. This did not surprise the Warden; she had her own reasons for being content to wait. She had been out at just after seven to inspect the remains of the bonfire, only to discover that George, aided by the odd-job man, whom he had pressed into service, had cleared up almost all traces of the incident. There might be rumours round the College of the goings-on at Athelstan on the first night of term; there was, Mrs Bradley noted gratefully, no evidence.

As she had no lectures to deliver that morning, she settled the household affairs in Athelstan, and then walked in the direction taken by the young men who had fled from the sound of George's voice on the previous night. From Athelstan past the bakehouse ran a wide gravel path, which, skirting on one side the garages and on the other the gymnasium, the laundry and the engine-room, passed the Chief Engineer's house and led into the lane which was bordered by the south wall of the College grounds.

'Easy enough, madam,' said George, joining her as she stood looking over the gate. 'That was the way they came in, and that was the way they went out. Over the top.'

'Yes. I wonder, George, who and what they were?'

'Gentlemen from Wattsdown College, three miles over towards Wattsdown Hill, madam. They had a challenge by post from the young ladies, and accepted it.'

'Ah, yes, of course,' said Mrs Bradley. 'I have to thank you for your timely assistance, George. We had to scatter them somehow. It would never have done for me to have caught one of them. I should have been obliged to report him, and then the fat *would* have been in the fire.'

'But I thought you *did* apprehend one, madam?'

'No, George, that was one of the young ladies. A very different matter, and one which I can deal with without troubling the Principal.'

*

The students lunched in their halls of residence at a quarter past one, and during the afternoon there were very few lectures until about half past four. Nobody turned up to interview Mrs Bradley after lunch, so she waited until tea-time and then sent Bella, the head servant, into the dining-room, to request that Miss Morris would favour the Warden with a visit as soon as she had finished her tea.

Not at all to Mrs Bradley's surprise, a tall, thin, spectacled student responded to the invitation to come in, and stood respectfully awaiting the Warden's remarks.

'Miss Morris,' said Mrs Bradley without preamble, 'you are a Second-Year Student?'

'Yes, Warden.'

'Did you put on a pair of dark-coloured trousers and dance round the bonfire in front of Hall last night?'

'No, Warden.'

'Thank you, Miss Morris. Are you the only Miss Morris in Athelstan?'

'Yes, Warden.'

'And in College?'

'There is a Miss Morris in the Second-Year in Bede.'

'Thank you, Miss Morris.'

'Anything more, Warden?'

'No, child. I hope you didn't hurry over your tea?'

'Oh, no, not at all, thank you.'

The student retired to collect her books for a lecture, and Mrs Bradley picked up the telephone and established contact with Bede.

'Athelstan speaking,' she observed. 'Have you a student named Morris?'

'Yes. A Second-Year.'

'Is she likely to wear trousers and dance around bonfires at eleven o'clock at night?'

'You'd better ask her,' replied the voice at the other end of the line. 'Half a minute, and I'll ask the Warden of Bede to bung her over. I'm answering the phone under false pretences. I'm only a visitor here. My name's Topas. I really live at Rule – at Columba. I'm the Sub. Do come over this evening and bring your baby girl.'

'To Columba?'

'Yes. But I'll see you get your Miss Morris. Is it true you had a Walpurgis Night at Athelstan?'

'You shall know all,' said Mrs Bradley.

CHAPTER 5

INTRUSION OF SERPENTS

MISS MORRIS of Bede proved to be a chubby, ingenuous student with a Midlands accent, and Mrs Bradley acquitted her at the end of her second sentence.

Rightly interpreting the reference to her baby girl, she took Deborah along to Columba Hall after dinner, and received her first impression of, according to Kitty, 'the live-est wire at Cartaret.'

Miss Topas made the coffee herself, explaining that she always made her own, that the Warden, fortunately, liked it made that way, and that, anyway, they hadn't a maid in the place who had any ideas beyond boiled water poured on to chicory, and that she had heard they had had a very fine first-night rag at Athelstan. She added that Mrs Bradley was to be congratulated, and that she wished she had been there to see.

In short, she babbled on until the Warden of Columba, a grey-haired, slightly deaf lady of nearly sixty, excused herself on the plea of two references to look up for her divinity lecture next day, and departed.

'And now,' said Miss Topas, coming back to the fireside after closing the door behind the Warden, 'let's hear all about poor Miss Murchan.'

"I don't think there's much I can tell you,' said Mrs Bradley. 'The police are going on the assumption that the grandfather of the child is the person responsible for Miss Murchan's disappearance. He went into a mental hospital after the inquest, you know, but he came out, apparently cured, about midway through last term – actually on the eighth of May.'

'Still vowing vengeance?'

'Well, the police don't claim that.'

'What about the man himself?'

'He has gone away for a rest and change.'

'Still, I don't see how he spirited Miss Murchan away at the end of a College dance.'

'You don't? I was hoping I should be able to find some evidence of how that could have been done.'

'Frightfully difficult. You see, that particular dance is different from the other end-of-term dances, because the students can invite men friends. The result is – or was, last term, as I can testify – that the whole of the College grounds are crawling with couples after about nine o'clock. You sit on them on the benches, you bump into them by the rockeries, and you tread on them on the field. Horribly embarrassing, poor things.'

'And you think that Miss Murchan, attended by a cavalier, would have excited attention?'

'Not a doubt of it. No man alive could have got Miss Murchan out of the College grounds on such a night without at least two dozen witnesses coming forward to testify to it. Either she left the grounds of her own accord and alone, or else the man had a – what do they call it – a female accomplice.'

'That is very clear,' said Mrs Bradley. 'By the way, would you mind giving me a description of Miss Murchan? I've seen her photograph at the school she came from, but I never think people look themselves surrounded by thirty children.'

'Miss Murchan? Well, she was about forty-two or forty-three, I should think. Rather a faded-looking person; fair hair going grey, withered skin, weak mouth, but rather arresting eyes – grey-green and alive-looking, which the rest of her certainly wasn't. She was very reserved, and not very popular, either with the students or with us. But I was only here one term with her, you know.'

*

'Demonstration lesson,' said Miss Menzies impartially, 'to Group A.1. on Poetry – capital P, by Miss D. K. St P. Cloud at 11.35 a.m. And very nice, too. Kitty, and thou, Alice, I think this merits our support and close attention.'

'I'm not going to rag Miss Cloud,' said Alice, mildly but with determination.

'And who says otherwise?' demanded Laura. 'I say we ought

to give Athelstan a good hand. And now, to change the subject to one of even greater importance: who's got any money for the cakes and ale at break?'

It was eight-fifty on the second Tuesday morning of term. Prayers (optional) were concluded, the Principal, and those lecturers who had elected to uphold her, had left the College hall, and the students who had attended the ten-minute ceremony were on the point of dispersal.

Deborah had attended prayers and had no lectures that morning now that her Demonstration lesson was in view. This Demonstration lesson, wished on her at short notice by the Senior English lecturer who had contracted a severe cold, was, she knew, not sufficiently prepared, and the poem was not one which she herself would have chosen. Since, however, thirty hectographed copies of it, and of the aim, material and method of the lesson, had already been circulated to the students, she had no option but to do the best she could. This, she thought miserably, would be surprisingly below the general standard of the College. She had become aware, as the term got into its stride and the students settled down, that Mrs Bradley's lectures in psychology and Miss Topas's lectures in medieval history were always crowded, even by students who had no particular reason for attending them, whereas her own lectures in English literature were attended only by those students who had neither the effontery nor the bad manners to cut them. Her Demonstration lessons, she felt, would be equally uninspiring.

She was feeling particularly depressed that morning, having had a passage-at-arms with a Second-Year student in Athelstan who had been discovered in the act of giving Lulu her shoes to clean, and whom Deborah had only been able to worst by threatening to report both her and Lulu to Mrs Bradley. The interview had left her feeling slightly like crying and with a notable diminution of her usual good-humour.

However, there was the set lesson, there were the students, and soon there would be the children. It behoved her to pull herself together and readjust her mind. She thought of the poem, groaned, picked up her hymn book and went dispiritedly out of the College hall and along to the Staff sitting-room. This happened to be next door to the Demonstration Room in which she would give her lesson.

Opposite this room was the cloakroom to which the children would be taken as soon as they arrived at the College. Deborah went out and had a look at it, and then she went into the Demonstration Room to see that everything there was in order. The room had been specially constructed and furnished for its purpose, and was a good deal wider than the other lecture rooms. At both sides there were benches to accommodate the students who would listen to the lesson, and between these two sets of benches were the desks for the children, so that the students were sideways on to both children and teacher. At the back of the room was a long bookshelf, there were a cupboard, a gramophone and the teacher's desk at the front, and the door was on the teacher's left as she faced the class.

Deborah fidgeted round this torture-chamber for five minutes or so, and then, having noted that the desks were supplied with pens, pencils and paper, for another Demonstration lesson which came before her own, she placed on the table some copies of the book from which the poem was to be taken, got a box of white chalk from the cupboard and then went back to the Staff sitting-room and tried to settle down to the business of correcting a batch of First-Year essays.

At ten minutes to ten Miss Harbottle, the lecturer in Mathematics, came in, dumped down her books and observed loudly and cheerfully: 'Thank God for an hour off. Nothing now until that stinking Dem.'

'Oh, are *you* the other one?' asked Deborah, who had been too much engrossed in her own troubles to think of those of other people. 'Do tell me something about it, and how one begins. I'm absolutely terrified.'

'Oh, Lord, so am I, my dear. After all, one can't help knowing that the majority of the students could make a much better job of it than we do. I don't see why the Mistress of Method can't do all the Dems. After all, Maths may be my subject, but I don't affect to be able to teach it to children of nine and ten. Arithmetic lesson, if you please, on simple areas! And to Second-Year students who've all given it on School Practice already!'

'I've got to take a poem with them – the children, I mean – for Group A.1. And I didn't even choose the poem myself, and I loathe it, anyway,' said Deborah.

'How come?' inquired Miss Harbottle, taking out her cigarette case and handing it over. Deborah accepted a cigarette and explained. 'Hard luck,' commented Miss Harbottle, fiddling with a lighter. 'Curse this gadget! Ah, that's it. Look here, I'll tell you what. Mine is supposed to come at five-past eleven, but I'll let you have first innings if you like. Both children and students are very much easier to handle first go off, and the children are apt to hot up for the second Dem. I've often noticed it.'

'Oh, I say!' said Deborah gratefully. 'Would you really change! If only I could wade in and get mine over, I'd be most terribly grateful. I'd be able to have the discussion directly afterwards then, shouldn't I? You know, before the brutes have got together and swopped ideas.'

'Righto. Look here, I'll waylay Fish as she comes out of her lecture and tell her to let the students know we've swopped. There's nothing more in it than that. It won't affect the time-table, as it happens.'

She lay back and finished her cigarette, then she went out to arrange with the Mistress of Method as she had promised.

'I must just make sure the students don't go giving out rulers until your Dem. is over,' she said when she returned. 'Children, even the mildest, always seem to think a ruler is a sort of animated drumstick. I have to have 'em out for my lesson, but you won't need 'em for yours. Done any teaching?'

'Oh, yes. I've done two years at the Elinor Gresham School in North London, and before that I was at Nixfield for a year.'

'You don't look old enough, but I suppose you are. By the way, you might invite me over to Athelstan when convenient. We poor tramps who aren't Wardens or Subs. have to go the rounds of the Halls for our grub, you know, and are supposed to spend a week at each in turn. I've had a week at Edmund, and I'd love to meet your old lady.'

'We've got Miss Murdoch at present,' said Deborah, 'but she moves on to Bede on Sunday afternoon. It seems an odd system to me.'

'Yes. It's supposed to keep us all in touch with one another or something. I know there's some theory about its being a good thing. The only thing I've ever noticed is that it encourages the students to dig stuff out of the Staff instead of looking it up for themselves, the lazy little beasts. Still, why should we worry? Glad I'm not a Warden, anyway. Has the Principal asked you yet whether you find yourself overburdened? If not, she will. Take my advice and say you can manage. What sort of lot have you got at Athelstan? I hear you had a very impressive first-night rag.'

They passed to happy and comfortable shop about the students until Deborah, coming to with a shock, realized that in ten minutes' time she was due to stand before a class of children for the supposed benefit of a group of students, and give a lesson on *When Cats Run Home and Night is Come*, by Alfred Lord Tennyson.

She could hear the children arriving. They had come by bus, and were cheerful and talkative. She took an apprehensive peep at them, but they looked nice little things and their teacher was young and pretty. The students, led, Deborah could hear, by Laura Menzies and Kitty Trevelyan, were helping them off with hats and coats and ushering them through the inner door of the cloakroom for the purpose referred to by their teacher as 'visiting the offices'. So far as Deborah could determine, their efforts were meeting with very little success.

'Silly, I call it, anyway,' said Laura loudly. 'After all, dealing with kids who shove their hands up in the middle of a lesson is all part of teaching, isn't it?'

'And deciding whether it's genuine, or whether the little blighters are simply bored stiff and want a bit of a change,' agreed Kitty. 'Yes, that's what I should think. Same with giving out pens and paper and apparatus and stuff. It's all done beforehand here, and by us. Actually, I don't see much use in these Dems. After all, any fool can get up and give a *lesson*. It *is* all the oddments that count.'

Deborah trembled. It was going to be even worse than she had supposed. She crawled back into the Staff sitting-room, but the Mistress of Method, who came bustling along the passage at that moment, saw her and grabbed her.

'I hear you've changed round with Miss Harbottle,' she said. 'I've told the students. Oh, and there's a wretched child with adenoids who *will* ask unintelligible questions. I thought I'd warn you. And if you don't mind my saying so, you *won't* snap at the children, will you? So bad for the students. Patience and gentleness, gentleness and patience, are what I try to inculcate.'

Deborah thought of saying that she was taking a cane in with her, but she did not want to make an enemy of the Mistress of Method, who, although excessively irritating, was one of the senior lecturers and had been at Cartaret longer even than the Principal, so she merely smiled weakly, and walked to the table on which was another copy of the book which contained the poem.

She picked it up and then walked as steadily as she could into the Demonstration Room. The children, unnaturally quiet, and as upright and stiff as little statues, gave her the unwinking attention of savages. The students whispered and rustled. The Mistress of Method said: 'Oh, someone give out the books.' This was done. Everyone then settled down. Deborah's mind was a blank.

'Good morning, children,' she said in a husky voice. One or two children giggled, but the others replied: 'Good morning, madam,' with the horrid automatic intonation of musical-boxes, and fixed her with their disconcerting gaze.

'We've come here this morning,' said Deborah, clearing her throat, 'we've – we are – I mean I would like you all to think about something very beautiful this morning before we begin, so that we – so that you – I mean I would like you – perhaps flowers, or the lovely trees, or – perhaps some of you can think of something even more beautiful for yourselves.'

She tried to smile, and felt that her face had twisted itself into some horrible grimace.

'Can – can *you* think of something beautiful?' she said nervously, addressing a child at the end of the front row, whilst she racked her brain to remember the beginning of the lesson as she had prepared it. What *was* the poem she was supposed to be taking? On what page of the book could she find it? She looked helplessly at the book as it lay on the table, and began to turn

over the pages. Surely, *surely* she had put a marker to show the·
page? Surely she hadn't been such a fool – What *was* the damn
silly poem, anyway? To her horror she discovered that she had
not the faintest idea.

She looked in hunted fashion at the class. One or two hands
had come up. What had she asked them? She had not the slightest recollection. Or did they want to go outside already, goaded
by the suggestions of the students? Or was one the dreadful child
with adenoids? She pointed to a child in the centre of the class.

'Biscuits,' said the child.

'I beg your pardon? I didn't quite . . .' said Deborah, glancing
helplessly at the students, who were beginning to look thoroughly
uncomfortable. Hastily she pounced on another child. This one,
to her horror, proved to be the one with adenoids. She got up and
made a long and possibly important contribution of which Deborah followed not one single word. A mist gathered in front of
her. Her eardrums pounded.

'What the *hell* shall I do?' she wondered; and, wondering,·was
suddenly conscious of the heartening voice of Laura Menzies,
speaking loudly, clearly and sanely.

'I don't see why they want to think about beauty, Miss Cloud,
when they are really thinking about cats running home and night
is come, and a lot of bally owls and things,' she was saying.

'Oh, dry up, Dog,' said Kitty. 'You can talk all that rot afterwards. You're not supposed to butt in on the lesson.'

Deborah's brain cleared. She smiled at the children who were
all staring at Laura, and said, in her ordinary tones:

'I wonder whether you can find the poem for yourselves in the
books? Come on. You heard it's about cats and the night coming
and the owl, and I believe . . .'

But by that time every child was searching feverishly, and an
outbreak of calling out, argument and self-justification set the
lesson triumphantly on its feet, where to Deborah's dizzy relief,
it remained.

She sent for Laura after lunch.

'I think you ought to know, Miss Menzies, that you saved
my bacon,' she said, with her shy, very charming smile. Laura
nodded, and grinned.

'It was Group B.2. who had the fun,' she said. 'Did you hear about the snakes?'

'What snakes?'

'Well, you know, when your lesson was over, we all squeezed out so that Group B.2. could have Miss Harbottle's lesson – Mathematics for the Million and all that. Well, how long would you say the room was empty?'

'I don't know. But it wasn't really empty at all, because the children were in it all the time.'

'No, they weren't. Miss Fishlock turfed them all out for a run whilst Miss Harbottle got the rulers given out. I wonder what my headmistress will say when I do same on School Prac.? Remind me to try it some time. Well, anyway, some time during that five minutes some sportsman must have nipped in and shoved a couple of assorted vipers inside the gramophone cabinet, and, apparently, about half-way through Miss Harbottle's exposition of When is a Square not a Square, out these serpents came, creating quite a sensation.'

'Good heavens!' said Deborah. 'How beastly! What did Miss Harbottle do?'

'Stood back and asked if anyone was willing to remove them, as she thought they were frightening the children. Kept her head pretty well, I hear from my spies.'

'And – ?'

'Yes. A selfless knight-errant named Cowley – know her? – doing Advanced Biology, so it was all very suitable – nipped out, collected the all manner of creeping things, and took them off to the lab. Then Fishy and Miss Harbottle between them blew out the flames, and Miss Harbottle concluded the most popular dem. since Pharoah kicked Moses in the pants for producing the plague of frogs.'

Nothing else, Deborah discovered, was talked of by Staff and students during the afternoon, for Miss Harbottle had formally reported the matter to the Principal, and Group B.2. had been 'put through it' – to quote Miss Harbottle herself – 'in no uncertain manner,' but without the slightest result.

'Personally, I wouldn't put it past Cartwright,' said Miss Topas, when asked for her opinion.

Deborah herself went to the Principal when she learned how much stir the affair had caused, and said abruptly that she was not at all sure that the little attention had not been intended for her.

'I was supposed to give my demonstration lesson at the time Miss Harbottle gave hers. We changed over, as a matter of – er – of mutual convenience, at the very last moment. I only mention it because I do think it is more likely that somebody new, like myself, would be ragged rather than Miss Harbottle, who is well established here.'

'I see. Thank you, Miss Cloud. It was a horrid thing to do, whoever it was intended to annoy. I shall interview Group A.1., then, and see where that will lead us. I am determined to track the culprit down. I had half suspected Miss Cartwright, of Group B.2., but what you say lends a different aspect. I am obliged to you. How are you getting on at Athelstan? Not finding yourself overburdened?'

The Principal got no further in her search for the person responsible for the snakes, and the excitement which the incident had occasioned would probably have been short-lived but for a more serious outbreak which, even in the widest sense of a very elastic word, could scarcely be looked upon as ragging.

In Athelstan Hall there were twin sisters called Carroway. Needless to say, they were always known as the Seeds, and were in their second year. Apart from their name and their twinship, they were in no way outstanding and certainly had not, so far as was known, any enemies.

But one afternoon, when Annet Carroway went to the box-room to get a dress out of her trunk, she discovered that all the clothes she had left there had been slashed and torn. These clothes included her new winter overcoat, which had had both pockets ripped right out and a great piece chopped out of the back. Further, the trunk itself had had the lock burst open, and the top looked as though someone had jumped on it.

Her immediate reaction was to sit down on the box-room floor and cry; her second to find her sister. Margaret Carroway gave one look at the damage and then threw open the lid of her own trunk. Here the damage was even worse. Her dance frock had been torn to shreds, and not only her winter coat but two pairs of heavyweight winter pyjamas had been cut and torn until they were quite beyond repair.

Margaret kicked the lid of her trunk to close it, took her sister by the hand, and went off to lay the facts before the Warden.

Fortunately, although it was Saturday, the Warden was in. She accompanied the tearful Annet and the white-faced Margaret downstairs, and inspected the damage. She said very little. These were poor girls whose family, at some sacrifice, had allowed them to come to College. Infuriating and inconvenient as the loss of the clothes must have been to anyone, to these two girls it was something not far short of tragedy.

'The College,' said Mrs Bradley, when they had returned to her room, 'will, of course, make good the damage. In fact, unless you have any very definite plans for this afternoon, I should suggest that you take a 'late leave' from me, your fare and some money, and go into York – or Leeds, if you can get a train – and see what you can do in the way of a little shopping. And – may I ask this of you, my dear students? – please don't tell anybody else about this until I have spoken to the Principal. She is away for the week-end, so I shall not see her until Monday.'

They promised, murmured against taking the money but had it forced on them, and were hustled out of the house with time to catch the train which Mrs Bradley had looked up for them. When they had gone she went very thoughtfully down the stairs again to the basement, and stood for a long time looking at the door which led into the box-room. Then she went along the passage towards the bakehouse, then walked back, through the basement of Athelstan, towards the next Hall. There was a door to separate Athelstan from the bakehouse, another to separate Athelstan from the connecting piece of corridor, and still another, she knew, to separate this connecting corridor from the next Hall. All these doors were locked, as usual.

She took out her keys – a formidable bunch – unlocked the door to the bakehouse and the door to the passage, went down on hands and knees, and carefully inspected the floor. It had been so carefully swept, however, that nothing was to be gained by even the closest scrutiny. She went along to the kitchen to question

the servants. The floor had been swept that morning at nine o'
clock or thereabouts. It was swept every day. There were always
students in and out of the box-room to get things out of their
trunks or put things in. The wardrobe space in the study-bedrooms was so extremely limited that the trunks were continually
requisitioned. The floor was often muddy. It was washed over
twice a week. Students came down into the basement straight
from muddy walks or from the games fields.

Mrs Bradley locked the box-room door, returned to her room
and rang up Columba. To her delight, Miss Topas was in.

'Yes,' she said, in answer to Mrs Bradley's inquiry, 'I'll come
over at once. I wanted to go to York this afternoon, but I've only
got thirty bob and couldn't be bothered to go to the bank to cash
a cheque. How's Deborah?'

'Out,' replied Mrs Bradley. 'That's the only reason I want to
see *you*. Oh, and I want to try your keys, so bring them with
you'.

She hung up, and had not long to wait, for Miss Topas appeared in less than five minutes, having run, she explained, fall-
ing into a chair and puffing loudly, all the way. What, she inquired, had Mrs Bradley discovered?

Mrs Bradley informed her.

'And I'm sending a round robin to all Wardens and Sub-
Wardens to check up on their students at night, as far as is possible,' she added.

*

'Clothes-slashing?' said the Principal. 'Have you any theories?'

'None,' said Mrs Bradley, 'that you would wish to hear. For
instance,' she continued before the Principal could deny this, 'I
might say that I have a theory that it was not done by any student in my Hall, but you would reply, most justifiably, that it is a
dirty bird that fouls its own nest.' She watched, with bright black
eyes, the Principal's mental struggle, and then continued: 'Or I
might say that I have a theory that none of the students anywhere, in any Hall, is responsible.'

'That brings us to the servants,' said the Principal, in a tone of
relief.

'Or to the Staff,' said Mrs Bradley, with a loud chuckle. 'Or even to someone outside the College altogether,' she concluded kindly.

'Yes, but – ' said the Principal.

'I know. We have no proof, and we can do no good by formulating theories which at present are incapable of proof.'

'At any rate we can change the locks at Athelstan,' said the Principal. 'That should prevent any unauthorized person from breaking in. I am rather inclined to your idea that it must be someone from outside. All our students come with such very good records.'

Mrs Bradley sighed inwardly. There was nothing, naturally, the Principal would have liked better than to believe that the culprit would be found outside the College, but she felt compelled to point out that she had presented other theories.

'The Staff? Oh, nonsense, Mrs Bradley,' said the Principal. 'The servants, if you like!'

Mrs Bradley pointed out that the servants came with even better records than the majority of the students. She added, to the mystification of the Principal, that she did not want the locks on the doors at Athelstan to be changed.

'I don't quite see your point, but I must agree, I suppose,' said the Principal. 'It is a very unfortunate occurrence, but if you don't suspect your own students I can't see why you are determined to appear to lay the blame on them. At least, that is the interpretation which will be put on it by the College. Why are you?'

'Because the hunt is up,' Mrs Bradley replied, 'and although it is not yet well-nigh day, I do begin to see my way a little more clearly in the matter of Miss Murchan's disappearance.'

'I don't really see that destructive ragging can have much to do with poor Miss Murchan, and I am seriously concerned about this clothes' slashing. But, still, we cannot expect you to take breaches of the College peace as seriously as we do ourselves, I suppose,' said the Principal. 'But if you have already come to some conclusions about poor Miss Murchan, that is most satisfactory.'

'Conclusions is not perhaps the best term,' said Mrs Bradley. 'But I am at the point of having thought out one or two questions which I ought to ask you. It appears that Miss Murchan can hardly have been spirited away from the end of term dance without her knowledge and consent. It also appears that if she had a companion when she left the College, that companion must have been a woman, at any rate in the immediate environs of the building.'

'It is very easy to get into and out of the grounds on such a night,' remarked Miss du Mugne. 'A great many of the visitors come by car and motor-cycle, owing to the distance from the station, and so the gates are left open until half-past eleven, half an hour after the official ending of the dance.'

'Do you know that they were closed at half-past eleven that night?'

'Oh, yes. In view of the unusual nature of the proceedings, Charles, the garage-and-groundsman, has orders to make sure that all except the Staff cars are off the premises by that time, and then he brings me the keys. It is the only occasion, I may say, on which we lock the main gate. Charles made his report as usual. Further, he declares that no car left before eleven, and Miss Murchan, of course, was not seen, so far as can be discovered, after half-past ten, when she went off to tidy her hair.'

'Thank you. I suppose there were some women visitors?'

'Oh, yes, quite a number. We can scarcely restrict the students in their choice, and some who have no men friends invite sisters or old school-fellows. Each student is allowed one guest, for whom a fee of two shillings is payable to cover the cost of supper, printing of programmes, decoration of the hall, a little extra remuneration to the servants, and so forth.'

'Do the Staff invite visitors?'

'Yes, sometimes. Miss Topas invited a famous novelist who was very charming, but who contrived – by what means I do not know – to become somewhat inebriated during the course of the evening, and Miss Harbottle invited her cousin, a Mr Tallboy, who is a professor of chemistry at Wattsdown. A great many of the students' visitors came from Wattsdown, too. It is the large training college for men which you see from the train as you come through from Moors Cross.'

'Did any of the Staff invite women friends?'

'No one. Miss Fishlock invited her old father. He is nearly eighty, and does so love to come. We give him a seat on the platform, out of harm's way, and the students take him in to supper. He is the most delightful old man, and always looks forward to "the party" as he calls it.'

'Miss Murchan, then, had no visitors?'

'No. Neither year she was here did she invite anyone. In fact, she seemed rather a friendless woman. I can't think why. She got on very nicely with everybody here.'

'Was she a timid woman?' asked Mrs Bradley.

'Timid?' The adjective appeared to puzzle the Principal. 'In what way timid?'

'Not in any particular way. Generally speaking.'

'Well, she was, perhaps, somewhat deprecating in her attitude.'

'How often did she receive letters?'

'Really, I have no idea. Her letters would have been sent direct to Athelstan Hall. I should have no means of knowing anything about them.'

'Thank you. Who else is new to the College besides myself and Miss Cloud this term?'

'Nobody. Miss Topas came at the beginning of the summer term, but everybody else has been here for at least four years. We had a good many changes between 1924 and 1931, but everybody has settled down nicely now, except for one or two marriages or appointments to Principalities.'

Mrs Bradley liked the last word immensely, and thought it over for a minute.

'Miss Topas won't fit the bill,' she said at last, as though she were talking to herself. 'But if ever I am obliged to absent myself from College for a day or two, I wish you would send Miss Topas along to take my place in Athelstan.'

'It would be more in order to send Miss Harbottle or Miss Murdoch,' replied the Principal. 'They are our usual deputies.'

'Never mind that. I must have Miss Topas. She is intelligent. Besides, she and Deborah get on.'

'They get on much too well!' said the Principal, with sudden irritation. 'I don't approve of these violent friendships on the Staff.'

Mrs Bradley nodded slowly and rhythmically for a long time; but not, the Principal suspected, in agreement with what had been said.

CHAPTER 6

HIGH JINKS WITH A TIN-OPENER

'Go on, Alice; shove your name down,' said Laura. 'I'm not going to sweat alone, and Kitty's much too lazy to play games. Besides, Fat Finnigan in your Group told me you were wizard at gym.'

It was true. The pale and diffident Alice, denuded of her shabby coat and skirt, and clad in the half-sleeved shirt and the brown shorts which were regulation wear in the gymnasium, became a different being. She was seen to have muscle and wiry strength, and to have overcome the handicap of being very light by her agility, balance and poise. Whatever was the work, with or without the use of the gymnasium apparatus, she was among the foremost, and at the end of three weeks had been singled out by the lecturers in physical training as being, in the words of Miss Wootton, the junior of the two, 'one of Cartaret's Young Ladies'.

'Means a Dem. for you, my duck, as soon as we start them,' said Kitty. At these fell words poor Alice turned pale, but her Group noticed, all the same, that she had a crisp word of command and possessed that uncanny sense of being able to have the whole class in her eye which marks the born practitioner. The Group were encouraged, at the beginning of every lecture, to take turns at giving a few commands, and these were criticized, not verbally, but by the reactions of the squad to the voice, manner, personality and choice of words of the embryo instructor. Thus Kitty had contrived to get a whole Group lying on their backs with their legs in the air, bicycling away to the point of incipient apoplexy, and then had been obliged to turn to the lecturer and observe that that seemed to be that and for the life of her she didn't know how to get them standing on their feet again.

'I mean, I could tell them to do it, but that wouldn't be right, would it?' she had continued earnestly. The lecturer declined to assist her, and the students, after risking heart-failure by carrying on with the exercise as long as they could, one by one restored themselves to an upright position and began to dust themselves down.

'A well-behaved class. I congratulate you on your discipline, Miss Trevelyan,' said the lecturer, with her usual irony. The students took the hint, raised pandemonium, dusted each other down instead of themselves, and were ultimately called to order by the lecturer herself, who thereupon addressed the crestfallen and perspiring Kitty in these terms:

'Now I want you to imagine, Miss Trevelyan, that I am a Board of Education Inspector, and that you are on probation at your first post. What have you to say for yourself? Is there any reason why the Government and the ratepayers should support you?'

'No, Miss Wootton. I'd better learn up the book of words,' replied Kitty with her usual amiability.

'And so you'd better,' said Laura afterwards. 'I might tell you that in the general mêlée – which certainly *was* of a sumptuous kind – I got home a couple of juicy clouts athwart the beam of that toad in Edmund who swiped my hockey stick last week, so we didn't lose all along the line. But to get a mob of kids round your neck in a P.T. lesson is no joke, young K., and don't you forget it. You'd better get Alice to put you through your paces beforehand if ever you click a Dem.'

'I shan't click a Dem.,' said Kitty. 'It's only the star-turns that get Dems.'

'Don't you believe it. Some achieve Dems., but a darned sight more are apt to get Dems. thrust upon them. One of the Second-Years told me that sometimes they pick the names out of a hat.'

'I should go sick,' said Kitty with simple omniscience.

'Not in Athelstan you wouldn't,' retorted Laura meaningly.

'Why not?'

'Mrs Crocodile is a doctor, fully qualified. She'll give you the once-over and sling you out into the cold and dreary night as soon as look at you. You'll be Little Orphan Annie in two shakes of a lamb's tail if you try that game on with her. Minnie Poppleton, that Second-Year golumph on our floor, tried it on last week to get an essay written for the Deb., and out she came like a bullet. The old girl threatened her with a stomach pump. Yes, as sure as

I'm standing in front of this notice-board. You know, that bunch keep cocktails in their hat-boxes, and apparently Mrs Croc. is wise to the goings-on.'

'It isn't forbidden,' said Alice, sharply.

'Only because the Principal hasn't thought of it as being a possible thing to do. Don't tell me, my dear d'Artagnan, that we cherish a secret drinker in our bosoms.'

'No, of course not. Only I don't see that Mrs Bradley has any right to interfere when there isn't a rule.'

'Don't thump tubs, duck. It don't become a young woman. After all, if it comes to that, there isn't a rule to say that you mustn't go over to Wattsdown after dark and dance on the College dining-table when the boys are asleep in their beds, and yet, strange to say, the Principal sent down, for the duration and without a character, a bright girl named Billings some four years ago for doing just that same.'

'Was *she* tight?' inquired Kitty, interested in this exploit.

'Tight? No. She did it to win a bet. No harm in the girl whatever. But the Principal took a Grave View, as, after all, who would not? Anyway, it didn't matter. She went in for journalism and has never looked back. Billings, I mean. My sister knows her quite well.'

*

Alice and Laura did put their names down, and, the College having retained five of its netball team from the previous winter – two Third-Years, one of whom was staying on for a special course in P.T., and three Second-Years – there were only two vacancies, of which Alice obtained one without difficulty, and treated Laura and Kitty to doughnuts and coffee at the College buffet on the strength of it. Laura, whose game was hockey, scraped in, she informed the others, by sheer ability to chuck her weight about, *finesse* having no place, so far as she had been able to gather, in the operations of the eleven.

Kitty made one or two abortive efforts to shed lustre on herself and her friends, but without success, her most notable effort being an attempt to become a member of the Twenty-Nine Club, a highbrow society which read Russian plays and discussed the ballet.

'But I can't see what the devil you would have done if they *had* admitted you,' said Laura frankly.

'Why, of *course* you do ! I should have given my impression of Hermione Baddeley giving her impression of a prima ballerina.'

'It's a wow, as a matter of fact. I've seen her do it,' said Laura confidentially to Alice. 'And if we have a smoking concert, or its equivalent, in Hall, at the end of the term, we must have it. It's hardly for a mixed audience.'

In consequence of Laura's and Alice's inclusion in College teams, Kitty was sometimes left to her own devices. It happened that the College had fixtures for every Saturday in October, and it was on the last of these, the Saturday before Half-Term, that the next of what were referred to later by Laura as the Athelstan Incidents took place. There was an optional study-period on Saturday mornings, but it ended at noon. Lunch was at twelve-thirty on Saturdays so that students could get away early for afternoon excursions. As it happened, both Laura and Alice had matches. Kitty – to whom a period of optional study was merely time spent in happy and, in a sense, profitable idleness, for she devoted most of the study-periods to designing those fashions in hairdressing for which, five years later, she became famous – volunteered to sneak out of Hall at ten and make her way snakily into the town in order to purchase doughnuts, ginger-beer, fruit, chocolate and potato crisps. She accepted commissions from about a quarter of Athelstan, and abstracted a small suitcase from the boxroom, which was no longer locked up.

Alice had no money, except the return fare for the match and her Sunday Church collection, for it was the end of the month. Nearly everybody else was short, but Laura had had a windfall, and had floated a succession of small loans. In response to what she termed a Grade A blood-sucking letter, her people had sent her November allowance in advance, and, in addition to this, a brother who had received promotion and a rise in salary, 'came up big,' as his sister observed contentedly, and had sent a couple of pounds.

By half-past eleven Kitty was back, and at twenty-five to twelve she encountered the Warden on the back-staircase.

'Ah, Miss Trevelyan, well met,' said Mrs Bradley. Kitty, who was making valiant efforts to hide the bursting suitcase with which she was burdened, responded politely and began to make conversation about the weather, the close atmosphere of her study-bedroom, and the probability of the College winning their matches that afternoon. Mrs Bradley listened attentively. Then she stretched forth a skinny hand for the suitcase, and asked permission to inspect its contents.

'Doughnuts,' she pronounced. 'How many, child?'

'A – well, I got a couple of dozen, actually,' said Kitty, who, with all her gifts, was no liar.

'Threes into twenty-four goes eight. Is it wise, do you think, for Miss Menzies and Miss Boorman to eat eight doughnuts each before they play games?'

'Well,' said Kitty candidly, 'I shouldn't think Dog and Alice will have doughnuts. I mean, you see – well, it was for several of us, actually.'

'I'll come up with you and see fair play,' said the Warden. So she did, and ate two doughnuts and two-pennyworth of crisps. Of the fact that one of the Principal's rules relating to Saturday morning leave had been broken, she seemed blandly unaware.

'You know,' said Laura, later, 'I *like* the old girl, and I don't care who hears me say so. That was the one o'clock news, loves. In other words, the gong for lunch. And I might tell you that, from what my spies mutter, the Second-Years think the grub here has improved at least two hundred per cent since *La Belle Dame sans Merci* took it over. Fat Finnigan stated that if Miss Murchan got appendicitis, it was probably from eating College stew.'

'The improvement may be due to the Deb.,' said Alice loyally.

'The Deb. my foot!' said Laura. 'All personalities aside, and allowing fully for Samivel, my son, my son, bevare o' the vidders, the improvement noted by our revered seniors is due simply, solely, wholly and completely to Mrs Crocodile. Besides, we've kept the same servants in Athelstan for nearly half a term, and that, it appears, not counting Cook, of course, is a College record.'

After lunch she and Alice went off, and Kitty decided to go down to the field to watch the Second Eleven match. The match ended and the teams went in to tea. Kitty returned to Athelstan to get her own tea from the Servery, for on Saturdays and Sundays no evening meal was provided, and the students supplied their own suppers at half-past nine.

Hall was deserted except for a couple of Second-Year students who were spending Saturday working. One was a tall, thin girl with round shoulders who appeared to have no friends; the other was a rather too popular member of her year who had been told by the Principal at the end of the previous term that unless she did some work she would be sent down for good. Her name was Cartwright. The thin student's name was Giggs. Both were already at the Servery when Kitty arrived, but neither spoke to the other. Kitty spoke to both. As she was fond of explaining to Alice and to Laura, she was not proud, and would much rather talk to seniors than to nobody.

To Miss Giggs she said: 'Well, what's the pot of poison this time?'

Miss Giggs laughed dutifully, but did not supply any information. To Miss Cartwright Kitty said: 'Anybody else staying in this afternoon?'

'Shouldn't think so,' replied Miss Cartwright. 'I say, can you lend me a bob until Thursday?'

Rather reluctantly Kitty permitted this inconvenient loan to be floated out of money she herself had already borrowed from Laura.

'Thanks tremendously,' said Miss Cartwright. 'Do the same for you later. I must say,' she continued, scanning her plate with an indulgent and even slightly enthusiastic eye, 'that the old serpent does us a lot better in Hall than Miss Murchan used to. By the way, when you take your crockery back, look out where you put your feet. There's a kind of creosote or something all over the box-room floor. I went there to get another frock out of my trunk . . . Why, what the devil has Giggs got on her feet?' she added, staring at the retreating form of the friendless student as, having come out from the Servery, she walked along the passage towards the stairs.

Kitty, who often acted upon impulse, put down her plate and hurried after her.

'The footwear,' she said. 'How come?'

'Oh, my slippers?' said Miss Giggs, looking at a pair of scarlet satin evening shoes in an embarrassed manner and tilting her full plate dangerously. 'I – well, it was just to rest my feet while I did my Advanced English essay.'

'Very tasty,' said Kitty; and, before Miss Giggs knew what had happened, she had left her and was tearing up the front staircase as hard as she could go. She knew Miss Giggs' room. It was on the same floor as her own. Miss Giggs occupied Number Thirty-three, next to the bathrooms.

Actuated, she stated later to the grinning Laura and the scandalized Alice, by the highest motive of all, that of pure detective fever, she burst into Miss Giggs' room and dragged open her hat-box. These receptacles were large and square, and were made of wood, forming an extra seat in each study-bedroom. In Miss Giggs' hat-box was a pair of shoes so sticky that the newspaper on which they had been placed came up with them. The smell given off by the hat-box was undoubtedly that of strong disinfectant.

Kitty knew that it would be some seconds before Miss Giggs, carrying a full plate, could reach the cubicle, so she stole, with her prize, back to the front staircase, and descended to the first floor. She knew that Mrs Bradley and Deborah were both out, so she nipped round the first corner she came to, entered the Warden's bathroom, and placed the shoes, still on their newspaper, at the far end, underneath the bath. Then she descended the front stairs to the Servery, retrieved her plate, and went pensively into the Common Room. Once there, she ate the food as quickly as she could, did not go back to the Servery for cakes or a cup of tea, but paid a hasty visit to the boxroom.

At about half-past six Alice came back to Athelstan, and a quarter of an hour later Laura arrived. Both were tired; Laura disgruntled.

'Got a goal; a beauty,' she began.

'Offside,' concluded Alice and Kitty in chorus. Laura grinned.

'Win?' inquired Kitty of Alice.

'Eighteen, three. Good game, though. Better than it sounds,' Alice replied. 'Have you enjoyed yourself?'

Kitty seized the opportunity.

'Is Mathers back in Hall yet?' she inquired.

'No. Why?' inquired Alice; but Laura, who had been acquainted with Kitty for some years, seized her by the sleeve and said: 'Spill.'

'Somebody's been assing about in the boxroom again.'

'What? Not more clothes chewed up?'

'Not this time. At least, I don't think so. I want to get hold of Mathers, though, and tell her to shove up a notice warning people not to go paddling about down there. It's in the most frightful mess.'

'Blood?' asked Laura, rolling her eyes at Alice.

'No; as a matter of fact it is that creosote stuff the odd man uses for disinfectant. Somebody has kicked a tin of it over, deliberately I should think, and what's more, I know who, and she doesn't want it known, so I've swiped her shoes as evidence.'

'Be yourself, dear,' urged her friend. 'You befog me. Does she befog you, Alice?'

'No, I don't think so,' replied Alice seriously. 'She means someone's been assing about again, and this time she knows who it is.'

'Considering that in the Matric. paper she didn't know Hamlet was the hero of *Hamlet*, I doubt that very much indeed,' retorted Laura. 'But, come on, K. Don't leave us agonizing like this. Tell us all. Come on upstairs, anyway. Why are we wasting strength propping up this beastly Common Room?'

'I can't tell you anything upstairs, because it's Giggs,' returned Kitty. 'Come closer. I don't want to shout.'

*

'But we ought to find out more about it,' said Deborah. 'After all, if it isn't carelessness it's some more of this horrible destructiveness, like those clothes belonging to the twins, and I do think we owe it to the innocent students to find out the guilty ones, don't you?'

'I suppose so,' said Mrs Bradley. 'I want you to come with me to have another look at it, now that they're all in bed – or, at any rate, upstairs.'

The inmates, as Laura preferred to call herself and her fellow-students, had been duly warned about the state of the boxroom floor, and had been particularly requested by the Warden not to tread the disinfectant about the house. The warning and the request had been observed, and the boxroom was in about the same condition as when Kitty had seen it.

'And now,' said Mrs Bradley, stepping delicately, 'for our most interesting exhibit, which is not, as you seem to imagine, the dark and treacly fluid which is crawling over the floor, but the reason for its egress from the tins.'

The tins were large, green and rectangular. Each had a small handle on top, after the style of those on petrol cans. There were six tins. Each one had a small circular perforation in the middle of one side.

'Quite deliberately done, you see,' Mrs Bradley went on. 'No fumbling; no having several shots, as many people do when they attempt to open a tin; just a neatly-drilled hole expressive of a determined and bold personality.'

'Expressive of a man, not a woman,' suggested Deborah.

'I don't know. Some of the games-playing young are surely capable of a smack like that on a tin.'

'Do you think Miss Giggs is our man?'

'No, child. But it would be interesting to know, all the same, why Miss Giggs, instead of complaining bitterly about the damage done to her shoes, should have gone off and hidden them in her hat-box.'

'I think one of us ought to interview her. After all, several of the students know about the shoes. We ought to accuse her and let her make an explanation.'

'Very well, child. Suppose you interview her tomorrow morning immediately after breakfast?'

'I thought perhaps you'd be the better person.'

'Yes, I should be. But you are more sympathetic,' said Mrs Bradley grinning. 'Well, Oates will have a very pleasant task cleaning up all this mess tomorrow. Come along, child. Time you went to bed.'

Deborah interviewed Miss Giggs in the morning, as Mrs Bradley had suggested. Although in a sense she felt sorry for the friendless girl, she could not shake off a feeling of acute dislike, an unpleasant impression of repulsion, when the student came into her room. She appeared armed with the Book of Common

Prayer, Hymns Ancient and Modern, and was wearing gloves and a hat.

'Oh, I'm going to make you late for Church,' said Deborah, apologetically, afflicted immediately by a sensation familiar to her at her last post, that of being, somehow, put in the wrong by a culprit before she could begin an unpleasant interview. It was one of the reasons why she had given up a teaching post.

'It's quite all right,' replied Miss Giggs, 'It's about my shoes, of course. Well, I do think the Warden ought to have a rule about people going to other people's hat-boxes, especially Juniors. I mean to say ...'

'Yes,' said Deborah, 'that's what we're going to talk about. Now, first ...' The student tried to interrupt, but Deborah held on firmly. 'Now, first,' she repeated, 'let me assure you, Miss Giggs, that the Warden has your grievance in hand, and it and the offender will be dealt with. Please don't let us refer to that again for a while. What I want to know is what made you put those shoes into your hat-box?'

'There's no rule against putting shoes into a hat-box. I kept mine there all last year.'

'Miss Giggs,' said Deborah, beginning to feel desperate, 'more lies behind this than you seem to realize. Your shoes were dirty, weren't they? You had been in the basement, hadn't you? Don't you think it would be best, if you have nothing to hide, to tell me, just straightforwardly, what your idea was?'

'Nobody likes me here,' began Miss Giggs.

'I don't think that can be true. But go on.'

'I got my shoes all messed up, and I thought it was one of their senseless practical jokes. It's nothing but silly ragging, and I don't see we're here to rag. I want to work, and I don't see why a lot of jealousy should upset it.'

'Neither do I,' said Deborah uncomfortably. 'But it wasn't – it couldn't have been – directed at you, don't you see? It was all over that part of the floor. Anybody might have trodden in it. It couldn't have been – have been specially meant.'

'I don't see that. They know I always stay in and work on a Saturday afternoon. And they know I keep – well – biscuits in my trunk. And because I don't hand them round, I suppose they don't like it. But my father can't afford biscuits for everybody. He sends them to me – he can't afford that, really – but he wants me to keep up my strength. You see, when I leave College and get a job, he'll be able to give up *his* job. We've got it all planned out. I'm going to have a little country school – you can get those when you first leave College – and he'll do a bit in the garden, and I shall help him, and . . .'

She broke off, looked vaguely at Deborah, and then added :

'Does the Warden think I spilt the paint?'

'No, she doesn't. She knows you didn't, and she wanted to give you a chance to make your explanation about the shoes before she speaks to the rest of the students. I feel that you have made your explanation, Miss Giggs, and, if I were you, I shouldn't think about the ragging and the jealousy. I should just be as nice to the others as I could, and go on working, and – and thinking about the future.'

'Yes,' said Miss Giggs, as she blew her nose, 'that's all very well, Miss Cloud, but if it wasn't intended for me, why should somebody have run up the back stairs just in front of me? If I hadn't stopped to take my shoes off, I should have seen who it was.'

'Oh, dear ! Have you *any* idea?'

'No. I sort of felt it was someone I'd seen before, but whoever it was had on quite a long dress, I saw it swish round the bend of the stairs as she ran.'

'A lie,' thought Deborah, grimacing as the door closed behind the student's back.

'She didn't do it,' she said to Mrs Bradley, after she had detailed the conversation. Mrs Bradley grinned, but offered no other comment. She touched the bell, and Lulu appeared.

'Ask Miss Trevelyan to come and see me,' said Mrs Bradley; adding, when Lulu had gone, 'You'd better sit in on this. We must look horribly official.'

'Oh, dear !' said Deborah, who was very much attached to Kitty. 'You're going to chew her up.'

'Duty must be our watchword,' said Mrs Bradley, with a fiendish, anticipatory grin. Kitty entered nervously.

'Warden?' she said.

'And Sub-Warden,' said Mrs Bradley, indicating Deborah, who was sitting on the very edge of a chair and was looking thoroughly scared.

'How do?' said Kitty, clearing her throat. At this Deborah had a sudden desire to giggle, and, to conquer it, she reverted to the formula of her youth, that of thinking about her dead grandmother whom, incidentally, she could not remember at all clearly.

'Miss Trevelyan,' said Mrs Bradley, 'you had better sit down.'

'Yes, Warden.'

'Now, Miss Trevelyan, what have you to say for yourself?'

'I – I don't know what you mean.'

'Don't you try those schoolgirl gambits on me!' said Mrs Bradley, more bolt-upright than before. 'Search your conscience, Miss Trevelyan, search your conscience! When you have done so, excuse yourself if you can.'

'Oh – breaking and entering,' said Kitty, giving way at once in this battle of nerves. 'Yes, I – I did do that. It seemed sort of necessary at the time.'

'And now?'

'Well, I can see why I did it.'

'So can I,' said Mrs Bradley deliberately. 'You were actuated by what, for want of more original wording, I can only call sheer, vulgar, spiteful curiosity.'

'Oh, no, Warden!' wailed Kitty, stung to the quick by this uncompromising view of her detective faculties.

'How *dare* you enter another student's room without her permission?'

'Oo, Warden!'

'I say nothing about prying and probing into her private affairs...'

'Oh, I say!'

'Abstracting her property...'

'Oo, but...'

'As to the hiding-place you chose in order to get rid of the evidence of your crime...'

'Oh, I object to crime, Warden! No, honestly, I do call that a bit thick, I mean! No, really, dash it, Warden, I *say*!'

'What *exactly* did you think you were doing?' concluded Mrs

Bradley mildly. Kitty looked at her, gulped, and then grinned.

'I knew you were kidding,' she said. At this ingenuous statement Deborah broke into a sudden squeal of laughter. Mrs Bradley stared at her disapprovingly, with a look which Deborah, with
an absurd little shiver of anticipation, translated as 'I will deal
with you later.' All that Mrs Bradley said was: 'Come on, Miss
Trevelyan. If you can give me any sort of reasonable explanation, I am prepared to overlook your really outrageous conduct.' 'O.K., Warden. Well, you see, it began with that string. I
knew, and Dog knew – I don't know about Alice – that when
you came in and busted us that first night, you knew we jolly
well didn't know anything about it. Well, Dog put two and two
together, as you know she's fairly well given to do ...'

'Yes. I do not underrate Miss Menzies' intelligence,' Mrs Bradley admitted.

'Good old Dog. Well, *she* said if *we* hadn't done it, who had?
Because you'd hardly put that kind of thing down to the servants, and as for suspecting the senior student – well, that's all
rot, whatever you may say.'

'I have never suspected the senior student, Miss Trevelyan, of
tying pieces of string across doorways.'

'No, of course not. Well, then, who are we left with? The lecturers, etc.,' concluded Kitty dramatically. 'So Dog said: "How
about some silly – some lecturer who'd hoped to be made Warden
of Athelstan, and hadn't clicked?" Some women are very funny,
you know.'

'Yes, I had noticed it,' Mrs Bradley drily agreed. 'Go on, Miss
Trevelyan, please.'

'Well, then, the – er – the What-Names, all piled up during
the Second-Year rag ... Remember?'

'Perfectly, Miss Trevelyan.'

'Well, that was another case of Oo-dun-it. Or was it?'

'It most certainly was, if I understand your idiom correctly.'

'So said all of us. Well, there's one thing I can tell you, Warden. It's this: those What-Names were abstracted before dinner.
I know, because we'd investigated ours, and – er – '

'Yes. I seem to remember an impromptu game of Rugby football,' said Mrs Bradley, 'in which one of the promiscuous vessels

figured as the ball. Am I right or wrong in supposing that Miss Menzies scored a try with her vessel at the top of the students' staircase?'

'Perfectly right, but – well, anyhow, I can swear to it they were there at five-fifty-five, pip emma. And nobody came into any of our three study-bedrooms while the Second-Year rag was in progress. That means those things were sneaked out of the rooms just before dinner. Was anybody absent from dinner?'

'No, child. I am prepared to swear to that, and so is Miss Cloud.'

'Me, too. Miss Mathers came round with a Hall list, and ticked off all the names. Well, what are we back to, again? The Staff. Q.E.D.'

'Or some outside person or a servant. It's not a very good point, Miss Trevelyan. All the same I can't see why you suspected poor Miss Giggs.'

'Oh, well, that was kind of by the way,' said Kitty. 'But, Warden, you remember the snakes? You do, anyway, Miss Cloud. You know, the snakes in Miss Harbottle's Dem.'

'What about them?' said Deborah, shortly. The snakes were still an uncomfortable subject for her.

'Don't you see? The Dem.-room being next door to the Staff Common Room ... ?'

'Oh, nonsense!' said Deborah sharply. 'The snakes were just a silly rag, and came out in the wrong lesson.'

'That will do, then, Miss Trevelyan, very nicely,' said Mrs Bradley. 'You will, of course, apologize to Miss Giggs for any annoyance or inconvenience you may have caused her. And you might return her shoes. And now,' she said to Deborah, when Kitty had gone, 'what makes you so certain that there is no connexion between the snakes and the activities in the boxroom, child?'

'Well, I can see the point of snakes in a Demonstration lesson, and, dimly, that some idiots might think the, – the First-Night rag screamingly funny. I mean, there *is* a school of thought – but the coat-slashing and the disinfectant seem quite different, somehow. Of course, I'm not a psychologist,' she added.

'Oh, yes, you are,' said Mrs Bradley. 'There *are* two sets of rags being carried on. You are perfectly right.'

CHAPTER 7

REVENGE UPON GOLDILOCKS

'AND how does it go?' asked Miss Topas. 'I hear you had a Common Room meeting of an unusual kind this afternoon.'

'Yes. Some students were out, but it seemed unfair to expect the poor things to lose their Sunday pleasures for the doubtful privilege of hearing me address the whole of Athelstan for the first time.'

'About the disinfectant?'

'Yes. We made it clear – I think, Deborah, don't you? – that we suspected nobody in Hall of having performed such a childish trick as stabbing cans of disinfectant so that the stuff ran out and made a mess...'

'And Laura Menzies was sharp enough to ask us whom we did suspect, then,' said Deborah.

'And what did you say to that?'

'We told her – and all the rest – that their lectures in psychology ought to supply the answer, whereupon Miss Menzies took it upon herself to observe "Tut, tut, Warden," ' said Mrs Bradley, cackling. 'I like that child. She is intelligent.'

*

The next Athelstan incident took place at the beginning of the half-term break. This lasted from a Thursday evening until the following Tuesday evening. Most of the students left College during this time, and only one of the five Halls was kept open to accommodate those who remained.

Kitty saw the notice-board first.

'I say, it's Athelstan's turn to be Half-Term Hall,' she said.

'Nothing to me. I'm going to see my relations in Scotland,' said Laura.

'Well, I shan't be here, either. Wish I could, in a way, but the family would expire if I didn't go home and tell them how I'm getting on, and let them see what a big girl I've grown in six weeks,' replied Kitty. 'You going home to London, Alice, my duck?'

'No; to my aunt in Lincolnshire,' Alice replied.

Further inquiry proved that all the Athelstan students, except Miss Giggs, Miss Mathers and a First-Year South African student named Firth, would be out of Hall during the long week-end. Miss Giggs made her usual excuse of wanting to work when the Warden inquired, gazing like a benevolent snake at the assembled students on the Saturday evening preceding the half-term week-end, how many of them proposed to remain in Hall, but in her case, as in the case of Miss Mathers, it was a question of a heavy railway fare. Poor Miss Firth had nowhere to go. During the vacations she would inhabit a dreary little room in London and go to all the shows, visit the museums and picture-galleries and generally acquaint herself with the various resources of the capital city, but the half-term break was too short, she informed Mrs Bradley, for so long a journey. Deborah had once attempted to obtain some light on the colour problem in South Africa, but Miss Firth's reply was so uncompromising that she had abandoned the attempt and had changed the subject of conversation.

'Colour problem?' Miss Firth had said. 'There is no colour problem in the part I come from. If the blacks and ourselves don't find the pavement wide enough, well, *they* just walk in the road.'

Asked by Mrs Bradley how she proposed to spend the week-end, she revealed that she had purchased an Ordnance map of the district, had arranged to hire a car, and was going to explore 'a few counties' and embody her findings in an article for a South African paper.

Contemplation of this enterprise left the Warden speechless with admiration. Miss Mathers, it appeared, was going to be 'called for' at College each day by one or another of the students who lived near enough, and would be taken out for the day. She was, in a quiet way, very popular. Mrs Bradley was glad that her senior student was going to have a good time.

'That poor wretch Giggs!' said Deborah, on Thursday night, when 'the tumult and the shouting having died,' as Laura Menzies expressed it, and those students who were not going to leave until the morning having been persuaded to go to bed, she and Mrs Bradley were enjoying a midnight peace in Mrs Bradley's sitting-room. 'I hate to think of her stewing here all alone.'

'She won't be all alone,' retorted Mrs Bradley. 'We are to expect five students from Bede, three from Edmund, two from Beowulf, and no fewer than eight from Columba.'

'I say!' said Deborah, dismayed. 'Not much of a picnic for us! That makes twenty-one counting our own three!'

'It will be a very great treat for *me*,' said Mrs Bradley. 'You, my love, are going away for the week-end. The car will be here for you at half-past ten tomorrow morning.'

'But – '

'My nephew, Carey Lestrange, is coming from Stanton St John, in Oxfordshire, to take you to his pig-farm. He has thousands of pigs, a son aged three, a daughter of twenty months, a nice, quiet, friendly, well-disposed, tractable, quite pretty wife, the best servants in England, and a heart of gold. Now don't be rude about it. Besides, it's not an invitation. It's an order.'

'But – '

'And Miss Topas is going as well. She can't possibly go home for such a short time, and she says she has no money or she would go to Penzance. Now don't argue, there's a good child. I am not equal to quarrelling. And why Penzance I don't know, so don't ask. And Carey's servants are called Ditch.'

'Now look here,' said Deborah. 'I'm not going to be packed off for a rest and change, as though I were an invalid or – or a baby or something. If you've got to stay, as this is our bad-luck term, I'm going to stay, too. You can't turn me out. I won't go.'

'Well, you must please yourself, of course, child,' said Mrs Bradley, solemnly wagging her head. 'It is extremely awkward, because my nephew's wife has invited two men, and I really don't see that Miss Topas can be expected to take *both* of them off her hands. Besides, she told me she wouldn't go if you didn't, and I really think that young woman needs some sort of a break. She works extremely hard, and she has been looking forward to your company for the week-end. Still, of course, you must do exactly as you like. I am sorry I didn't mention it sooner, but I had my reasons.'

'I bet you had,' said Deborah, setting her jaw.

'There, there! Go to bed,' said Mrs Bradley. 'I thought you might do me a favour, and go down with Miss Topas, whose young man, an archaeologist, is going to be there. She told me all about him last week. I don't wonder she didn't confide in you. You're an unsympathetic hussy.'

Next morning Carey came, and Mrs Bradley, to her great relief, was able to wave Deborah good-bye and go back into Athelstan grinning.

The drive from the College to Carey's place in Oxfordshire was a long one, and they stayed not for brake and stopped not for stone, as Laura Menzies would have observed, except for a brief halt at Leicester for lunch. They reached Stanton St John at six, and were welcomed by Jenny, Mrs Ditch and an enormous supper. Jenny was Carey's wife.

Seated at table with them were the two men referred to by Mrs Bradley. One, who immediately adopted Miss Topas, and, regardless of the rest of the company, talked archaeology to her in low tones until midnight, was introduced – or, rather, warmly introduced himself – as Professor Sam Dallas, lecturer in history at the State University of Corder, U.S.A. The other, a big, untidy, dark-haired man of thirty, turned out to be Mrs Bradley's nephew – one of many, he explained to Deborah, over supper – and was named Jonathan.

'In the morning,' said Jenny, giving Deborah her candle, 'you'll be able to see the pigs and the babies.'

'In that order of importance,' said her husband, glancing amusedly at Miss Topas and her American professor, who were disagreeing about Cnossus.

'In the morning,' said Jonathan Bradley with finality, to Deborah, 'all pigs and babies notwithstanding, you're coming out with me to see Iffley Church. It's the place I always wanted to be married in. It's the duck-bills do it, I think.'

Deborah laughed, said good night all round, and went out to ascend the dark stone staircase. She found her candle firmly confiscated by Jonathan, who escorted her to her door, and remarked, as he gave the candle back to her: 'You're nervous, aren't you? You'll hear lots of noises in this house. They don't mean anything. Be sure to bring a hat in the morning. I know the cleaner at Iffley. I should like to kiss you good night, but I suppose you wouldn't like it.'

She did go with him to Iffley in the morning, and by the following Monday night was in the vortex of the most idiotic, exasperating, wholly unsatisfactory love affair that could be imagined. At least, she found it satisfactory up to, but not including, the Monday night. It became serious then, and she no longer knew what to make of it, of herself, or of Jonathan.

Miss Topas enjoyed herself hugely. She and the American professor spent most of their time in the house, seated at Mrs Ditch's enormous kitchen table, on which they spread maps and plans, sheets of cartridge paper purchased in Oxford, coloured pencils, rulers, dividers and books, books and more books. Thus equipped, they spated forth volumes of learned argument which caused Our Walt, Mrs Ditch's son, to observe: 'I say, young Our Mam, do ee thenk their brains, like, ull stand et? Tes like so much wetch-craft to I.'

His mother agreed, brooded darkly awhile, and then said: 'They do be getten on very noice, though; very noice endeed. But I do wesh I could do sommat to gev t'other uns a lettle bet of a shove up. Made for each other, they be. But the Mess Young-I-say, her hangs back. Shy, I reckon, poor maid. Mester Jonathan ded ought to make a bold bed there, and breng her to et violent. Tes the only way. Her'd gev en, easy enough, ef he act forceful.'

*

When she had arranged for the students' lunch, Mrs Bradley walked across the grounds to speak to George, who had been given temporary quarters at the Chief Engineer's house, where he found congenial company, lavish and well-cooked food, and a boy of twelve whose idol he had become during the first week of his stay.

'George,' said Mrs Bradley, 'would you have any objection to taking parties of students out during the week-end?'

'Certainly not, madam,' replied George respectfully.

'Not on Sunday, or on Saturday afternoon, of course.'

'I shall be pleased to take the young ladies out *any* day,

madam. The car could do with a run. I haven't driven her for weeks, except to bring up the young convalescent lady from the station.'

'Ah, yes. Miss Vincent,' said Mrs Bradley. This unfortunate student had been rushed to hospital on the fourth day of term to be operated on for appendicitis. She had been three weeks in hospital, a couple more in the College sanatorium and, to release the nursing sister for a short break, she was to be shipped over to Athelstan for a long week-end. She was to be brought along the communal passage from one extreme end of the building almost to the other in the wheeled carriage, and then the nurse was to go off duty until Tuesday afternoon. This arrangement had been made possible, said the Principal, because Mrs Bradley was a doctor, and had kindly offered to remain at Athelstan for the week-end.

Mrs Bradley herself had been more than a little perturbed when the Principal suggested this arrangement, but she saw no graceful way of objecting, and so had announced her pleasure at the prospect.

Twenty-one students lunched in Athelstan, the twenty-first of them, the sufferer, being served in her room. Mrs Bradley had given her a bed in the Guest Room, which was on the ground floor between the Servery and the Junior or North Common Room. The Sub-Warden's sitting-room was directly opposite, and Mrs Bradley felt that no objection would be lodged by Deborah if she herself used it as a bedroom whilst she had the convalescent student under her care. Miss Vincent could stand, and was allowed to walk a little, but even the one flight of stairs from the basement up to the room which had been prepared for her was quite as much as she seemed able to tackle. The Guest Room, too, was larger and more pleasant than a study-bedroom. The convalescent Miss Vincent seemed very pleased with it.

The twenty students, who comprised First-Years, Second-Years, Third-Years and One-Years, made themselves into groups to go out in the car. Sometimes they gave George the route, sometimes he worked out an interesting drive for them. Those who did not go out in the car spent Friday afternoon at the pictures or in walking over the moors. By about half-past six most of them were back in Hall, and some had taken their own gramophone records over to the Demonstration Room – for the College building was open to students until seven – and were dancing in the space cleared of desks.

At seven came dinner. Mrs Bradley, on this first evening, elected to dine in Hall, and had asked the Third-Year and One-Year students from Columba to sit at her table. Judging by the laughter which came from the group throughout the meal, the students enjoyed themselves, and there was slight consternation, followed by general approval, when, with the pudding, a very sweet white wine was brought in by the maids and served in what one excited student diagnosed as 'real wine-glasses.'

Lights-Out was translated broadly by the Warden-in-Charge during half-term week-ends, but by midnight the house seemed comparatively silent. One or two quiet flittings from room to room were still going on, but noise had ceased and most of the guests were asleep.

Mrs Bradley stayed up until one, occupying herself with Hall accounts, and when she was ready for bed she had a last look at her patient. The girl, a fragile-looking child of nineteen with a long golden plait of very pretty hair, her eyes deeply shadowed, lay asleep, one hand out on the pink counterpane, the other beneath her cheek. The night was chilly, the room unheated except for one small radiator. Mrs Bradley put out a yellow claw and gently placed the arm under the bed-coverings. Beneath that experienced touch the girl did not even stir.

Mrs Bradley went out quietly again, carrying the electric lamp she had brought in with her and crossed the passage into Deborah's sitting-room. She left the door ajar when she went to bed. In about ten minutes she was asleep.

She slept lightly but soundly until about seven o'clock. She always woke at approximately the same time each morning. She got up immediately, put on her dressing-gown, and went across to look at the convalescent student in the Guest Room. The girl had altered her position, and was now lying on her left instead of on her right side. Her arm was again flung outside the bedclothes. But Mrs Bradley's black eyes gazed with curious intentness upon the plait of golden hair; for this was no longer attached to the small and delicate head it had once adorned. It lay on the pillow, certainly, but it had been cut off close to the nape of the little white neck, and, somehow, had become thus more a thing of horror than of beauty.

Mrs Bradley stood for about three seconds looking upon this scene of devastation. Then she turned about very sharply, but still silently, and went upstairs to the study-bedroom of the head student.

'Miss Mathers, dear child,' she said, waking her. Miss Mathers woke without either surprise or resentment.

'Oh, good morning, Warden,' she said. In place of the genial cackle she anticipated, Mrs Bradley said urgently :

'Who, among these students, is particularly friendly with Miss Vincent, the student who had appendicitis?'

'Oh – er – Miss Smith, from the same Hall, I think, Warden.'

'Miss Smith's number?'

'Number Three.'

'Go and rouse her. Tell her to put on her dressing-gown and report to me on the ground floor immediately. Reassure her. I don't want her descending on me in a state of nerves or peevishness.'

'I see, Warden.'

'I'll tell you all about it later on. Bless you, dear child. Be just as quick as ever you can.'

'Is Miss Vincent worse, Warden?'

'No, not worse. Just in need of an affectionate friend.'

'I understand.'

The admirable girl leapt out of bed, and, pulling her dressing-gown about her as she went, made her way to Miss Smith's room and roused that somewhat lymphatic student from slumber.

'Miss Vincent's taken a funny fit. Nothing serious, the Warden says, but she's got a bit nervy, or something. Will you tazz down to the ground floor? Quicker the better. It's nothing much. Don't worry.'

Miss Smith, a good soul, thrust back counterpane, blankets and sheet, abandoned, without a sigh, the laze in bed she had promised herself that morning (for another student had volunteered to bring up her breakfast) and went down to the ground floor, a trifle flummoxed by the sudden awakening and the summons, but anxious to do what she could.

'Ah, Miss Smith, my dear,' said Mrs Bradley, 'you are fond of Miss Vincent?'

'Oh, yes, we're bosoms,' observed Miss Smith, eagerly extending her chest.

'Right. Well, now, Miss Smith, I don't need to tell you that people under the influence of a single, terrifying idea can sometimes contrive to do extraordinary things. Miss Vincent has had in her mind, poor girl, for some time now, the terrifying idea of an operation – *cutting, cutting, cutting.* The consequence is, that (quite unconsciously, of course), she has cut off, in her sleep (a kind of sleep-walking we should call it), all her beautiful hair. It is a perfectly natural reaction, but, as you can imagine, it will be a very considerable shock to her to find out what she has done. You are well-disposed enough to bear the brunt of that shock for the poor child. Go in to her, and when she wakes up, break the news to her, and comfort her, as I know you certainly can.'

'Oh, Warden!' said the dismayed Miss Smith. 'I shall make a mess of it!'

'No, you won't,' said Mrs Bradley. 'You're fond of her, you see.'

*

'Oh, I do wish I hadn't left you!' said Deborah, on Tuesday evening, when she heard of it. 'I knew I ought not to have gone.'

'You look the better for the change,' said Mrs Bradley, 'and you couldn't have done anything if you'd been here, I'm sure. And Miss Smith managed beautifully, bless her heart! They had a nice little cry together, and then, of all things, Miss Vincent admitted that she'd wanted to have her hair off for years, ever since she was nine, and her parents wouldn't hear of it. So we sent straight away for a hairdresser, who trimmed up the hair, and later on she's going to have it waved, and she's perfectly happy about it, and has written home to break the news. So all has ended very nicely, except for me.'

'How . . . for you?'

'*She didn't cut her own hair, child.*'

'I should have thought it would have been quite a natural thing. I read of a case just like it. The girl had had a serious operation . . .'

'Nonsense, child.'

'No, really.'

'I don't think so. Do you mean the case of Miss E., as the psychologists so enthrallingly put it? Miss E. of Attleborough?'

'I think it was.'

'Well, she cut off her hair *before* the operation. She knew she'd got to have the operation, and it preyed on her mind.'

'Oh, yes, you're right. You mean that Miss Vincent would have got over all the horror . . .'

'Yes. You see, in the case of acute appendicitis the whole thing is over and done with in a few hours. In goes the patient and out comes the appendix, and that's all there is to it, except a certain amount of inconvenience afterwards.'

'Then . . . ?'

'Yes, I'm afraid so. Somebody is determined to make my stay at Athelstan as uncomfortable as possible.'

'Miss Murchan's disappearance . . . ?'

'I imagine so. It should not be difficult to put one's finger on the mischief-maker.'

'You don't mean that you know who is at the bottom of all this business?' asked Deborah.

'Well, child, let us ask ourselves a few questions. Ah, here is Lulu with the coffee.'

The negro maid, her broad face beaming, put down the tray and began to pour.

'Hullo, Lulu,' said Deborah. 'Had a good holiday?'

'Yes, Miss Cloud. Ah nebber work so hard in *ma* life! C'lectin' up dem coconuts Ephraim knock down, until he was warned off three shies, and nobody else wouldn't let him have no balls because dey'd had word from de udders dat he was a one ball one coconut man.'

She went out, beaming proudly. Deborah turned to Mrs Bradley for enlightenment. Mrs Bradley grinned.

'I have become Lulu's confidante,' she observed. 'She has a young man named Ephraim Duke, a mulatto. He can hit anything he throws at, up to a distance of thirty yards, twenty times out of twenty. I told Lulu I had a passion for coconuts.'

'You haven't!'

'Actually, in the sense you mean, no. Well, she brought back two suitcases full. I told her to take a taxi to the station at the other end, and George went to meet her with my car at this end. Very good of Ephraim, wasn't it?'

Deborah looked at her suspiciously, but Mrs Bradley's face told her nothing at all.

'I suppose it makes sense somewhere,' she admitted. 'But what were you saying when Lulu came in? Do you mean you've decided which student it was who gave the wrong name when you collared her out of that circle of young men who were dancing round the bonfire on the first night of term?'

'No, child. But I can find her when I want her. She's in Columba, I should say, on present evidence.'

'How do you know?'

'I deduced it. You see, she can't be on the Staff, unless she is Miss Topas. She can't be Miss Topas – or can she?'

'How do you mean?'

'Has Miss Topas an alibi for the night of last Saturday, child?'

'Well, she was talking to your nephew, his wife and myself up to midnight. Does that give her an alibi?'

'Yes, child. It must be quite two hundred miles from my nephew's pig-farm to this equally remote spot. Yes, I think we may say *Pass, Miss Topas; all's well.*'

'But you have never thought Miss Topas had anything to do with all these ridiculous goings-on, have you?'

'No, child; but it is as well to eliminate our friends as soon as we can.'

She grinned again.

'Besides,' said Deborah hotly, 'Miss Topas wouldn't go about cutting off people's hair.'

'Miss Topas is very intelligent,' said Mrs Bradley, 'and if it was thought that there was someone sneaking about Athelstan at night cutting off people's hair, there would be immediate panic. In fact, among girls of the age of these students I cannot think of anything more likely to cause disquiet, except . . .'

'Yes?'

'Have you ever seen a ghost?' asked Mrs Bradley.

'No, and I don't believe in them.'

'Lulu does.'

'I suppose so, yes. Negroes always do, even if they don't admit it.'

'She does admit it. I asked her.'

'Wasn't that – you know best, of course, but I should hardly have thought – wouldn't she immediately fancy she could sense a ghost in this Hall?'

'Yes.'

'I'm sorry, but I don't see the point.'

'Perhaps there isn't one, but I shouldn't be surprised – and you mustn't be, either, because I should need your help – if Athelstan produced a ghost before the end of the term. That is why Lulu is exchanging with my sister's Cambridgeshire kitchen-maid next week. I shall miss her, but that can't be helped. I don't want a hysteria-patient on my hands when the spirits walk or – much more likely – talk. How did you like my nephew Jonathan?'

'I – he – he's rather clever, isn't he?' stammered Deborah, who had been anticipating and dreading this question. 'But, really, I hardly saw enough of him to know much about him.'

'Would you call him clever? He's inclined to be impulsive, rarely a sign of the highest mentality,' argued Mrs Bradley, eyeing Deborah solemnly. Deborah got up.

'I hope you're wrong about the ghost,' she said, walking away. She did not reappear after dinner, but sat correcting a set of lecture notes and verifying references until about eleven. Then she went to bed without seeing Mrs Bradley again; for on the Monday evening, finding her alone, Jonathan had proposed marriage again, and Deborah had refused him. The trouble was that she had so much wanted to accept the offer, but it seemed to her ridiculous to agree to marry a man she had known for exactly four days.

She had told no one about it, not even Miss Topas. She thought that perhaps she might have confided in Mrs Bradley, but the fact that Jonathan was Mrs Bradley's nephew made such a confidence, to Deborah's way of thinking, impossible. However, College would soon fill her mind again, she concluded, particularly if Mrs Bradley was right, and the Athelstan Horrors were merely in their infancy.

She went over them mentally, whilst her pillow seemed to get more and more like something made out of wood. Taken separately, there was nothing very terrifying about them. Of course, things like the coat-slashing and the stabbing of the tins of disinfectant could have, as everyone had pointed out at the time, an unpleasant connotation, and if Mrs Bradley should be right about the hair-cutting, there was, somewhere loose, a devilish agency which it was not very pretty to brood on.

She continued to brood, however, and, when she slept, met Jonathan's dark face in her dreams.

CHAPTER 8

SKIRLING AND GROANS

THE term went on for a week or two without incident except for what could be accounted for by the normal course of events. Deborah, who was now enjoying her life at Cartaret, began to wonder whether, after all, everything which had occurred at Athelstan since the evening of her arrival at the College had not been magnified, or even falsified, into bearing an interpretation which it did not warrant or deserve.

She argued that Mrs Bradley's views on some subjects probably were determined – 'warped' was the word she first used – by her professional training as a psycho-analyst and by her past experiences as a criminologist.

This point she put to Miss Topas. It was the Monday of the week before School Practice, and Miss Topas, having done nothing all day except give one lecture and a couple of Demonstration lessons in English history, had spent the afternoon in Columba with her shoes off, her feet up, chain-smoking, and debating within herself (she told Deborah, who had been bidden to afternoon tea) which of two invitations she should accept for Christmas.

Deborah knelt on the hearthrug, removed ash from the fire, and began to toast the scones which were lying in a bag, a plate beside them, on the hearth.

'Debating within oneself is an unprofitable pastime,' she pronounced seriously. Miss Topas took her feet down and put slippers on them, hitched her chair closer to the fire, flung away the stub of her cigarette and observed:

'We are all attention. Unveil your past. Is the choice to be made between Tom and Dick, or is it complicated by the introduction of Harry?'

'You're as bad as the students,' said Deborah. 'That's the only way their minds work.'

'Rebuke noted and digested. Go on. Tell me all. By the way, how are the Athelstan Horrors?'

'That's the point. We've had nothing since that hair-cutting business at Half-Term, and, you know, Cathleen, I still think Miss Vincent did that herself. You know what a light sleeper Mrs Bradley is.'

'Is she?'

'Yes, and she was sleeping in my sitting-room opposite the Guest Room where this girl lay, and yet she didn't hear a sound.'

'That does seem odd if she really is a light sleeper, unless the person climbed in through an open window, or knew the house very, very well. Even then ... is Mrs Bradley certain Miss Vincent didn't do it herself?'

'She seemed perfectly certain, I thought, but these people get bees in their bonnets. Then, take the first affair – would you like to butter these as I do them? – that stupid rag. We didn't find the student she dragged out of the circle, but it doesn't seem to me that it's necessarily the same girl each time. Of course, she did say herself that two different people were at work.'

'I agree. Piling up the jerries and getting some young men to do a war-dance round them doesn't tally with cutting off a sick person's hair with the possible intention of frightening her into a fit. I think I'm with you both so far. Of course, we must remember that Mrs Bradley thinks there is a scheme to make Athelstan too hot to hold her, and, if that is the case, then the thing does hang together. But go on. And you might blacken one or two of those scones a bit more for me. I'm rather partial to charcoal.' .

'Well, how would you account for the snakes in that Demonstration lesson Miss Harbottle gave? Granted that they were intended to upset me and not her, I can't see in that affair anything more than another rather stupid and malicious rag. Can you?'

'Well, there, don't you see,' said Miss Topas. 'I say, you've done enough, I should think. Come on. Let's eat 'em while they're hot. Can't understand people who don't take sugar. If I don't get my three lumps per cup I become depressed – I was saying that that's where Mrs Bradley scores, it seems to me. Stupid and malicious. Doesn't fit students' ragging, you know. I was at a big mixed Training College before I came here, but it was just the same. The men, particularly, ragged a good deal, but it was seldom stupid, and as for malicious – not a bit. As a matter of fact, girls, particularly, don't like to hurt one's feelings. And the misses like you quite a lot, you know. They wouldn't want – but don't let me interrupt you. Proceed with the evidence.'

'Well, those tins of disinfectant. Wasn't that malicious?'

'Yes. Makes the argument even more sound. It simply *was* malicious, unless it was something Much Worse. You've read some morbid psychology, I suppose?'

'Yes, of course. But isn't it a boy's or a man's trick – that stabbing business?'

'Yes, it is. Connects up with Jack the Ripper, of course. You could connect the hair-cutting in the same way, you know, and that coat-slashing, too.'

'You don't think it could have been a *man* that Mrs Bradley pulled out of that dancing lot on the first night, when she said it was a girl? The rest were men, you know.'

'No, I don't. Besides, the voice. Although possibly that could be faked. But I should imagine that it was a woman all right. Mrs Bradley wouldn't make that kind of mistake. I shouldn't myself. The queer thing is – where did the wretched person get to?'

'This Hall,' said Deborah, laughing. 'At least, Mrs Bradley says so.'

'Does she, by Jove!' Miss Topas put a buttered finger on the bell. 'Elsie,' she said to the maid, 'bring me the Hall list from the Senior Common-Room notice-board. I'll brood over the question,' she went on, when the maid had gone, 'and get out a selection of felons for Mrs Bradley to choose from. Of course, in a Hall like this, where all the students are well over the average age and so forth, an ill-disposed person could hide under the spotted, unless she was unlucky enough to run into somebody who already knew her.'

'Yes, I can see what you mean. As a One-Year anybody could

take up residence here. Do let me know what conclusions you come to.'

'Not a word to the Warden, then. She'd have a fit if she thought I was snooping into the antecedents of the students here, poor wretches. Imagine having spent a blameless and patriotic existence as an Uncertificated Teacher for ten or fifteen years, and then being hounded by the authorities into getting your Certificate, complete with College training, in twelve miserable, uncomfortable, fish-out-of-water months! Because, they *are* fish out of water, many of the poor wretches here – except the Third-Years, of course. *They're* bred and born in the briar patch, but t'others hate every minute of it, and those who live near enough to go home leave us most week-ends, even if it means going back to digs and the motherly bosoms of their landladies. My heart bleeds for them. It does, really.'

Deborah giggled unfeelingly at this soulful picture, and then licked butter off her thumb.

'By the way,' she said, 'I've been notified that I'll have to do School Practice supervising. What exactly does that entail?'

'Fancy reminding me of what exactly it entails!' said Miss Topas with a hollow-sounding groan, 'but, if you must know, I'll tell you. Bend closer.'

' "Come on my right side, for this ear is deaf," ' said Deborah. 'Shades of Laura Menzies,' she added apologetically.

'And before I tell you about School Prac. I would say one word of warning,' Miss Topas continued. 'Your Mrs Bradley has a nice choice in words. She didn't say *girl*. She said *woman*. Therefore, presumably, she *meant* woman.'

'Yes. Well, your students here –'

'All right. Let it go, please. Now, then: School Practice ...'

She leaned forward and poured into Deborah's terrified but receptive mind the hateful and exacting nature of the task which would confront her during the ensuing weeks.

'And don't forget,' she added earnestly, 'that you are not responsible for keeping order. If you go into the classroom of a student who's obviously got the class completely round her neck, you take care it stays there. Don't help her. I recollect the case of a lecturer at my old shop who went into a Craft lesson –

she was a geographer, by the way, and ought to have known better than to interfere in a mystery which was outside her scope, but some of these people are apt to be conceited – and found the usual howling mob and an unfortunate student trying to give out scissors. Not only did she end up by bringing the headmistress into the room to quell the disturbance, but it was discovered that one child had cut two other children's frock's, that two others had cut each other's hair, and that another had been sick after eating most of the paste prepared for the lesson.'

'Golly!' said Deborah, laughing. Miss Topas wagged her head.

'I'm speaking for your own good,' she admonished her. 'Never rush in where angels fear to tread. And never let yourself in for critting a P.T. lesson. You'll probably have to watch one or two, but that doesn't matter. Step stately out of it, and leave it to Pettinsalt or Betsy. They can't bear having the uninitiated initialling their students' notebooks.'

'Really?'

'Really. Always something a bit inverted about these P.T. wallahs. I don't know why it is, but they always get it up the nose, with a few exceptions I could quote you. There's something horribly unnatural about physical training. Too much muscle warps the intelligence, I expect.'

As though this were her last word, she consumed the last piece of toast at a gulp, kicked off her slippers, put her feet up, lay back and closed her eyes. Deborah prodded her suddenly and painfully with the toasting fork.

'Wake up, slacker, and continue your idiotic but, possibly, invaluable remarks,' she said.

'No, no. You tell me why you've turned down your young man,' said Miss Topas firmly.

*

The ghost of Athelstan commenced operations on the following Friday night – a well-chosen time, Mrs Bradley was compelled to admit, taking into consideration both day and hour.

It had been an exasperating Friday. Deborah had had a very full time-table, and to add to it and to her troubles, she had been compelled to deputize at six-thirty for the Senior English lecturer, who had contracted another of what Deborah called, unjustly, to Miss Topas, one of her 'useful colds.'

This lecture, which was the third and last of a series on *King Lear*, lasted until twenty-past seven, and left Deborah exactly ten minutes in which to get back to Athelstan, wash, change and arrive in the dining-room. She was, of course, late. Mrs Bradley looked sympathetic and ordered her to avoid the cottage pie and to concentrate on soup and fish. Deborah, determined to be contrary, asked for cottage pie, did not care for it, left more than half, and got up from table hungry and irritable.

At half past nine she went to bed; not because she wanted to, but because there was no alternative except to sit up and correct English essays, which she was determined not to do.

She went to sleep remarkably quickly, and was awakened by the ghost at precisely two-fifteen in the morning.

She did not realize, at first, what sound it was that she had heard. All she knew was that she had been dreaming about pigs, and that one must have been killed. She started up, sweating with the horrible heaviness of nightmare, and, to her extreme horror, heard the sound again. To her credit, terrified though she was, she leapt out of bed, switched on the light, and, opening the door, called out: 'What's the matter? What's going on?'

Mrs Bradley's voice replied in comforting accents, and the head of the house appeared, electric torch in hand, just as more than half the students came crowding on to the landings, asking, as they huddled together, what was the matter, what had happened, who was it, and making other and similar useless and irritating inquiries. Even as they were asking the questions, the horrible sounds came again.

'Disconcerting,' remarked Mrs Bradley. At this inadequate comment Deborah began to protest, but her observations were terminated by a banshee wail which put all the previous disturbances in the shade. Deborah unashamedly clutched Mrs Bradley's dragon-strewn dressing-gown, and there were excited and frightened exclamations from the students.

Mrs Bradley, alone among those present, seemed entirely unimpressed by the manifestations.

'Put on coats or dressing-gowns, and come down to the Common Room,' she said. 'If there are any students still asleep, please wake them and bring them with you.'

There was some laughter at this, and the students came trooping down. Mrs Bradley called the House Roll when the assembly was complete, found that there were no absentees from the muster, and then gave instructions that no one was to go out of the room on any pretext until she herself had returned and granted permission.

Deborah followed her to the door, but Mrs Bradley whispered to her that one of them had better remain in the Common Room. Leaving Deborah, she descended alone to the basement. Outside the servants' rooms she stood and called the maids by name.

'We're all here, madam,' said the cook, opening one of the doors and appearing in curlers in the doorway. 'The girls didn't like the sounds, so we all collected ourselves in here. Did you wish to speak to anyone, madam?'

Her tone was not definitely impudent, but it was not, on the other hand, that of the trusty domestic, whether alarmed or otherwise. Mrs Bradley was interested.

'I should like to speak to you alone, Cook,' she said loudly, knowing that Cook was rather deaf. 'Come out here, please. Shut the door. Now, are the maids alarmed?'

'We was all frightened out of our seven senses.'

'Where did the noise seem to come from?'

'Right outside these very doors. You'll get my notice in the morning. I'm not stopping on in an 'aunted 'ouse. There was none of these goings-on when poor Miss Murchan was here.'

*

Nothing more was heard of the ghost that night. By the following midday, however, the story was all over College, and 'the ghost of Athelstan' was freely discussed. Various explanations were offered by students from the other Halls, but each, as it was presented to the Athelstan students, was rejected by them as being out of conformation with the facts.

'You ought to have heard it! I thought I should have fainted!' was the burden of the Athelstan chorus. The talk during the daylight hours was amused, speculative and ribald, but when dinner was over in Hall and the sun was beginning to set, there was a marked disinclination among the students to go about the house, or to remain alone in study-bedrooms. The group which assembled in Miss Mathers' room was typical of others on both floors. It consisted of the senior student herself, two or three of her year, three First-Years, and even the ostracized Miss Giggs, the mild Miss Morris and the ticket-of-leave Miss Cartwright.

'What do you think the Warden will do if it happens again?' asked Miss Morris.

'I can tell you one thing she's done already. Sacked Cook,' volunteered Miss Cartwright. Like a great many of the more adventurous spirits, she was extremely popular in the servants' hall, and so was in receipt of this bit of, so far, exclusive information.

'Sacked Cook? But who cooked dinner?' demanded Miss Morris.

'The ghost,' Miss Cartwright answered frivolously. 'No, as a matter of fact, Mrs Croc. has promoted Bella. She "knows the apparatus," as Mrs Croc. puts it.'

'She made a very good job of the dinner,' said Miss Mathers critically. 'And now, if it's all the same, I've got to get out some notes of lessons for next week.'

The guests departed unwillingly, keeping close together. Miss Giggs came back.

'I wish you'd let me sit in here until supper,' she said abruptly. Miss Mathers got out her notebooks and then looked up.

'All right,' she said. 'To be perfectly truthful, I'm not over and above anxious to be left alone, any more than you are.'

'What do *you* think it was?' asked Miss Giggs, lowering her voice and speaking hoarsely.

'An owl caught up in one of the chimneys, or something of that sort, I fancy.'

'Has the Warden said anything more?'

'No, but I happen to know she thinks it was some of the Wattsdown men playing the fool. I heard her telling Miss Cloud so.'

'What did Miss Cloud say?'

'Oh, I think she agreed.'

'It would be a good thing if it could be proved, though, wouldn't it? Did she think Cook was bribed to open the door or something?'

'Yes. Cook was rude to her this morning.'

'I shouldn't have thought anyone would dare.'

'Yes. She told Mrs Bradley that there had been none of these disturbances until Miss Murchan's illness.'

'Where is Miss Murchan? Is she at her own home?'

'I think she must be, but she is forbidden to have letters, Mrs Bradley said, so it isn't any use our writing, and Mrs Bradley won't give the address.'

In the study-bedroom apportioned to Kitty, the Three Musketeers were seated on the bed.

'So you can't take it, young Alice?' said Kitty. 'And, to tell you the truth, Dog,' she added, before Alice could reply to this derogatory estimate of her powers of endurance, 'I don't blame her. Where's the sense, anyway, of losing our beauty sleep? Suppose it *is* some of those silly goops from Wattsdown playing the fool, ten to one they won't risk it again tonight, or ever any more, come to that. They might not get away with it another time.'

'I didn't sleep a wink last night,' said Alice.

'Don't see how you could, with three of us trying to share your bed,' said Laura. 'So don't make that an excuse. Now I've got my hockey stick, you've got a cricket-stump each, and if we can't manage, between us, to knock any ghost for six, I shall be surprised.'

'Don't you believe in ghosts, Laura?' Alice inquired. Laura grinned.

'I don't, but my Highland blood believes with its every drop,' she confessed. 'Nevertheless, reason still holds sway.'

'Yes, until it gets round about midnight,' said Kitty pointedly. 'What I say is, I'm going to bed and to sleep, and you'll see there'll be no disturbance.'

She proved to be perfectly right, and by the following Sunday night the fears engendered by the ghost had given place to the less nebulous and more reasonable fears of School Practice.

Unlike some training colleges, Cartaret believed in getting School Practice over for all the students at the same time of year so far as this was possible, and for the last fortnight of the Christmas Term each student was assigned to a school.

Laura and Alice had been assigned to an establishment named immediately by the former the Village Institute.

It was an old-fashioned Church School, consisting of one main building with an annexe. The main building had been divided into classrooms by the expedient of putting partitions, mostly of glass, at intervals across the width. Thus the original three east and two west windows still lighted the whole of the building. The annexe consisted of a brick-built classroom and a cloakroom. Physical training, when the weather was too bad for it to be taken out of doors, took place in the Church Hall, on the opposite side of the playground.

Kitty's lot was both more and less enviable. She had been assigned to the Council School from which children were brought to College for the Demonstration lessons. What she gained upon the roundabouts was lost upon the swings, for the Church School came under the heading, in Supervisors' notebooks, of Special Difficulty, whereas the Dem. School, as the students called it, was given a mark of Alpha, and those unfortunates who were allotted to it for School Practice were expected, in the words of Miss Cartwright, to make good or bust. She herself had busted, she told an apprehensive and interested audience, on the Sunday night before The Terror (Laura's name for School Practice) began.

When Monday dawned, students in various degrees of anxiety and nervousness arose (many of them before the rising bell had rung in the various Halls) and began to put ready the impedimenta (Laura's carefully-chosen collective noun, much appreciated by Mrs Bradley when she heard it) for the day.

Of the Three Musketeers, Alice was the most nervous, Kitty the most ill-prepared. The latter set out at a quarter-past eight armed with her School Practice notebook, her time-table, a roll of large-scale paintings of various kinds of embroidery stitches, a stuffed fox (borrowed from the gardener's drawing-room for a Nature lesson) and a twig of poplar. This last was in case the fox gave out on her half-way, she confided to the grinning Laura and the apprehensive Alice. She knew she couldn't keep a lesson going for three-quarters of an hour, she concluded.

'Old Kitty will break her own record if she keeps it going ten minutes,' said Laura philosophically, as she and Alice walked to the bus stop, half a mile down the moorland road. In this estimate of Kitty's powers of entertainment she did her friend grievous wrong, however, for Kitty's first lesson, delivered with that aplomb and explosive energy which only the last stage of desperate fright can produce, went particularly well.

'And just my luck,' said Kitty, detailing the pleasures of the day when she encountered the others before tea, 'not a Supervisor on the horizon. I bet I fluff next time, and someone is sure to walk in.'

'We had the Deb.,' said Alice, smiling happily. 'She just walked into my Arithmetic lesson and said: "Cheer up, Miss Boorman. I'm twice as frightened as you are." And then she marked me – look!'

A red star, mark of extreme approbation, blazed, albeit smudgily (for Alice had wept over it in secret joy during the major part of the dinner hour), on the front page of Alice's notes.

'She told me off,' said Laura. 'Reminded me the teacher is the stage-manager, not the chief actor. Devastating, I call it. Besides, she's a perfectly rotten teacher herself.'

Her friends giggled unfeelingly, and neither they nor the recipient of Deborah's uncharitable advice allowed it to interfere in the slightest with their tea.

Between tea and dinner there were no lectures during School Practice. Some of the students commenced their preparation for the next day's work; Alice was one of them. Laura took Kitty apart, and they walked up and down the gravel path between Athelstan and Beowulf deep in conversation.

'But I'd be scared stiff, Dog,' Kitty protested, at the end of ten minutes' earnest monologue by Laura. 'Besides, there's Alice. We can't leave her on her own. And then, I've got P.T. tomorrow. I must swot a beastly drill table. What comes after Group Four?'

'Lateral,' Laura replied. 'But you'd better mug it up, in case I'm wrong. And don't let 'em do Forward Punching. They only edge up and hit one another in the back.'

'We've got a whale of a P.T. specialist in our school,' continued

Kitty. 'One of those hags from Rule Britannia's. She must be at least thirty, but she's marvellous. Name of Cornflake. I suppose she's Uncertif. and has come for a year to get the doings.'

'Name of what?'

'Cornflake.'

'Rot.'

'But I've seen it written down.'

'Then it can't be pronounced as it's written. You couldn't be called Cornflake.'

'I don't see why not. Look at *your* name.'

'Less about my name. I'd have you know, you wretched Anglo-Saxon, that the Clan Menzies was out in the Forty-Five, and on the right side, too!'

'I'm not a wretched Anglo-Saxon,' said Kitty, wounded. 'The Trevelyans are a very old Cornish family, as anybody but a half-wit would know.'

'All the more reason why you should live up to your family traditions and assist me in my ghost-hunt. Don't tell me a Tre-velyan ever turned his back and neglected to march breast-for-ward.'

'Oh, all right, but I shall be a rag tomorrow, I warn you. And I *have* got this wretched P.T.'

'All right, don't fret, then. I'll hunt alone.'

'No, you won't. But I think we shall have to tell Alice.'

'I have other plans for that jolly old nurse of ninety years. She's got to check up on the personnel of the students, to make certain it's nobody in Athelstan playing silly tricks.'

'We know it isn't. Mrs Croc. called the roll.'

'Like hell she did! After giving plenty of time for everybody to assemble in the Common Room, no matter where they'd been. I know for a fact that Cartwright was having a surreptitious bath in the maids' bathroom below stairs when the siren sounded.'

'Was she?'

'Of course she was. She said that from where she was it sounded like seventy devils whistling the "Soldiers' Chorus".'

'Was she scared?'

'Not a bit. Said she thought some fool was pulling a stunt. She just wrapped herself in her bathgown and toddled upstairs, prepared with explanations if asked for; which they weren't. Now do you see what I mean?'

'What did she have on her feet?'

'I don't know. What's it matter?'

'Mrs Croc. is a detective, don't forget.'

'I'm not forgetting. Even Sherlock Holmes could slip up. She probably wore her rubber shoes, and put them out on the window-ledge to dry. That's what I should have done.'

'I don't believe you could get away with it without Mrs Croc. knowing, all the same. What's the odds she knew all about Cartwright and her bath, anyway? Maybe she even gave her time to get to the Common Room in time for Roll-Call. Think *that* out.'

'I have. Ad delirium tremens. So what?'

'Well, she knows it was nothing to do with Cartwright, and she wasn't going to let her get mixed up in any subsequent inquiry.'

'Golly,' said Laura, respectfully. 'Your own idea?'

'You're not the only person who can add up two and two,' said Kitty, with the sunny good temper which characterized her. 'Anyway, if she was wise to Cartright she'll be wise to us if we go poking about down there. That's my point.'

'And, granted your premises, not a bad one,' said Laura thoughtfully. 'Look here, then, I'll tell you what we'll do. We'll give the ghost another chance, and if we hear that whistling row again we'll go into action, young Alice and all. She's game, all right, although her teeth are apt to chatter. How does that strike you?'

'Alice wouldn't tackle a ghost.'

'Ghost your old goloshes. Have you seen young Alice play netball? If she can't jump on a ghost from behind and bite pieces out of its neck, I'm a cow's grandmother.'

'That's still in the future,' said Kitty, with happy inspiration.

*

On the following morning, Tuesday, Miss Topas put on her coat and turned the collar up. Then she checked the contents of her attaché-case, added an extra fountain-pen, glanced regretfully at the neat files of her lecture notes on their shelves in the warm, cheerful room, and then looked out of the window.

Students in groups were walking across the grounds. There was a thick autumn mist which might turn to fine weather later in the day, or might, Miss Topas gloomily concluded, turn to rain. At any rate, she did not want to go out into it.

Her assignments for that morning were to supervise three history lessons; one by Miss Holt, a brilliant student in the Second-Year, a resident of Bede Hall; the second by Miss Pinkley, a doubtful stayer, also in her second year, and the third by a First-Year student from Athelstan, Miss Priest.

Sandwiched between the second and third of these lessons came a physical training lesson by – for Kitty had read and pronounced the name aright – Miss Cornflake, a One-Year student from her own Hall, Columba.

Like many of the lecturers, Miss Topas, as she had already indicated to Deborah, objected strongly to supervising lessons in physical training. She knew nothing about the subject, she protested – nothing at all.

'You used to play hockey for the County,' said Miss Rosewell.

'And since when has hockey-playing become a qualification for judging neck rest and arms upward stretch?' Miss Topas demanded. Gently supplied with a copy of the Board's syllabus, she refused to look at it.

'If she keeps the little brutes on the move and cuts out Country Dancing she'll be all right, so far as I'm concerned,' she said.

'If the students can take P.T. they can take anything,' said the drawling voice of Miss Pettinsalt, throwing in a bone of contention at which she knew all the Common Room would snap.

Miss Topas, picking up her traps preparatory to departure into the misty morning, went over points in the debate that had followed. Deborah, she remembered, had made one contribution only.

'I never know why, with some of these students, the children don't break their necks,' Deborah had observed.

'They probably do,' Miss Topas herself had answered, 'but it isn't found out until later.'

She left her door open for Carrie to clear away breakfast, and descended the front steps of Columba to cross the grounds in the direction of the garages. The school she was bound for was two and a half miles from College, and it was her practice to pick up two or three of the students in her car, for, although there was a bus service, it was infrequent, and those who caught the bus arrived either much too early or (as was already becoming the rule by which Kitty conducted her life during this trying period) slightly late. The headmistress had remonstrated with her on the point, but Kitty had remained firm.

'I suffer from asthmatic wheezing,' she explained, 'and the school is too cold for me at twenty-past eight. By five-past nine it is much safer.'

'I don't know how you dare be late on School Prac.,' Alice had remonstrated.

'Well, the sooner I'm chucked out, the sooner I can begin hair-dressing,' argued Kitty. With the cussedness usually displayed by Fate, however, she was not chucked out, but was permitted, instead, to continue in her outrageous line of conduct.

Miss Topas, who, beneath a flippant attitude, concealed a strong sense of duty and responsibility, was always at the school of her assignment in very good time. Sometimes she talked to the headmistress; sometimes she asked permission to see the 'stock list' of history textbooks in use at the school; sometimes she inspected such things as the surface of the playground and, from the outside, the homes of the children.

On this particular morning, however, she did none of these things, because she was held up by the police, and was forced to make a long detour to reach her destination. Her usual road ran south-east from the College, downhill and through the woods, until it met a major road at which Miss Topas turned almost due west for a hundred yards or so, and then south-west until the road crossed the canal. Once across, another hundred yards brought her to another main road, and this, turning north-east, ran alongside the river from which the canal had been cut.

It was as she was driving, at a respectable twenty-eight miles an hour, along this pleasant bit of riverside road, that Miss Topas was held up.

She prepared to show her driving licence, but the sergeant merely said politely : 'Afraid you'll have a good way to back, miss. Nobody allowed this way this morning.'

'Oh, something wrong with the road?'

'Be all right by lunch-time, miss. I should sound your horn as you go. The mist's a bit tricky along here.'

It was very thick alongside the river. Not more than a couple of yards of the silvery water could be seen from the edge of the bank. The haze of mist hung over the rest like teased wool. There was twenty yards' visibility on the road. Miss Topas put the car in reverse, and, thankful that she had come, comparatively speaking, so short a distance off the main thoroughfare, backed carefully, sounding her horn.

It seemed as though, on such a morning, most of the students had preferred to take the bus rather than to walk, for she passed nobody going her way, and arrived at the school at twenty-five to ten, for the first lesson, that to be given by Miss Holt.

She allowed Miss Holt five minutes to get going, and then went in. Good notes, good illustrations, pleasant voice, attentive class – Miss Topas gave a very high mark, wrote a couple of lines of criticism, stayed in for the next quarter of an hour, and then drifted out.

Miss Pinkley, in the crude but apt vernacular of the profession, had got the class round her neck. Miss Topas, who invariably rushed in where she had forbidden Deborah to tread, came a little nearer the front desk and began to 'collect eyes'. The miserable and terrified student so far had not noticed her, but the gradual silencing of her tormentors gave her the clue, and she turned round, blinking nervously.

'Carry on, Miss Pinkley,' said Miss Topas. 'Don't mind me. You're the important person.'

She remained with Miss Pinkley for the next eight minutes, sighed inaudibly, initialled Miss Pinkley's notebook but added no comment, wrote a brief report, and then went into the next classroom. Here was Kitty, initiating such as permitted the process into the mysteries of decimal fractions.

'So you see,' said Kitty, 'all you do – hey, you, in the back row, stop pulling that girl's hair! No, dash it, you weren't doing up her slide. You were pulling her hair; I saw you. Oh, don't argue. You listen to me. Oh, hullo, Miss Topas. Take a seat, won't you ... Now, you perishers – that is children – look here, this is the point. No, *not* the decimal point, haddock! The point of my remarks. In other words, what I'm saying, Oh, all right, if you won't listen, you won't. Sit up, and we'll do some Pence Table. Don't know it? Don't know Pence Table? How does your father make out his betting slips, then? Come on, all of you. Twelve pence are one shilling. Eighteen pence are half a dollar. No, I'm wrong, at that.'

She got the class laughing. Then she rolled her eyes at Miss Topas, and went back to multiplying decimals. Miss Topas gave her an average mark, prayed inaudibly for her soul, and passed out, highly appreciative, but, she feared, wrong-headedly so, of Kitty's capabilities as an instructor.

At half past ten a bell rang to denote that it was time for the mid-morning break. This break lasted for a quarter of an hour. The younger and the more frivolous supervisors (the terms were not necessarily synonymous) divided the Practice Schools into those that made coffee in the morning break and those that did not. Sometimes a school would make afternoon tea instead. One or two schools made hot drinks both morning and afternoon.

Kitty's school happened to have a headmistress who liked coffee and tea, so that there was always a good chance of being invited into the staff-room and of being provided with coffee and even, possibly, a biscuit. The students were not invited in. Miss Topas could see them in the end classroom when she glanced through the glass top of the door.

The headmistress also came into the staff-room for the coffee. She was what Miss Topas, who had her own system of classification for the various professional types, called the White Knight sort of headmistress. She was elderly, kindly, and laid down minute rules and regulations with regard to duties and to the methods of teaching the various subjects, marking the books, punishing misdemeanours, keeping registers and records and dealing with consumable stock, and she always wore a black alpaca apron in school, and was festooned with little ornamental and useful gadgets of all descriptions.

She fussed round Miss Topas who had supervised students at this school once before, and, applying the technique of doing and saying absolutely nothing, Miss Topas contrived to get the fussing over and done with in the minimum of time, got rid of her, and was able to hear a thrilling account of what had been happening down by the river from one of the teachers who had had it from a bus conductor, who had had it from the policeman who lived next door to him.

'A woman found in the river – dead. Murdered, they think, although I don't know how they knew. More likely to be suicide or accident, I should think, in a neighbourhood like this.'

Lively discussion of this view was interrupted by the bell which indicated that the break was at an end. Miss Topas went out into the playground. The school, except for the class which was to have physical training, led into the building. In charge of the class left outside was a lank-haired student in glasses. Her blue serge skirt hung badly, and dipped lower at the back than at the front. She had changed into rubber-soled shoes, but had made no other difference in her dress. She gave Miss Topas a sickly smile, and then took off her glasses and put them on a window ledge. She gave an order to the class and got the children running, then she took off her skirt, displaying well-cut shorts not of the College pattern. Then she gave one of the most interesting and remarkable physical training lessons that Miss Topas ever expected to supervise.

'Why, Miss Cornflake, I had no idea you were such an expert! May I have your notebook, please?'

Miss Cornflake, putting on her skirt, her glasses and then a heavy coat, handed over her notebook.

'Don't star it, whatever you do,' she said. 'It was, actually, rather dud. Didn't you notice . . .'

She proceeded with technicalities until Miss Topas, glancing at her watch, decided that she would never get in to Miss Priest's history lesson. She was feeling slightly irritated with Miss Cornflake. She sat in on Miss Priest's lesson on the Conversion of the English to Christianity and wrote a slightly acid and decidedly unfair report of it. Then she crossed that out and wrote a snappy comment in Miss Priest's own notebook advising her to remember that a class does not consist only of the middle of the front row. Then she crossed that out, too, and gave Miss Priest a better mark than she deserved – or, at least, than the lesson warranted – to compensate herself for her evil feelings.

'I shan't come back this afternoon,' she said, at the end of the morning. 'You can tell the other three.'

'Four, Miss Topas,' said Miss Priest.

'Yes, four,' said Miss Topas.

'I wish I could have you for that wretched Nature lesson to-morrow, instead of Miss Mount,' continued the student, gazing raptly at the mark upon her notebook.

'Well, you can't,' said Miss Topas. 'I don't know a single natural order – except fools,' she added irritably. Miss Priest looked slightly taken aback. 'And you *must* remember that you've got a class of forty, not a class of six. You talk to nobody but the middle of the front row, you know.'

'Oh, do I? Oh, *thanks*, Miss Topas. Now that I remember, I *do* do that, and you're quite right. It's a jolly good tip. Thanks *ever* so !'

'Go and have your lunch,' said Miss Topas, 'and for God's sake don't bolt it.' She went out to her car and raced back to College, determined to suborn Deborah and make her spend the afternoon in the car on the moorland roads.

CHAPTER 9

EVIDENCE OF THE SUBMERGED TENTH

DEBORAH, however, was not available. The police were in possession of Athelstan, for the dead person proved to be the cook whom Mrs Bradley had dismissed. Why she should have been walking by the river-side, either by dark or by daylight, was not yet clear. The police were anxious to get it clear.

Miss Topas, disgruntled, went back to Columba, got out the manuscript of a textbook for schools which she had been threatening (her own word) to finish and publish whilst she was at Cartaret, and, settling down to work, soon became quite cheerful and forgot all about the body, the police, School Practice, Deborah and the afternoon's outing.

Deborah cursed her own decision to return to the College for lunch. If she had had lunch in the town she would have missed the major part of the police proceedings, she decided, for the police cleared off at half past three and did not show up again for the rest of the week. As it was, they insisted upon interviewing her, although she could tell them nothing which seemed to her of the slightest importance. They also interviewed Miss Cartwright, who had to leave her Practice School in the middle of a geography lesson because she was requested, over the telephone, to report at Hall forthwith.

Mrs Bradley's first intimation that the police were in the front passage and were seeking an interview was from the newly-returned Lulu, who had remained two days and one night in her new service, and then had come back by motor-coach, explaining that she 'didn't like dem strange victuals down thar' – a statement which Mrs Bradley could scarcely credit. The following dialogue ensued.

'Well, Lulu, I'm very glad to see you back, and the other maid will be very glad to see her own mistress again.'

'Sho', sho', Mis' Bradley.'

'But, Lulu, I ought to tell you that since you went two things have happened which you won't like at all.'

'Mis' Cloud been run home away from you?'

'No. I'm not as cruel as that!'

'Ah knows dat, Mis' Bradley. Dem gentlemen from Watts-down College done some'un foolish? Just like boys!'

'Well, it might be that. The fact is, Lulu, we have begun to hear peculiar noises at night.'

'Noises?'

'Noises.'

'Lor, Mis' Bradley, what kind ob noises?'

'Ghostly noises. Furthermore, I have had to dismiss Cook.'

'For making noises?'

'No. Just for the ordinary reasons.'

'Sho', sho'. I know. Sass. Dat cook sho' is po' trash!'

'That is correct. Well, now, if you stay, and you hear any noises, you mustn't let them frighten you, that's all.'

'Won't frighten *me*, Mis' Bradley. Ah ain't an ignorant pusson. No, *sir*! Walk under a ladder don't frighten me, break my mirror, see de moon t'rough a window, spill de salt – don't turn a single har!'

'Well, that seems very satisfactory. This noise sounds rather like a lot of whistling. It is very difficult to tell where it comes from.'

'Dat's all right wid me, Mis' Bradley. Ah reckon ain't no ghosts nor devils neither, care to meet *you* face to face!'

With this dubious compliment and a happy chuckle, she went downstairs to release the Cambridge maid and send her up to Mrs Bradley for her fare.

It was at about half past nine that the police arrived at College. They came in by way of the gate near the Chief Engineer's house, and obtained the information they wanted from his wife, who was washing up after breakfast.

They went over to the main College building, and interviewed the secretary. She went in to the Principal.

'The police are outside, Miss du Mugne,' she said. 'There has been an accident – drowning – the river – and they seem to think that the woman is one of the College servants.'

'I'd better see them,' said Miss du Mugne. 'You might go through the rest of these, and you might let Mr Carter know that I can't ask the students to do Play-Centre activities during School Practice.'

'Very well, Miss du Mugne. Will you have the inspector in here?'

'Yes, in here.'

The inspector came straight to the point in a hearty manner which disconcerted Miss du Mugne considerably. She felt that she was being invited to confess all.

'I am Inspector Bingham, of the County Police, madam. We were given information of a body in the river, and we dragged it out this morning at half past eight. I can depend on you to see this goes no further, madam, but it looks like – well, not an accident. I can't go into details, as you will appreciate. Now from letters in a waterproof packet found on the body, it seems that the woman had some connexion with this College. The letters are all addressed to the same party, Mrs Castle, Athelstan Hall, Cartaret College. Would the name convey anything to you?'

'No, but I can have you directed to Athelstan Hall, which is one of the hostels for students, and you can pursue your inquiries there, inspector. It *sounds* like one of the College servants, but each Hall is a self-contained unit, and the servants are the business of the Warden-in-charge.'

'Thank you, madam.' He rose as Miss du Mugne rang the bell.

'Get someone to take the inspector over to Athelstan Hall, Miss Rosewell, please.'

Miss Rosewell, whose neat, adult appearance and sophisticated, finished manner concealed the average share of childish curiosity, took him herself, and adroitly learned the facts which he had just committed to the Principal's guardianship. As all the newspapers would have them in the morning, this signified very little.

The sight of Lulu's black face and happy grin seemed to surprise the inspector, but, reassured by his companion's unperturbed explanation of his business, he took off his hat, and, carefully wiping his boots, followed her into the hall, where both females immediately deserted him, Lulu to find Mrs Bradley, the secretary to return to College.

'The police?' said Mrs Bradley. 'Very well. Show them in.'

'Him, Mis' Bradley.'

'Him, then.'

'Mrs Castle was cook at this establishment until last Saturday morning,' she told the inspector. 'She left, at my request, with a week's wages in lieu of notice and a good reference.'

'We found the reference, madam. That's why, to be frank, and knowing of you from up above, so to speak, we suspect murder, and not suicide.'

'Dear me! That was very careless of somebody,' said Mrs Bradley. 'No question of accident, inspector?'

'Well, it might be, madam. But what would she have been doing, wandering down there at night? Time of death proves quite a lot, you see. She went in off Caddy Old Bridge, we reckon. It comes as a kind of a funny business after the disappearance of the other lady who was in charge here before the holidays. You've heard about that, of course?'

Mrs Bradley said that she had, but added no comment, so the inspector set to work on his 'check-up', as he called it, requiring minute details as to the reasons for Cook's having been dismissed, the time she had left the house, her probable destination and any other information which could be supplied.

It was at the end of this interview, and whilst the inspector was questioning the servants, one by one, that Mrs Bradley telephoned Miss Cartwright.

'Golly,' said that lady, when she was sent for to receive the message, 'the balloon's gone up at last!'

Mrs Bradley received her very kindly.

'Ah, Miss Cartwright! Now, dear child, that bath you took on the night the ghost walked. You remember?'

Miss Cartwright gurgled, blushed slightly, and replied that she remembered.

'Good. Who suggested that you should have it?'

'Nobody. That's to say, I often have one down there after hours.'

'In Miss Murchan's time, too?'

'Oh, yes. I – I had a key cut.'

'Have you ever had reason to suppose that the maids enter-
tained nocturnal visitors without the knowledge of the head of
the house?'

'No, of course not. Anyway, I shouldn't give away the maids.'

'None of that nonsense,' said Mrs Bradley firmly. 'Your answer
is no, is it?'

'Certainly.'

'And it is the truth? Don't bluff me.'

'Yes, it's the truth – except for this last time.'

'That's better. Listen, student.' Miss Cartwright flinched before
the brilliant black eyes and nervously crossed her fingers. 'Cook
is dead – drowned. The police are here. They are anxious to hear
about this bath of yours. Take my advice, and be perfectly frank.
Don't hide anything. I may say that there is no breach of the
rules of this Hall, so far as I am aware, in your choosing to take a
bath at two o'clock in the morning, or at any other time, so do
not hesitate upon that score. Authority is not involved. On the
other hand, Cook's death is a very serious affair indeed. How
much noise does the water make, running out of those downstair
baths?'

Mrs Bradley did not wait for a reply. She patted Miss Cartwright kindly upon the shoulder, picked up the house telephone,
and informed Bella, the head maid, since promoted to cook, that
she was at liberty whenever the inspector was ready, and also
that she had another witness for him.

'I don't – I don't know anything except about having the baths,
you know,' said Miss Cartwright, now thoroughly cowed and
frightened.

'That is all the inspector will want to know about,' said Mrs
Bradley gently. 'Now, sit down, my dear child, and we will get
Lulu to bring us some coffee and a biscuit.'

*

Deborah's share in the inquiry was limited to two answers.
Where had she been, the inspector inquired, on the nights of the
previous Sunday and Monday, and had she seen or spoken to Mrs
Castle after the cook had left College employment?

Deborah, astonished by both questions, answered composedly that *(a)* she supposed she had been in bed and *(b)* that certainly she had not.

The inspector appeared to be satisfied by these replies, and then consented to interview Miss Cartwright.

'Baths at two in the morning, miss? Was that allowed?'

'Yes, apparently. I mean, nobody objected!'

'But why in the servants' bathroom, miss?'

'Because I should wake the other students if I had a bath upstairs.'

'Didn't you wake the servants, miss?'

'They didn't seem to mind. They'd soon have complained if they *had* minded, I should think.'

'Very good, miss. Now, did you see or speak to Mrs Castle, the last time you had one of these late baths?'

'Yes.'

'Did you usually see her on these occasions, miss?'

'No.'

'Were you surprised to see her?'

'Yes.'

'Why?'

'Well, without meaning any – anything, I'm bound to say she was a miserable old blighter – luckily as deaf as a post, or she'd have heard me before.'

'Oh, she was deaf, miss, was she?'

'Good Lord, yes. Everyone knew that.'

The inspector picked up the house telephone and asked for Mrs Bradley.

'Did *you* know Mrs Castle was deaf, madam?'

'Yes. Everybody knew that.'

'Thank you, madam ... You were saying, miss, that you saw Mrs Castle?'

'Yes. She – she kind of popped out on me, and said she'd draw the bath while I got warm by the kitchen fire. She felt my hands and said I was cold and that it wasn't a good thing to get into a boiling hot bath if you were cold. Then she shoved me into the kitchen, where there was still quite a bit of fire – burning out, you know, but the room was warm – and shut the door. Then I heard the bath water rushing in, so I toasted myself until she came and lugged me out and told me the bath was ready. All very odd. She was a crotchety old thing as a rule. Bella was my pal down there.'

'And did you see any unauthorized person on the premises while you were down there, miss?'

'Did Mrs Bradley tip you off about that?'

'If you would kindly answer the question, miss.'

'I didn't *see* anybody, but I heard someone. At least, I don't know about unauthorized. I thought it was another student, and later on I was sure it was, only it seems it really couldn't have been.'

'Explain that statement, please, miss.'

'Oh, didn't they tell you we had a ghost in the place that night? Yes, I'd just got out of the water, and it was making the – making a noise running out, so that you couldn't hear much else, you know, when I heard a most frightful sort of screeching, wailing whistle – most weird. So I shoved the plug in the bath and listened again, and really it was most grisly. And then I heard this person whispering, and decided it must be a rag. So I shoved my wet feet into tennis shoes, wrapped my bath sheet round me, and floated upstairs, because I thought if there was a rag in progress, I'd better be among those present in case they counted heads. They did, too. Roll-call in the Common Room. But I was there with them, answering up with the best.'

'Can you add anything more to that statement, miss? We should find it very helpful, I may tell you, if you could.'

'No, I don't think I can tell you any more. How awful, though. Do they really think Cook was – '

'Now, miss,' said the inspector, cutting her short. 'I've not used that word, and you mustn't, not until after the inquest. And then perhaps we shan't need to.'

He asked to see Mrs Bradley again before he left.

'Of course,' he said, 'we've got nothing really to go on, nothing at all. But it's suggestive about this visitor in the kitchen regions while the young lady was having her bath. But what would be the object of anybody alarming the house by whistling like that in the dead of the night, do you think, madam?'

Mrs Bradley shrugged.

'There is a school of thought which is determined to get me out of Athelstan,' she said. 'This is not surprising, considering the reason for my presence. I seem to be endangering somebody's peace of mind. So far, the incidents have been slight, silly and spiteful. The death of Mrs Castle marks a more ambitious stage.'

To what extent the inspector accepted this interpretation of the facts she could not tell. He asked for details, and she gave them. If he thought them negligible he did not say so, and he and Mrs Bradley parted with great cordiality, Mrs Bradley asking only one question.

'Have you finished down by the river? Is the road open now?' she inquired.

'Oh, yes. The young ladies can get along that way this afternoon, if they want to,' said he.

'Ah,' said Mrs Bradley.

'Are you prepared to come along and identify the body, madam? The only letters on her were addressed to the College. It would be easier than trying to find her relations.'

'Oh, I can give you the address she left with me for holidays, but I'll come along, by all means.'

She was, in fact, particularly anxious to see the body, although not for the sole purpose of identifying it.

Cook had certainly met her death by drowning. It needed less than Mrs Bradley's expert knowledge to determine that. She was permitted, upon production of her credentials, to examine the body. It showed no marks of a struggle.

'One can deduce accident or suicide; scarcely murder,' she said. The inspector nodded.

'All the same, murder it was, madam,' he said. 'We're pretty sure of it. But what did she know, that somebody had to do her in? And another thing, madam. Where was it done? Because it wasn't done on the river bank. That seems clear. I didn't tell you before, but the body, although clothed to some extent, wasn't fully clothed. No corsets on it, madam.'

'Miss Cartwright's baths may have a clear significance, I presume,' said Mrs Bradley.

'That young lady could do with an eye kept on her, you think?' said the Inspector.

'Miss Cartwright? Good gracious, no! But her habit of taking these nocturnal baths in the servants' quarters may have put an idea into somebody's head, that's all. Now, I want you to come back to College with me, inspector. The place will be fairly quiet, and quite denuded of students, since all are out on School Practice.'

George drove them back in Mrs Bradley's car. The inspector was as interested as Mrs Bradley had thought he would be in the passage that ran from end to end of the hostel buildings, and spent an hour and a half examining it.

'I'd advocate a burglar alarm on this door and a mortice lock, madam,' he said, 'although it's a case of shutting the door when the horse is stolen, I suppose. And now, if you've no objection, I'm going to have another talk with some of your maids. One of 'em surely must know what Mrs Castle was up to, to get herself into such a mess as this.'

The maids, however, were either guiltless of knowledge or obstinate in retaining it. Bella was again questioned closely by Mrs Bradley after the inspector had interrogated her, along with the other servants. When he had gone Mrs Bradley said: 'Bella, I want you to tell me exactly what happened on the night we heard the ghost.'

Bella, eyeing Mrs Bradley frankly, answered: 'Well, madam, I don't think I can say any more than I *have* said. Cook had a visitor, but I didn't see who it was. They whispered, in Cook's room, so I couldn't recognize the voice.'

'And this was at half past eleven?'

'About then, madam. We'd all been in bed half an hour, just about, I should think.'

'And you know it couldn't have been one of the other maids whispering with Cook?'

'Well, madam, May was in with me, and Flossie was in with the other maid that came in Lulu's place for the day or two, that's all I know.'

'You didn't think it could be a man with Cook?'

'Gracious, no, madam! Cook wasn't that sort at all.'

'No, I don't think she was. But could you swear that it wasn't a man?'

'You mean at the inquest, madam? Well, I don't know that I could. But, all the same, I'm just as sure it wasn't.'

'And then you remember nothing more until the ghost woke us all up?'

'Nothing at all, madam. When that happened, it was just like I told the inspector. May put on the light by the bedhead switch, and said: "Oh, Lord, what's that?" And I jumped out of bed because I thought perhaps the new maid might be having a night-mare.'

'You recognized the sounds as human, then?'

'Well, I didn't stop to think, madam. I just went into next-door, with May keeping close behind me and holding on to my dressing-gown, and I saw the other two with their light on, sitting up in bed with their eyes sticking out of their heads and Flossie with her fingers in her ears. Then Cook came along and took us all into her room, like you found us, madam.'

'Did she mention her visitor?'

'No, madam.'

'And nobody asked?'

'Nobody liked to say much to Cook at any time, madam.'

'Tell me, Bella, did you ever suspect that somebody broke into Hall at nights?'

'No, I certainly never did, madam. I should have been the first to report it to you.'

'Yes, I'm certain you would. Ah, well,' said Mrs Bradley, ter-minating the interview.

*

No matches were arranged for the two Saturdays of the Christ-mas Term School Practice, so, Laura and Alice being officially un-occupied, they, with Kitty, decided upon a walk.

It was a wonderful day, crisp, sunny and cold, and the three students, wearing short skirts, blazers and scarves, stepped out from Athelstan, paused a moment to watch a goal-shooting prac-tice on the hockey field, and then walked on to where, on the east side of the College grounds, a wicket-gate opened on to a small public park.

They passed several groups and couples of students as they went through the park, but encouraged no one to join them.

'Business is our pleasure this afternoon,' said Laura to tentative hangers-on; and she spoke so determinedly that she shook off all potential companionship.

'What's the big idea, Dog?' asked Kitty plaintively. 'Why do we act as though we've got the plague or something?'

'We're going down to have a look at the old bridge,' Laura replied. 'And then I'm going to have the inside out of that mermaid Cartwright.'

As she vouchsafed no more, but seemed intent upon reaching Caddy Old Bridge in the shortest possible time, the others asked no more questions, and were soon warmed through by the pace she set.

Caddy Old Bridge was thus named to distinguish it from Caddy Swing Bridge, which had been built some centuries later, and spanned not the river but the canal.

A few yards upstream from the Old Bridge was a weir, and the three students stood on the bridge for some moments, absorbed in watching the foaming water.

'I suppose,' said Laura, 'the murderer's idea was that the force from the weir would carry Cook's body further downstream than where the police actually found it.'

'But we don't know where they found it. It didn't tell that in the papers,' objected Alice.

'Bobby Breen told me,' replied the leader of the expedition. (Constable Breen received inevitably this soubriquet.)

'He ought not to have said. He might get into trouble,' said Alice.

'Well, I asked him, casually, and he did say. Anyway, all the errand-boys know, because I checked the information with Miggin's Albert, and he said exactly the same thing. We're going along there in a minute to have a look, and then I'm going in, *à la* the corpus, to see what really does happen. Mrs Croc. isn't the only pebble on the beach when it comes to a spot of detection.'

'I call it very grubby and little-boy, to take all this morbid interest,' said Kitty, witheringly, forgetting her past.

'Do you? We're on to a big thing here, if I mistake not,' replied her friend. 'Don't you see that Cook simply went the way of all flesh – to wit, the way Miss Murchan went last term?'

'Oh, rot!' said Kitty and Alice with one accord.

'And how will you go in? You can't undress on the bank, and you haven't even got a towel, let alone a bathing costume,' said the former. 'You're an ass, Dog!'

'And you'd catch your death of cold,' said Alice. Laura patted herself on the stomach.

'Costume on under my clothes; towel round my waist to hide it from our smirking acquaintance as we came through the park,' she announced. 'And what's the use of a pub if you can't ask permission to use the summer-house on their bowling green as a dressing-room?'

This amount of generalship took away speech from her companions. Moreover, by some gift known to herself but not to them, she did indeed obtain permission to use the summer-house.

'Here, hang on to my watch, Kitty,' said she, emerging on to the bank, tall and big-limbed in her scanty bathing suit.

'I wish you wouldn't do it, Laura,' said Alice. 'You've no idea how cold it will be.'

'Sez you!' retorted Laura, dancing up and down on the grass. 'Well, here goes. I'm going to wade in and try it for depth and currents first. Then I'll come up on the bridge and drop in off the parapet. "When I am dead, my dearest, Sing no sad songs" – Ow! Wow! It's freezing! – "for me! Plant thou – "' She thrust in, waist deep, and then struck out into midstream, waved to the watchers, and began to thresh down-river. Kitty remained where she was, but Alice, herself a swimmer, walked anxiously along the bank, after having loosened her shoe-laces and unfastened all but a single hook on her skirt. She knew the cramping effects of extremely cold water, and was on hand to render assistance.

Laura, however, needed none. She turned after about a hundred yards of strong, swift crawl, and began to come upstream in a series of duck-dives, testing the depth of the water. It was amusing to watch the white legs and the very white soles of the feet breaking water at every seven or eight yards, and after a few minutes Alice realized that she and Kitty were not the sole observers of the scene. Several of the other students, also out for walks, had come up, and one or two villagers, mostly from the inn, were also upon the bridge or upon the bank.

Having carried out the first part of her experiment, and taking no notice of the spectators, Laura waded through shallow, very muddy water to the bank, climbed out, and trotted up to the bridge.

'Do hurry up and come out, Dog. We're attracting attention,' urged Kitty. But Laura briefly invited her to pass the hat round, and, climbing on to the parapet of the low bridge, breathed deeply and – a martyr to her thirst for knowledge – fell awkwardly and painfully in.

'No good diving. Wouldn't have the same effect as tipping in somebody with their hands tied,' she told the others later.

The current was fairly strong because of the rush from the weir. It carried her, half-drowned (for she did not like to mar her experiment by coming to the surface to breathe more often than she could help), past the inn and towards the right bank of the river. At last, exhausted, and beginning to feel that warning cold which seems to strike internally, she came up, breathed deeply once or twice, and then began to race about to get warm. The patient Alice kept pace along the bank, the public-house portion of the audience offering bets among themselves, meanwhile, as to what it was all about; one section holding that it was for a wager, the other certain that the young lady was in training for something, and that Alice was her trainer.

It was Alice who saw the corsets; at least, it was Alice who, suddenly cupping her hands round her mouth, yelled:

'Laura! Something pink! Laura! Look, Laura!'

Laura did not hear at first, and was amazed to see Alice come down to the water's edge as though she were going to wade in. So she would have done, had not Laura's attention been attracted just in time.

Laura, treading up mud, handed her the corsets. Alice rolled them up, but the watchers had seen what they were, and, having no idea at that moment of connecting them with the body which had been dragged out by the police, now cancelled all bets and assumed, with beery joviality, that they were the object of Laura's

researches. There was some crude chaff, at which the girls grinned
and Alice also blushed, and then Laura trotted off to get dressed.

The others accompanied her, and Alice, offering money which
was not accepted, obtained the use of two more towels from the
publican, and whilst Laura, now shaking with cold and with
hands too numb to dry herself, fumbled with the towel she had
brought out from College, Alice and Kitty got to work on her
like ostlers working on a horse, and, deaf to her protests that
they were taking all the skin off, had her, except for her hands
and feet, quite warm again by the time they had crammed on her
vest and heavy sweater. Then, taking her by the arms, they
trotted her up and down the stone-flagged path which bordered
the bowling-green until she pronounced her circulation fully
restored. By this time the watchers had dispersed, and the three
went back to College.

*

'And didn't you scold her?' asked Deborah. She and Mrs Bradley were having tea in Mrs Bradley's sitting-room.

'No. Why should I? I gave them all some parkin, and Miss
Menzies a cup of Bovril,' said the head of the house composedly.

'But she might have got pneumonia!'

'My scolding her would not prevent that, dear child. And look
at the prize they brought in! Although I must say I can't imagine how the police came to overlook it. Something to do with
the action of the current, I suppose.'

'But what did they bring in?' asked Deborah.

'Haven't you heard? I feared it was all over Hall. Perhaps
they've kept their mouths shut after all. They found Cook's corsets in the river!'

CHAPTER 10

THE FLYING FLACORIS

'WE'VE traced her movements over the week-end, madam,' said the inspector, 'and although we can't find anybody who actually saw her enter the College grounds, she *was* seen, acting in a furtive manner, between the two stiles leading to the backs of your five houses of young ladies. That was at half-past nine on Monday evening. She was seen by Mr Titt, of the Watch Committee.'

'I bet she was!' said Miss Topas, when she heard this. 'That man ought to be in prison!'

The two stiles referred to by the inspector were on College property. Behind the five Halls ran a drive, and behind the drive, and parallel with it, was a fairly high wall. Midway in this wall, and behind Beowulf Hall, there was a gap closed by a stile. A short footpath ran from this stile to another stile across a waste piece of ground used by the lecturers in botany as a kind of research-station for wild plants. The second stile was also set in a high wall, and beyond it stretched open fields which, in their turn, gave place to the moor. One of these fields was used by the College for hockey, but all the others belonged to farmers, and there was a right of way across to the College stile from the moorland highway, now an almost unused track since the stone-quarries there had been abandoned.

'She went to Bradford,' the inspector went on, 'to her relations there. Respectable people; a man and his wife and three children. Nothing against them in any way. She stayed with them over Sunday, and then on Monday morning she told them she'd got a letter about a situation in York. They didn't see any letter, but as she'd gone to the door herself to collect the post, they couldn't question it.

'And now, madam, comes a funny item. On Friday morning she went to the Post Office in Wantley – not here in the village, you'll notice, nor anywhere near the College – and put fifty pounds into her Savings Bank account. Further to that, she put another fifty in on the Saturday before she visited her relatives, and *not* in Wantley this time, but in Bradford itself; and, even then, not at the branch office where her relations, living in the part they do, would be most likely to go. What do you make of that?'

'At any rate, I know what you make of it, inspector,' said Mrs Bradley. 'She received half the payment before she performed some task, and the other half when the task was satisfactorily completed.'

'Question is, what was she bribed to do?' inquired the inspector. Mrs Bradley would have enlightened him if it had been in her power to do so.

*

'A woman like Cook,' argued Laura, 'would have put her stays on, chance what.'

As there was no dissenting voice, she glared militantly round her small circle of listeners and then lit a cigarette and smoked it half through before she continued her argument.

'So what do we get?' she went on. 'I'll tell you.'

'Bad teaching, Dog,' observed Kitty. 'If you ask a question, you shouldn't answer it yourself.'

'I'll tell you,' repeated Laura firmly. 'We get this: somebody drowns poor old Cook in the bath; the other servants, used to the goings-on of that idiot Cartwright, don't take any notice; the body is then dried and clothed, but the murderer, like a chump, doesn't put on the corsets.'

'Why not?' Kitty inquired.

'Ass! Can you imagine Cook without them? I bet the murderer gave one goggle-eyed look at the mass of adipose tissue, then took a despairing flip at the corsets, decided two into one won't go, and slung the corsets into the river after the body, never dreaming that they'd fetch up where they did. You see, allowing for drift, current, prevailing winds, seasonal variations, present height of river, mean annual rainfall and the character of the local vegetation, that garment ought to have floated down ever so much farther than the body; instead of which, it got caught in weed, and hardly drifted at all. So when the police found the body at Spot A, they didn't bother too much to search the bank at Spots A minus x, x being the unrecorded distance between the bridge and the body. Do I make myself clear to the lower division of the class?'

'You're an ass, Dog,' said Kitty.

'I see what you mean. I wish I could work things out,' said Alice.

'Old Dog made up most of that,' said Kitty. 'What a hellish day Sunday can be. Let's go out and sweat at something, shall we?'

'Let's go into the gym,' suggested Laura, who was still childish enough to delight in forbidden pleasures.

'May we?' inquired Alice. Her friends regarded her anxiously, and Kitty felt her pulse.

Entrance (unofficial) to the gymnasium was gained by means of the gallery, for the wall-bars prevented ingress by the lower windows. It was not a difficult matter to obtain possession of the groundsman's ladder, and Laura and Alice soon reared it against the gallery end of the building. The long windows of the gallery were always open, and even if the groundsman came up in search of his ladder and removed it, it was possible (for Alice, the most agile of the three, had tried it as a test exercise once, under the eye of the lecturer) to leave the building by one of the downstairs windows behind the wall-bars. It was tricky, and required, besides a certain amount of careful judgement, the sinuousness of a cat, a monkey or a little boy. Nevertheless, it could be done.

'Better not make a row going in,' said Laura, as they eyed the ladder before commencing the ascent, 'because you never know when Miss Pettinsalt isn't in there, having a private practice. I suppose these lecturers have to keep up to scratch, and maybe they find Sundays boring, too.'

She led the way, but, upon gaining the window-sill, she signalled the others to be silent. She herself stepped cautiously over the ledge, and made an almost soundless landing on the wooden boards which formed the gallery floor. There was certainly somebody practising in the gymnasium. If it was another student, they could proceed without fear, but if it should prove to be the india-rubber Miss Pettinsalt, then it would be better to give up the attempt and find some other way of getting through the day until tea-time.

She crept to the gallery rail. There was the performer; pretty agile, too, thought Laura, watching the smooth work and beautiful timing.

'Golly, she's *pukka*,' she thought. She could not, however, recognize the figure, although Miss Topas would not have hesitated. It was not, at any rate, a lecturer. Laura crept back to the window and beckoned her henchmen to mount.

'Somebody here,' she whispered. 'I don't know who it is, but it ain't Staff. You have a look, Alice. Don't let her hear you, if you can help it.'

Alice went forward with the stealth usually associated with Red Indians, gave one glance, and then returned.

'Oh, that's Thingummy,' she remarked. 'Wizard, isn't she?'

'What, that – ?'

'It's only that woman from Rule Britannia's. The one at our Practice School. Cornflake. She looks different without her glasses.'

They watched Miss Cornflake as she finished her wall-bar exercises.

'She's coming up a rope,' said Laura. 'We don't want to give her a fit of the vapours when she looks along and sees us all parked here like Tom Sawyer at the funeral. Might fall and break her neck. Better get on down.'

This humane suggestion was immediately carried out, so that when Miss Cornflake came level with the gallery it was empty, the Three Musketeers having descended by way of the staircase which came down at the left-hand side of the gymnasium.

Miss Cornflake did not notice them until she reached ground-level. Then her eyebrows shot up and her lip curled back like that of a snarling dog. Her whole demeanour thoroughly alarmed Alice, for whom the wrath of authority had always held that peculiar terror which is the hell of the law-abiding when, by chance, they fall from grace.

'And what are you people doing here?' demanded Miss Cornflake.

'Well, I'm damned!' said Laura, with a round frankness which astonished two of her hearers and was silently approved of by the third. 'And who on earth might you be?'

Miss Cornflake was visibly taken aback by this spirited challenge. She appeared to be confused.

'You startled me. You see, I haven't permission to be here.'

'Neither have we, so that's all right,' said Laura, climbing out of her skirt, beneath which she was wearing her gymnasium shorts. She climbed the rope which Miss Cornflake had just left swinging, slapped the metal fastening at the top, reversed slowly and gracefully and came down head-first until she was within five or six feet from the floor. Then she reversed again, and dropped to the floor.

'Good,' said Miss Cornflake, condescendingly. 'Well, I'll just have a short skip and a shower, and then I'm through. I take it you people don't want your presence advertised?'

'Up to you,' said Laura coolly. 'Our hands are clean.'

This odd expression appeared to disconcert Miss Cornflake. She opened her eyes wide, then opened her mouth as though to reply, but walked off, in the end, without a word. Laura, still holding the rope, gazed after her and watched her take a skipping-rope from the box under the gallery. Miss Cornflake, with lowered gaze, walked past her, and, going to the far end of the hall, began to skip to a measured rhythm and with the automatic concentration of an athlete in training.

Laura, without saying anything more, walked over to the 'horse' and began to push it out into the middle of the floor. Alice and Kitty went to her assistance. Miss Cornflake put back her skipping-rope and went off to have her shower.

Laura, however, was thoughtful. When she and her companions had taken their showers, put their towels in the drying cupboard, and gone back to Hall for tea, she would not listen to the chatter about her, but sat with hunched shoulders and ate large quantities of bread, butter and fish paste, obviously brooding so darkly that no one dared interrupt her thoughts.

At five she went abruptly to Mrs Bradley's sitting-room and found Miss Topas there.

'Come in,' said the Warden's exceptionally beautiful voice. 'Ah, good afternoon, Miss Menzies! I hope you have come, as is meet, to confess your sins.'

'Confess my – oh, you don't catch me that way, Warden,'

responded Laura, grinning. 'You name the sin, and I'll confess it.'

'Unlawful entry into the gymnasium by means of the grounds-man's ladder and by way of the gallery window,' said Mrs Bradley, closing her eyes and reciting in a police-constable's righteous but carefully expressionless voice.

'Golly!' said Laura, over-awed by this display of omniscience. 'Anyway, Warden, it cuts the cackle, that's one thing.'

'You know,' said Mrs Bradley, 'you should not allow yourself to fall into Miss Trevelyan's slip-shod methods of speech.'

'I know. Never mind that now. Come back to it later. Warden, do you know anything about a Columba student named – although you won't believe it – Cornflake?'

'I'd like to,' said Mrs Bradley. 'Can you talk in front of Miss Topas?'

'Yes, if *you've* no objection. Anyway, as she's in Columba, perhaps Miss Topas ought to know. Mind, I've got nothing to go on, but these various little stunts which have cropped up from time to time during the term are obviously inside work, and, in my opinion, this bird Cornflake could bear watching. She isn't what she seems. Moreover, she's a red-hot gymnast, and can do all the things the average fly can do, and more. If she couldn't oil into Athelstan, nobody could. Come over to the gym., if you don't mind. There's something I'd like to show you.'

Miss Topas supplied footnotes to Laura's description of Miss Cornflake, and, when Miss Topas had gone, Laura said, a little shyly:

'I say, I don't want to put ideas into your head, Warden, but I wish you'd ask Miss Pettinsalt what *she* makes of our friend.'

'Good idea,' said Mrs Bradley, whose thoughts were moving even faster than Laura's, for the reason that Miss Cornflake, if what she suspected was a fact, would make so complete a missing link that she seemed too good to be true. She rang up Bede, which had the honour, at that time, of Miss Pettinsalt's company.

'Out,' said Mrs Bradley. 'But it is only a pleasure deferred. We'll get her later. Now, let's have the rest of the information.'

'Some of it's in the gym. The rest isn't information; it's merely surmise. The three of us – as apparently you spotted from your window – got into the gym. this afternoon to do a turn on the ropes and rings, and this woman Cornflake was there.

'Well, granted we may have startled her a bit, would you expect a student – even from Columba, where, granted, they're all as old as the hills and most have done teaching before they came here – but would you expect the following?' (Here she gave a passable imitation of Miss Cornflake's tones and bearing.) ' "And what are you people doing here?" This, Warden, being said haughty, as indicated.'

'Curious,' said Mrs Bradley, her opinion crystallizing into certainty.

'More than curious, Warden; a dashed give-away. What's a Secondary School mistress doing at Columba? And a P.T. specialist at that? And why does she go about, according to Miss Topas, practically dumb and half-witted, and yet does that most amazing P.T. in School Prac.? Dirty work somewhere, Warden. That's what I think.'

Mrs Bradley cackled, and suggested that they repair forthwith to the gymnasium.

'But how are we to get in, if you haven't a key?' demanded Laura. 'And that's another thing. How did that blighter get in? Because we had the only ladder. Likewise, how did she get out? These are deep waters, Warden.'

'You certainly seem to be up to the neck in them,' Mrs Bradley remarked, with a chuckle. 'Let us go across to Bede Hall, and see whether Miss Cornflake did not borrow a key.'

'She *said* she was there without permission.'

'Ah, well, there are ways and other ways of borrowing, are there not?'

'If that's a dirty dig, Warden, then I'm justified in saying I don't know.'

'*Touché*,' said Mrs Bradley, with a polite grin. 'By the way, I may have to commit assault and battery on Miss Cornflake. There might be some point in having witnesses. Bring Miss Boorman and Miss Cartwright.'

'Not Miss Trevelyan?'

'Not Miss Trevelyan. She is one of my favourite students, but she has little or no discretion.'

'Has Cartwright, then?'

'Miss Cartwright's standing with the Principal is, fortunately, so questionable that I can terrify her into silence,' replied the Warden, with a leer of evil joy.

'Hot dog, Warden!' said Laura; and went to beat up the escort.

'But why not me?' wailed Kitty.

'You've got the morals of a sieve,' responded Laura. 'At least, that's what she said.' Leaving her friend to fathom the implication of this allusion, she took the meek but excited Alice in tow, and went off to find Miss Cartwright.

That amphibious lady was lying on her bed, smoking and reading. She rose with alacrity, and put on her frock, a coat and some shoes.

'What's she want *me* for?' she asked.

'Spot of bother about the gym.'

'Nothing to do with me. Hate the place, anyway. Why should she pick on me?'

'How should I know? She merely sent me to find you.'

Miss Cartwright's anxieties were not diminished when the party, instead of bearing south-west towards the gymnasium, turned due east for Columba. Mrs Bradley had vouchsafed no explanation, and offered none as they walked along, herself and Laura in the lead, Miss Cartwright and Alice following.

'Miss Cornflake?' said the Warden of Columba. 'I'll send for her at once. I expect she's in her study-bedroom.'

'Look here, Warden,' said Mrs Bradley. 'It would be less embarrassing, both for you and me, if you were officially out of this. I have to make some accusations against Miss Cornflake, but as they do not come strictly under the heading of College discipline, perhaps – '

'Oh, dear,' said the elderly Warden of Columba. 'It seems a little irregular. Can't I know – ?'

'Certainly, if you'll agree to take no action. It's nothing very serious in itself. She's a keen gymnast, and makes entry into the gymnasium for practising, at times when the students are not expected to be in there. I've caught these wretches of mine' – she met Laura's eye squarely – 'and I thought I'd find out whether Miss Cornflake has unauthorized possession of a key. It's really a question of the discipline of my own Hall, rather than yours.'

'Oh, in that case – ' said the Warden of Columba. 'Look here, have this room, and I'll go and sit with Miss Topas.'

It was clear that the visitors were not at all welcome to Miss Cornflake. She knocked, came in, and, casting one swift glance about her, seemed inclined to back out again, but Laura had placed herself, gangster-like, with her back to the door.

'Ah, Miss Cornflake,' said Mrs Bradley. 'I wonder whether, by any chance, Miss Pettinsalt happened to leave the key of the gymnasium with you before she went out this afternoon?'

'Yes, she did,' replied Miss Cornflake, after a slight pause.

'Then may I borrow it?' Mrs Bradley inquired.

'Yes, I suppose so. I'll go and get it. It's in my room.'

'Thank you,' said Mrs Bradley.

'But she said she was there without permission,' said Alice, under her breath. Mrs Bradley caught the whisper and smiled.

'Do not mention that fact,' she said. 'Now, students, I am going to do some very curious things. Ready, Miss Cartwright?'

Before Miss Cartwright could reply, the Warden had slipped behind her and was holding her in a firm grip.

'Do you mind struggling quite hard? I'll try not to hurt you,' went on Mrs Bradley. 'Harder, Miss Cartwright. Try to get away.'

Miss Cartwright, inhibited at first by a mixture of chivalry and awe, was very soon fighting her hardest. Mrs Bradley released her, pushed the panting girl into an arm-chair in a dark corner, and waited for Miss Cornflake to return. She had to wait for two or three minutes, and once or twice glanced at her watch. When Miss Cornflake came back, key in hand, Mrs Bradley gripped her round the waist, imprisoning her arms. Then, holding her firmly, she said: 'Now don't be alarmed, Miss Cornflake. Repeat after me these words: "For heaven's sake, Warden, don't report me! It was only a rag. I shall be sent down for certain if you report me."'

The victim, standing perfectly still, said quietly: 'I don't understand all this. Have you all gone mad?'

Mrs Bradley began to haul her towards the window.

'Open that window, Miss Menzies,' she commanded. 'I'm going to throw this student out.'

At this Miss Cornflake began to struggle violently. Mrs Bradley exerted a good deal of strength to hold her. Then she let her go.

'What *is* all this?' demanded Miss Cornflake, panting.

'Psychology tests,' said Mrs Bradley unblushingly. 'I am sorry to have inconvenienced you. I shall award your reactions a mark of Beta.' She grinned ferociously, took up the gymnasium key, which Miss Cornflake had dropped in the struggle, and which had been picked up by Alice, and led her myrmidons away.

'And now, Miss Cartwright, not a word of this to a soul,' she said, when they were out on the drive once more. 'I suppose, by the way, you wouldn't care to confess to me that you were the Miss Morris in trousers whom I captured on bonfire night, and the snake-charmer who so much annoyed Miss Harbottle? – Never mind, child. But, remember, these tests of mine must be secret, or I can learn nothing from them at all.'

'I shouldn't dream of saying anything, Warden,' said Miss Cartwright, giving a half-glance at Laura.

'Very well, child. And I shouldn't smoke quite so much, if I were you. You make odd, gasping sounds, which displease my medical ear, when you become short of breath, as you did just now when we struggled.'

'She took long enough to get the key, Warden,' said Laura, as she and Mrs Bradley, having sent the other two off, walked briskly towards the gymnasium.

'The inference is that she took it off a key-ring.'

'Not to lose it, I suppose; although you'd hardly think she'd bother, just for an hour in the gym. Anyway, why not lend you the whole caboosh?'

'She may have keys on the ring which she didn't want us to see, including a key to the doors of the passage that runs from Hall to Hall,' said Mrs Bradley. 'And, of course, this key may be one she had cut for herself when she *did* borrow Miss Pettinsalt's key one day.'

'Shall you ask Miss Pettinsalt whether she lent it?'

'Not at present, child. It isn't necessary. Here we are. I don't think I've been in here since I went all over the College when first I came.'

She opened the door, and they went in by a door which led into a short passage past the dressing-rooms and shower-baths.

'Better put these on, Warden, not to spoil the floor,' suggested Laura, handing Mrs Bradley a pair of rubber-soled shoes. 'They'll be pretty big for you, but I daresay you can slop about in them. I can go in in my stockings.'

Mrs Bradley changed her shoes, and Laura led the way to the space under the gallery where the movable apparatus was stored.

'You'll want a clean handkerchief, Warden. I brought one in case. See that skipping-rope? The one with my shoe-lace tied round it? I haven't touched the handles. Those are Cornflake's prints. Superimposed on a good many others, I expect, but an expert might do something with them. On the top of the wall-bars – here – they ought to be good. Nobody's used the wall-bars since yesterday, except her, and they get cleaned on Saturday mornings. On the shower-tap, cleaned yesterday with metal-polish, hers again. I wouldn't let Kitty or Alice touch the tap. Gave them their showers with the fire-bucket and we used the tap from the floor, and I took my shower the same way. We've done it before, and it's more fun, actually, so they didn't tumble to the true inwardness of the proceedings.'

Mrs Bradley put her hand in her skirt pocket and took out her small revolver.

'Put it back, Warden. It makes me nervous,' said Laura. 'A rounders stick will do twice as well, and makes a lot less noise. Are you going to phone the police?'

'Why should I?' inquired Mrs Bradley. 'However, I am going to send Miss Trevelyan and Miss Boorman to keep you company, and the three of you will keep out all intruders. Here are your shoes again, child. On no account is anybody, even Miss Pettin-salt herself, to come in until I have given permission.'

'Atta-baby!' murmured Laura, going off to select the three heaviest sticks she could find.

CHAPTER 11

THE EVE OF WATERLOO

'I AM quite infinitely obliged to you, Miss Menzies,' said Mrs Bradley, when the inspector had brought his experts, and Miss Cornflake's fingerprints, 'for better, for worse,' as Laura expressed it, 'were upon record. 'Of course, we've nothing much to go on, except that a person in unlawful possession of one key may, as I suggested, be in unlawful possession of other keys. And, of course, there does seem something a little odd about her, as you say. And she's very strong.'

'Worst of it is, if she's got anything to do with the Athelstan Horrors, she's wise to you now,' said Laura.

'Yes. I intended that she should be, child. I now await her reactions.'

'Golly! But she may take a stab at laying you out, don't forget. If she *did* drown Cook, she's dangerous.'

'Don't jump to conclusions, child. I haven't mentioned Cook, and you must not. Now I should like to show my appreciation of your detective powers. What would you like me to do?'

'Well,' said Laura, after a moment's thought. 'I wish you'd keep the Deb – keep Miss Cloud out of old Kitty's literature lesson on Friday afternoon. She wants her to take a poem by Wordsworth, but if she wasn't coming in, Kitty would be able to read 'em a slab of the latest Tuppenny.'

'And they would prefer that?'

'Well, dash it, Warden, of course they would, poor kids. I mean, no one is a greater admirer of Willie Wordsworth than old Kitty. She actually told me this morning that she considers *We Are Seven* one of the funniest poems in the language. But when it comes to a few poor, innocent offspring, who don't even want to be in school at all, I do call Wordsworth, as ladled out by old K. on a Friday afternoon, coming it a bit too thick, especially as the poem isn't *We Are Seven*.'

'Well, child, I can hardly dictate to Miss Cloud which schools and classes she is to visit on Friday afternoon.'

'No?' said Laura with a cheeky and confident grin. 'Thanks a lot, Warden. Old Kitty will remember you in her will for this, I shouldn't wonder. I'll tell her to go ahead, then.'

Strange to say, Deborah did not visit Kitty on Friday afternoon, and that unwilling applicant for professional honours spent a pleasant last hour with a strangely attentive class to whom she had delivered the following homily at the commencement of the period:

'Now, look here, cads' – a form of address which the class accepted at its B.B.C. value, and liked tremendously – 'this is the very latest issue. I only got it at dinner-time, and I haven't even looked at it yet, so no interruptions, or else I shall jolly well set you some sums or something, and read it all to myself. Now anybody who wants to open a desk, or shut one, or say anything, or fidget about, or drop things, or break a ruler, or any other dashed thing, just jolly well go ahead and do it, and then I'll begin. All set? Righto. We're off. Keep your poetry books open at page eleven, and, if anybody comes in, never mind who I mean, mind you're reading that bally poem like billy-o. I'd better put mine ready, too . . .'

Some of the children cried when school practice was over and Kitty was compelled to say good-bye. She returned to Hall laden with late chrysanthemums, two hyacinth bulbs vouched for 'to come up' in the spring, and a collection of confectionery.

'Hullo, Kitty? Got a cold?' asked the slightly obtuse Alice, when she met her.

'No. I've been having a howl,' said Kitty, frankly.

'What on earth for? The Deb. didn't come in, did she?'

'No. But those blinking kids. You just get fond of them, and then you don't go any more.'

'You *are* an ass!' said Laura, when she heard it. But the words were comforting, for Laura, in her way, was as acute a psychologist as Mrs Bradley.

*

School practice having been concluded, and holiday reading having been settled by the various lecturers with their groups, work came to a close and thoughts turned pleasurably to the end of term dance. This was not exciting, in the sense that the summer term dance was exciting for no visitors were allowed, but it was anticipated eagerly by students a little jaded by the exigencies of school practice. The various committees met twice on Saturday and again on Monday morning, to have all the necessary arguments about an orchestra, Christmas decorations, the arrangement of the programme, printing, catering and the vexed question of whether the Principal would allow the proceedings to continue until midnight for once.

Laura was on the programme committee, and was, as she herself expressed it, 'lost to sight, to memory dear,' for most of Saturday. Alice had a pleasant voice, and was to sing from the platform in the interval, so she had gone off to the Music Room for a practice. Kitty went back to Athelstan and ironed the three dance frocks for Tuesday.

The week-end passed without untoward incident, the programme was settled, and willing hands rolled out copies of it by the score on the College duplicator, the supper was decided upon and the books balanced. Each student contributed one shilling and sixpence towards the cost of the festivities, and all lecturers were invited, free of charge. Decorators (the Advanced Art group, mostly, assisted by such gifted amateurs as Kitty, who insisted upon helping 'put up the stuff' and proved a practical and experienced workman, and a steady and even daring performer upon step-ladders) did their bit towards contributing to the success of the evening, and a ladies' orchestra was hired from Bradford and arrangements made to feed it and bed it down since it could not get back by train that night, particularly if the principal should relax the 'eleven o'clock rule' and allow the party to continue until midnight.

This she refused to do, although a deputation, made up of first years, second years and third years, waited upon her with eloquence, great respect and some special pleading.

'I am sorry, students,' she said, when she had listened patiently to all their arguments, 'but it will be *past* midnight by the time you get to your beds, and some of you are catching the seven-thirty train on the morrow. It isn't fair on the servants.'

This 'time-honoured gag,' as the disgusted Laura put it, clinched all arguments, and the deputation, completely deflated, filed out.

The next petitioner was Mrs Bradley, but upon a different matter.

'I want you to allow me, Miss du Mugne,' she said, 'as part of my attempt to account for Miss Murchan's disappearance, to supply the College with a band of Thugs. For one night only,' she added; and proceeded to supply footnotes. The Principal, without relish – in fact, with complete and awful disapproval – listened carefully to Mrs Bradley's plans, and, against her will, agreed to them.

*

'"Now it is the time of night",' observed Laura, gazing critically at herself in the mirror, ' "that the graves, all gaping wide..." Kitty, lovey, do up my zip, would you? If I bend, be it never so slightly, I can't get it to do its stuff. I seem to have put on flesh since I came to this glory hole.'

'And then,' said Kitty, 'I'd better just re-arrange your hair. I told you to be careful of it when you put your dress on, and you haven't been careful. You've completely mussed it up.'

She had been, needless to say, hairdresser in chief, not only to her two comrades, but to half of Athelstan. All those, as Laura observed, who had one lock of hair to lay beside another, had clamoured for her skilful ministrations. Kitty had responded nobly, and the Athelstan contingent formed 'a bevy of fashion and beauty unequalled in the annals of the College,' as Laura announced with pride, surveying the happy faces and 'gala get-up' – her phrase again – of the young girls 'ere Time's fell hand had touched them.'

'You seem in form tonight,' observed Miss Cartwright, who had attempted sophistication in a scarlet frock and a good deal of rouge, and was not too certain whether the end justified the means.

'Wait till you see the Warden,' said Laura mysteriously.

'I've seen the Deb, and I must say she looks too beautiful for a wicked world,' said Miss Cartwright. 'In fact, she makes me look quite Tottenham Court Road, and I rather relished the look of myself before.'

Kitty had waylaid Deborah on the previous afternoon.

'You've had it set,' she said, without preamble.

'Yes,' said Deborah nervously, conscious of a professional eye upon her coiffure.

'You come to me an hour before tea tomorrow,' said Kitty. 'It isn't bad. I'll be able to do something there.'

Deborah had laughed, but, in the end, was compelled to promise. But Kitty's great triumph was to come. Mrs Bradley, who had something to talk over with Miss Topas, dressed early, in an orange and royal blue evening frock which was then in its fourth season, and encountered Kitty, who was on her way to the bathroom, as she herself was about to descend the stairs.

Kitty's jaw dropped; her eyes opened wide. She made odd, gurgling noises. Mrs Bradley halted.

'Goodness me, Miss Trevelyan!' she said. 'Are you ill, child?'

'Well, you might call it that, Warden,' replied the sufferer.

'But what is the matter, my poor dear?'

'Warden,' said Kitty, with the desperate honesty of the artist, 'you can't go over to College looking like that.'

It was a statement which many of Mrs Bradley's relatives, notably her sister-in-law, Lady Selina, and her nephew's wife, Jenny Lestrange, would have given much for the courage to make.

'Why, what's the matter with it?' asked the head of the house, genuinely surprised by the passionate outburst.

'Well, nothing, of course, Warden. It's like my cheek . . . only, haven't you got something . . . ?'

'Come and rummage,' said Mrs Bradley, grinning. 'But I mustn't be long. I've got to see Miss Topas before the dance begins.'

Kitty accepted the invitation with alacrity, but, confronting the contents of Mrs Bradley's wardrobe, her face fell.

'No?' said the Warden, in Kitty's opinion unnecessarily and wrong-headedly amused by the proceedings.

'I might do something if you'd let me put on a touch of Miss Cartwright's rouge. It's perfectly horrible on her – wrong shade altogether – but it would make this dress quite wearable on you.

It's a lovely frock...' She took it down, and, laying it on the bed, brooded over it, and then looked critically at Mrs Bradley's raven hair, black eyes and yellow countenance.

'Don't mind me,' said the Warden; but she herself was surprised at the result, especially of a skilful and artful application of Miss Cartwright's rouge. 'Dear me, I don't think I've seen myself like this for thirty years.'

Kitty hung up the discarded blue and orange in the wardrobe.

'Well, you see, you've got the *bones* all right,' she said. 'And your hair – not a touch of grey. And that frock, now, with the rouge, and your shoes are nice. I wish I could afford expensive shoes.'

Mrs Bradley kissed her – a brush against the smooth, young, earnest brow.

'It's kind of you to take the trouble, my dear,' she said, and laughed again. 'Has Miss Cloud ... ?'

'Oh, the Deb's a beauty ... really a beauty,' said Kitty. 'Even at that ghastly little hairdresser's she goes to they can't really do much to muck her up. Of course, I took out their wave and re-set it ... Well, I had better have my bath, I think, or Dog will be yelling her head off.'

Mrs Bradley gazed after her, still struggling with laughter, but when she saw Deborah she did not laugh; she moaned (to Deborah's discomfiture) with appreciation of her loveliness.

'You know,' she said, holding Deborah off and looking her up and down, 'we shall have to make sure that that child doesn't waste her time teaching. Even the mouse-like Alice looks almost pretty tonight.'

Deborah looked at her suspiciously.

'You're up to something,' she said.

'I have been up to something,' Mrs Bradley corrected her. 'I have had Miss Cornflake put under guard.'

'Arrested, do you mean?'

'Not arrested, exactly; rather, illegally detained. Miss Topas, Miss Cartwright, Miss Menzies and Miss Boorman assisting, George and I have locked her up in the cellar of the chief engineer's house, where George and the chief engineer are mounting guard until midnight.'

'But won't there be trouble about it?'

'No. She thinks it is an Athelstan rag. George, Miss Topas and I did not appear. We merely made the plans to incarcerate her, and arranged for the necessary transport.'

'But what on earth was your object in preventing her from going to the dance?'

'I want to solve a mystery or two, and I want to be certain, for her own sake, that she is out of the way.'

'Do you really suspect her of the murders?'

'I don't suspect her because I don't know as much yet as I should like to. She may be as innocent as Miss Murchan was. And that, I may as well inform you, is a double-edged statement. But if she *is* innocent, it is as well to keep her safe and sound. Or don't you think so?'

'I think it's a good thing you are friends with the police,' said Deborah. 'And what on earth will the Principal say? All the same, if you want any assistance in solving your mysteries ...'

'No, thank you, not from you. The inspector is coming to help me. He is bringing the sergeant and the police doctor, so I shall be perfectly safe.'

'Can't you tell me what you are going to do?' asked Deborah, looking anxious.

'I had better not, child. The very walls have ears.'

'That's not the reason. But I can see you've made up your mind to be obstinate.'

'I've made up my mind I shall be late in meeting Miss Topas,' said Mrs Bradley.

*

The dance was mildly entertaining, Deborah thought. The students were enjoying themselves. She herself, although she did not know it, filled Alice's cup to overflowing by sitting next her at supper. Laura made a speech, and the Principal, at half past ten, 'saw the light,' as Laura insisted, and permitted announcement to be made of her permission for an extension to eleven-thirty. The students applauded. Miss Topas, dancing (very badly) with a clumsy-looking One-Year from her own Hall thought: 'Oh, so she hasn't found it.'

Mrs Bradley had withdrawn from the College Hall at half past eight as unobtrusively as she could, but the majority of the Athelstan students missed her before nine o'clock, and asked Deborah whether she was 'all right'.

Deborah reassured them, but felt anxious, as the young are apt to do when they feel responsible for the safety and well-being of the elderly. She said to Miss Topas, when they met in a Paul Jones: 'What's she up to?'

Miss Topas replied irritatingly: '*Elle cherche la femme*,' and grinned. Deborah scowled at her. 'No, really, it's completely hush-hush,' Miss Topas continued.

'Come into the staff-room and tell me, while I tidy my hair.'

'Nothing doing. Oh, Lord. The merry-go-round again! See you later!' And they separated into their respective circles.

She dodged Deborah the next time their orbits intersected in the dance, and seized a fat student from Bede. Deborah grimaced at her, but was almost swept off her feet by a muscular captain of hockey, who gripped her purposefully and swung her relentlessly into a polka which the orchestra, with what Deborah could only classify as a misplaced sense of fun, had suddenly introduced instead of the waltzes and fox trots with which the Paul Jones had, so far, got along so nicely. The muscular student then took Deborah out to the buffet for an ice, and when they returned to the dancing floor Miss Topas had disappeared. She reappeared again in the doorway at twenty-five past ten and went across to speak to the Principal. At half past ten the announcement was made of the 'first extension night in the long and glorious history of the College' (Laura).

Deborah buttonholed Miss Topas.

'What's been happening? What's come over Miss du Mugne? The Second-Years say she never extends the time.'

Miss Topas, who was looking pleased with herself, said brightly: 'Nothing. Come over to Columba with me for a drink.'

'On condition you tell me what has been happening,' said Deborah. Miss Topas took her arm and pulled her gently out into the passage.

'I've been to take some nourishment to the Athelstan prisoner,' she said. 'It's cold across the grounds. The wind's changed. It's in the east. Put your coat on, and tie something over your hair.'

'The Athelstan prisoner? What *are* you talking about?'

'Nothing. I'm merely babbling. Come on! What a time you take!'

It was dark, as well as cold, across the grounds, and seemed a good step from the College to Columba. There was a light, however, in the window of Miss Topas's sitting-room, which seemed to beckon and welcome, and Miss Topas had her latch-key and opened the front door wide.

'Come on. Don't stop to wipe your feet,' she said in a voice in which Deborah recognized excitement.

Miss Topas switched on the light in the passage, shut the front door and led the way to her sitting-room. A man rose from her most comfortable arm-chair as they went in.

'Hullo, Deborah,' he said. 'Aunt Adela sent for me, and told me to fetch up here.'

'Hullo, Jonathan! Whatever you're doing here, or think you're doing, I don't see why you have to explain yourself,' Deborah said, with a laugh to hide the fact that she was blushing.

'I'll go and get the drinks,' said Miss Topas, going on the instant, and closing the door behind her.

'Sit down, Deborah. Or, rather, don't. At least, not yet,' said Jonathan, advancing.

Before Deborah could avoid it, he had taken her in his arms, and, with a most disconcerting amount of enterprise, swinging her slightly sideways, so that her head was firmly against his upper arm, he kissed her with an enthusiasm which caused Miss Topas, coming in with the tray of drinks, to click her tongue regretfully and to observe that her sitting-room was not a film studio. She then put down the tray, seized Deborah (who seemed uncertain whether to launch an attack upon the intrepid wooer or whether to cry) and embraced her more gently and a good deal less disturbingly than she had been embraced by the ardent young man.

This action decided Deborah. She made a dash for the door, tore out, and they could hear her running up the stairs.

'A bit precipitate, weren't you?' said Miss Topas. 'Say when.'

'Make it a good one,' the young man responded. 'I've been obeying orders, that is all.'

'Whose?'

'Aunt Adela's. She told me she wanted Deborah in the family
– Oh, I say, *when* !'

'There you are, then. And did your Aunt Adela advise you on
procedure?'

'Well, no. But I've wanted to do that to Deborah since that
week-end – you remember? – at Carey's. Anyway, I seem to have
mucked it. Do you suppose I've put her off for good? She
wouldn't agree to marry me when we were there, so I thought I'd
try other methods.'

'Well, you'd better not have more than one drink. Women
don't like being made love to by a stink of whisky. You drink
that, and make it last, and I'll go up and bring her down again.
And you'd better be a little more gentle. Deborah's not a Rugby
football player, you know. She's nervous and highly strung, and
all those other things that you've probably previously connected
only with racehorses and prize pumpkins.'

With this delicate admonition, she went upstairs to her bedroom. Deborah was seated in front of the dressing-table tidying
her hair. Her hands were shaking.

'Let me,' said Miss Topas; but instead of taking the comb she
took Deborah by the shoulders, held her firmly for a minute and
then said : 'Well, and do you want him?'

'Of course I want him,' said Deborah.

'Come on down, then, and say so.'

'I can't meet him again tonight.'

'Rot. Don't be girlish.'

'I can't go down there. Tell him – tell him – '

'Tell him yourself. Come on. Don't be a coward.'

'I'm not. You don't – Look here, why did you ask him to come
here tonight?'

Miss Topas laughed, and made for the door.

'There's nobody at home to make scandal. I'll send him up,'
she said.

Deborah tried to detain her, failed, and, mistrustful of her sense
of humour, followed. She found Jonathan alone. He was seated
on the settee, staring gloomily at his whisky, which he had not
touched. He put it down and stood up when she came in.

Deborah backed away, but heard the key turn in the lock behind her. Miss Topas was taking no chances of her match-making going astray.

'Deborah,' said Jonathan. 'Look here, come and sit down. No, honestly, I won't do it again. At least, I won't do it without warning you! I'm sorry I rushed at you like that. Silly to frighten you, but my courage failed me. I say, Deborah, you will marry me, won't you?'

'But, it's so silly! I hardly know you. In fact, I don't know you at all!'

'Yes, you do. What about that Saturday afternoon at half-term? What about the Monday? Besides, you know my aunt, and what could be more respectable than that? You like Aunt Adela, don't you?'

'I love her. She's been a darling, but . . .'

'Well, you could love me, too. It's perfectly easy. My parents have managed it for years, and they're not terribly talented. And I'm more of a darling than Aunt Adela. And if you know her, you know me. We're exactly alike. The same noble, generous natures; the same acute psychological insight, the same brains, the same brawn . . .'

'Yes, you've got the same brawn,' admitted Deborah, beginning to laugh. 'But she hasn't your amount of classic impudence!'

'Hasn't she?' said the young man. 'Look here, giving you due warning, I am about to repeat my effects, after which, I will tell you just how much classic impudence my aunt *has* got! Ready?'

'No!' said Deborah, putting up an ineffective hand. The young man removed it.

'What are you afraid of? Not of me,' he said gently. 'Come on! Don't be a chump. It only messes your hair up when we fight, and I like it best as it is.'

*

Whilst these preparations were being made to enlarge her already wide circle of relatives, Mrs Bradley was putting in some grim work, with the assistance of George and the policemen. Athelstan was empty of servants, for all were helping over at the College, with permission to watch or join in the dancing. Mrs

Bradley had decided to put this clear field to the test. Did it, or did it not, she inquired of the police, conceal the body of Miss Murchan?

Having put in her brief appearance at the dance, she returned to the house to meet the inspector, and, having changed from the garment of Kitty's choosing into workaday clothes, she and the inspector commenced the search.

By a quarter-past ten nothing had been discovered by the inspector, although Mrs Bradley had made one notable find, and Miss Topas, who had been taken into her confidence and who had already 'popped over' once or twice 'to see whether there was anything doing', appeared again in time to take back a message to the Principal, and to give Mrs Bradley the news that Deborah was engaged to be married. She made this announcement in characteristic fashion. 'By the way,' she said, 'you are by way of adding a niece to your collection. Do you mind?'

'Deborah?' said Mrs Bradley, grinning. 'How did you manage it?'

'I invited Jonathan over to Columba, as you suggested, and prevailed on her to come over with me for a drink. All unsuspecting, she came. I told him he would have to work fast.'

'He must have taken you at your word. Is everything settled?'

'Oh, yes.'

'Well, heaven knows what her parents will think of him! But there! It's no business of theirs,' said Mrs Bradley. 'I'm glad Kitty did Deborah's hair,' she added, with apparent irrelevance.

'From what I saw, I don't really believe it made the slightest difference,' said Miss Topas. 'They'll make rather a lovely couple – he so overriding and Deborah so devilish obstinate.'

They contemplated this picture of married loveliness in silence but appreciatively. Then Miss Topas said briskly: 'Well, you'll have to pack up the researches. The students will be coming over in about a quarter of an hour, unless you want me to ask the Principal for another extension, but, if I do, some of the intelligent young will smell a rat, and you don't want that, I suppose?'

'No, I don't want that,' said Mrs Bradley. 'I showed the inspector the only result I obtained. He is greatly disgusted. Should you like to see what I found?'

'Is it gruesome?'

'Yes and no.'

'Then I'd like to see it. By the way, have Miss Menzies and Miss Cartwright their orders respecting Miss Cornflake, or shall I go along and let her out?'

'No. They will do it. How is she? Very angry?'

'No. She seems cheerful enough. Of course, I haven't spoken to her myself. I've been over in company with the Chief Engineer. He's been very good. He explained that he cannot let her out because the students responsible for the rag have the only key. I think she believes him all right. Did you have to tell him everything?'

'Well, almost. He's been in the Army, so it didn't excite him too much.'

'About poor Miss Murchan, do you mean?'

'No, I didn't need to tell him anything much about her. He decided long ago that she had been murdered, and he is firm that the grandfather did it.'

'I think myself it's quite a possible thing, you know, although I see the difficulties in the way of such a theory. Much depends now, I suppose, on your being able to trace a connexion between Miss Cornflake and the school where the child was killed.'

'Everything, I suppose, depends on that. I am going there to-morrow. The school does not break up until Wednesday week. Their term is longer than ours. Now where's this Sub-Warden of mine? Still over at Columba?'

'Yes. I'll send them both over. But what about your promise? Forward to the Chamber of Horrors, please.'

*

'Well, not a bad show,' said Laura, 'and the water's hot, thank heaven.'

'Well, come out, pig, and let somebody else have a go,' suggested Kitty. 'There's still Alice after me to have her turn.'

'And two more,' said Alice's voice from the landing. 'Oh! Hi! Let me in! Here's the Warden!'

Kitty obligingly unlocked the door. Alice slipped in, and the 'two more' scurried hastily into study-bedrooms.

'Good night, students,' said Mrs Bradley primly. This benediction was followed by a distinctly masculine laugh.

'Golly!' said Laura coarsely. 'She's taking a man to bed!'

'I bet it's the Deb, not her,' said Kitty, antedating by a mere couple of months an interesting and, to Deborah, a dreaded ceremony. 'Wonder what Mrs Croc. has been doing with herself all the evening?'

Laura, who knew, had too much loyalty and discretion even to look wise.

'Come on, young Alice,' she said. 'You'd better just take a shower. The bath water makes such a hell of a row running out.'

This order was well received by Alice, and the three were soon in their adjacent cubicles and in bed.

'What happened to Cornflake?' asked Kitty suddenly. 'I didn't seem to spot her at the revels.'

'Didn't you? Who cares, anyway?' said Laura, sleepily. Kitty took the hint, and turned over. Miss Cornflake was, as a matter of fact, in her own study-bedroom at Columba, having pushed under the Warden's door an ultimatum to the effect that she wanted an interview in the morning on a question of serious ragging.

The Warden granted the interview, and Miss Topas, brought into an affair with which the Warden of Columba felt incapable of dealing, observed that the matter was already under consideration by the Principal, the students concerned having confessed their crime.

'They were Athelstan students,' she added, soothingly.

'I am sorry for Mrs Bradley. There seems to be a most undesirable element in Athelstan this year, from what one can gather,' said the Warden, when Miss Cornflake, protesting still, had been ushered out of the presence, and bidden to catch her train.

Laura and Kitty watched her go. The students and their suitcases were all allotted to buses, and theirs was the fourth to go off, Miss Cornflake's the second.

'So that's that,' said Laura, climbing into the bus. 'What's the date we come back on, again?'

'Twenty-fourth of Jan.,' replied Kitty. Alice, whose train went a good deal later than theirs, was on bus fifteen. 'Happy Christmas, and all that.'

'Incidentally,' said Kitty, before they parted at the station, 'does it strike you that there is a certain sort of fat satisfaction on Mrs Croc.'s face this morning?'

'It hadn't struck me,' said Laura, torn between two loyalties, and therefore lying boldly. 'Don't forget the twenty-seventh at Charing Cross. *District* Station, mind, and the Embankment entrance. Bung-ho!'

During College vacations the servants stayed up for two or three days to clear up and scrub through, as Kitty put it, and then were put on board wages until three days before the return of the students. The Chief Engineer and the Infirmary Matron, having their own quarters, often stayed up all the time. The Principal usually stayed up for an extra day or two after the students had gone, and Mrs Bradley had decided to wait until the College was empty before communicating to Miss du Mugne her discovery. With this aim, she waited until the Saturday before producing her evidence. Then, with George's assistance, she carried up to her sitting-room the damaged trunk of the younger twin, Miss Annet Carroway.

'Let's lock the contents up in here, George,' she said, indicating a large cupboard. 'Then you can take the trunk down again.'

The contents surprised George, although he had been in Mrs Bradley's employment for some years. They comprised human bones.

'Pretty work, George, don't you think?' she asked, taking them out one by one. 'See how beautifully they were articulated before somebody took the skeleton to pieces.'

She showed him the ingenious wiring.

'Then I take it this is not the remains of the missing lady, madam?' George inquired.

'No. This is the skeleton of a man. Look at the length of leg, the magnificent jaws, the size and strength of the bones. Besides, this person has been dead for a good many years, by the look of him, and has been used, I should say, for demonstration lessons to students.'

'A kind of doctor's piece, madam?'

'Well, something of that sort; or possibly for physiology lessons to students in training here. If so, we shall soon get some information about him, I've no doubt.'

This information she sought immediately, by going to the Principal with her news. Miss du Mugne ordered coffee and talked about College affairs until it came. When the maid had gone she said:

'What exactly has happened, then?'

'I've found the wrong skeleton,' said Mrs Bradley; and proceeded to explain.

'It sounds like another of those silly practical jokes which have been perpetrated in Athelstan all this term,' said the Principal. Mrs Bradley agreed, with disarming meekness, that it did sound exactly like that. 'I suppose you've no suspicions of anyone?' the Principal continued. 'I know you don't like the suggestion, but I still think Miss Menzies, of your Hall, could be watched with advantage. She came up with a bad reputation.'

'For ragging,' said Mrs Bradley. 'And Miss Cloud came with a bad reputation for not being able to keep order. I've seen no evidence yet to support either contention. Besides, the disturbances of one kind and another which we have suffered at Athelstan since September have been directed chiefly at me, and in such circumstances that Miss Menzies can scarcely come under suspicion.'

'Well, you know your students better than I do, of course,' said the Principal, in a tone which indicated that she did not believe this, 'but such a business as purloining and breaking up the College skeleton certainly seems to me like a stupid, would-be joke on the part of some of the students.'

'Even so,' said Mrs Bradley, 'it would help considerably if we could prove that the bones I have found *are* those of the College skeleton. Would you be able to recognize them?'

'Oh, good gracious, Mrs Bradley!' said the Principal, losing her calmness entirely. 'You – you're not suggesting – ? I thought you said just now – ?'

'Not suggesting that these are Miss Murchan's bones? No, I am not. The skeleton is not only that of a man, but the bones have been wired to give articulation – so necessary in demonstrations to a physiology group, for example.'

The Principal sat down again. Her face took on a look of regret struggling with its customary expression of benign conceit. The look of regret – to the credit of her intellectual conscience – won fairly easily.

'I am sorry to say that I could not possibly undertake to recognize the College skeleton except as a skeleton,' she said. 'I mean that if you offered me a collection of well-articulated skeletons to choose from, I could not possibly pick out the one used here in the physiology or physical training classes.'

'Oh – you use the skeleton for the physical training classes, do you?'

'Certainly.'

'Let me congratulate you,' said Mrs Bradley, poking her in the ribs with a remarkably bony forefinger, and thus obtaining unintentional but indubitable revenge for the slights proffered, earlier in the interview, towards her students. 'But tell me,' she added, as the writhing Miss du Mugne eluded her torturing hand, 'when can I see the College skeleton and how unlock the cupboard in which it is kept?'

'I have a key.' The Principal, smiling wanly, produced it. Mrs Bradley thanked her, and rose to go. As she came out of the Principal's office she saw Deborah.

'Why, what on earth are *you* doing here, child?' she asked. 'I thought you went home two days ago, and took my nephew with you.'

'Well, what are *you* doing here?' demanded Deborah. 'I made him bring me back. What *are* you doing?'

'Oh – just clearing up,' said Mrs Bradley, vaguely, waving a skinny claw. 'What have you done with the young man?'

'He's in the lane with the car.'

'If Jonathan's there, go and get him. I may be able to give him a job, and you, too. Fancy coming back, after all the trouble I had to smuggle him off the premises that Wednesday morning without the students' knowing.'

'Poor lambs! It would have given them the thrill of their lives!' said Deborah, with the wicked, unamused glint which Mrs Bradley was interested to think of in connexion with her nephew Jonathan, whose conception of life from childhood, so far as she had ever been able to determine, was that he should have his own way in everything. She began to hum.

'I don't like you when you sing,' said Deborah, who recognized the tune as that of a light-hearted sea-shanty called 'The Drummer and the Cook', 'and I shall be obliged if you won't refer to Jonathan as the young man.'

'Well, go and get him, anyway,' said her aunt-in-law to be, with a propitiatory smile which gave the unfortunate impression of being a lewd and evil grin. Deborah hesitated, then said:

'Please tell me why you're staying up. If you're still hunting murderers we're going to stay and help you. I've absolutely made up my mind, and Jonathan agrees, so you needn't argue about it.'

'Now, don't be naughty,' said Mrs Bradley, placidly. 'Go and fetch Jonathan, and tell him I want him to carry a bag of bones across to College.'

'Not – not – ?'

'No, not Miss Murchan's bones. Quite accountable bones, in fact.'

'What's the argument?' inquired Jonathan, who had left the car in the lane and had come up to the building to find out what was keeping Deborah so long. 'I say, Aunt Adela, we've come to be your bodyguard. Deb's going to stand outside the bathroom door listening to somebody lifting up your feet and submerging you, and I'm going to stand outside on the gravel with a hatchet, waiting to bean the murderer when she crawls out over the sill.'

'So I understand,' replied his aunt graciously. 'Meanwhile, I want you to come over to Athelstan and help me with a skeleton. Comparisons are odious, but two sets of bones have to be compared, and I want witnesses to prove that I don't change over the skeletons when I've compared them.'

She took the two over to Athelstan, and, to her observant nephew's interest, stood for a second at the top of the basement steps before she descended. Deborah began to ascend to the first floor to get a book she wanted from her sitting-room.

'Come back, Deborah,' said Mrs Bradley. For a moment Jonathan thought that Deborah was going to disobey, and he leapt up to catch her, but she turned and they met face to face on the stairs.

'All right,' she said. 'I'm well trained.' She followed him down, and Mrs Bradley nodded.

'I don't want anybody to walk about alone in this house,' she said quietly, when the two had rejoined her. 'It isn't too safe.'

'Miss Cornflake?' asked Deborah.

'What do you know about Miss Cornflake?' retorted Mrs Bradley. She led the way down the basement steps, listened again at the bottom, and then pushed open the door which led into the box-room. 'There!' she said to Jonathan. 'That badly-battered trunk, if you don't mind. The bones are in my sitting-room cupboard.'

'I see.' Another thought came to him. 'By the way, you don't expect to find poor old Miss Thingummy locked up in the Science Room, do you? Because, if so . . .' He gave an eloquent glance in the direction of Deborah, who was looking out of the window.

'Don't be oafish, dear child,' retorted his aunt. 'Deborah is quite as capable of seeing a skeleton as you are.'

'A skeleton, yes, granted. But . . .'

Deborah turned round.

'You don't really suppose the College Science Room could have housed a corpse all this term without somebody complaining, do you?' she demanded coldly. 'Our students are not all idiots.'

'Oh, granted. I see. Then, in that case, may I ask . . . ?'

'No, you may not,' said his aunt.

'I beg pardon. Lead on, Patrick Mahon.' Mrs Bradley cackled, and no more was said until they had left Athelstan with 'the luggage,' as Jonathan termed it, and had mounted to the second floor of the College building.

'Now,' said Mrs Bradley, producing the Principal's key, and unlocking a cupboard.

The skeleton was in a long box, coffin-like, and yet with the indefinable austerity of hospitals rather than that of morgues. The three of them gazed upon it in silence. Jonathan, characteristically, broke this silence.

'Indubitably male,' he said. 'Pass, skeleton. All's well.'

'Hm!' said Mrs Bradley.

'Are you disappointed?' asked Deborah.

'No. One and one make two,' replied Mrs Bradley, 'not to speak of two and one making three.'

'Once aboard the lugger, and the girl is mine,' said her nephew, whose quotations were apt to follow the line dictated by his immediate preoccupations.

'The trouble will be to find some reasonable excuse for obtaining eye-witness's information about the girl in question,' said Mrs Bradley. 'There is no doubt now where she is.'

'Where, then?' asked Deborah, startled.

'Cast your mind back to our first-night rag,' Mrs Bradley replied. 'I suppose they have a new lecturer in Science, or perhaps in Physical Training, at Wattsdown College. At any rate, I think that rag is now seen in its true perspective.'

'But – ' said Jonathan. His aunt silenced him by cackling and shaking her head. Then she locked away the College skeleton, picked up the Athelstan bones and led the way out. Her nephew relieved her of her burden, and the three of them went back to Athelstan.

'Please tell me what you're going to do during the holidays,' said Deborah, before they parted.

'I shall carry out my original plan of visiting Miss Murchan's former school,' said Mrs Bradley. She watched the car as far as the first bend, and then put through a long-distance call to the school at Cuddy Bay. It was the dress rehearsal of the Christmas play, she was informed. She arranged to go on the Monday, and ordered the car for one-fifteen.

CHAPTER 12

IN AND OUT THE WINDOWS

THE Cuddy Bay Secondary School for Girls was a second-grade establishment compared with the High School of the same resort. The latter had a splendid position on the cliff-top, with views of sea and moorland; the former was back in the town.

Mrs Bradley was directed wrongly at first, but one glance at the notice-board beside the front entrance decided her that this was not the place she sought, and she then found the Secondary School without difficulty.

It was half-past two, and a practice game of hockey was being carried on in the school field, and was being coached by a short, broad young woman in a gymnasium tunic and heavy sweater, the latter bearing an impressive badge. Mrs Bradley watched the game for a few seconds, and then rang the front-door bell of the school.

'I have an appointment with Miss Paldred at half-past two,' she said to the prefect who answered the door. 'My name is Bradley.'

'Oh, good afternoon, Mrs Bradley. Will you come this way, please? Miss Paldred is expecting you. I'll tell her you are here.'

The headmistress's room was simply but very beautifully furnished. The headmistress herself was of medium height, freckle-faced, grey-eyed and very charming.

'This nasty business,' she said, when they had shaken hands. 'Have you found out any more about poor Miss Murchan?'

This propitious beginning to the conversation made Mrs Bradley's carefully-prepared opening gambits unnecessary. She agreed that it was a nasty business, and said that she had come to ask a good many nasty questions ... 'even more than last time,' she concluded.

'Yes, I expect you have,' Miss Paldred agreed. 'What do you want to see first again – the gym?'

'Thank you. Not that it will make any difference, I'm afraid. I think we explored its possibilities fully last time I was here.'

They saw the gym., which was like all other gyms., except that it had a long gallery running lengthwise instead of being, as at the College, at one end. Mrs Bradley evinced little interest, except in this gallery, which led from one set of classrooms and a corridor to another similar set and another corridor.

'Is it possible,' Mrs Bradley asked, 'that a person passing along this gallery would be unobserved by the people below?'

'It is probable,' Miss Paldred replied with a slight smile. 'I myself have been a frequent passenger when the girls have been quite unaware of my presence. If one keeps alongside the wall there is no reason whatever why one should be observed.'

'I see. Yes. There seems reason to suppose, then, that Miss Murchan could have seen what happened here in the gymnasium if she had happened to walk along the gallery at some time after seven o'clock on the evening the child was killed?'

'Yes, but . . .'

'What did you think of Miss Murchan?'

'Personally, do you mean?'

'Yes, and as a member of your staff.'

'Personally, I found her rather colourless. She was inclined to be timid and deprecating.'

'A "burglars under the bed" sort of woman?'

'An apt description. Also – we must be perfectly frank, I take it – I regretted having felt obliged to make her Senior Mistress, as she detested and feared responsibility. But she was so much the oldest member of the staff that I felt I had no option, particularly as I enjoy very good health, and there was little reason to suppose that I should have to be away from school for any length of time, and leave her to cope, as it were.'

'Thank you very much. So that, if Miss Murchan had been in possession of a very horrid secret, you think she would have become very nervous about it?'

'Good gracious, yes. But what are you telling me, Mrs Bradley? The verdict at the inquest . . .'

'Suppose she knew – having walked along your gymnasium gallery after school that evening – that one of the staff was responsible – directly responsible – for that poor child's death, what do you suppose would have been her reactions?'

'I see you are determined to ask questions, but not to answer them, but you will forgive me if I disagree completely with your premises. However . . .' She hesitated and then added: 'One cannot, of course, be certain, but I should think she would go to that member of the staff – she was a very loyal comrade, I am sure – and tell what she had seen, and suggest, I feel, that they should both come to me about it.'

'But that did not happen? I know you will be frank. I am to take it that you know nothing except what actually came out at the inquest?'

'That is true. But you have no evidence that Miss Murchan did see the accident, have you?'

'Except that I cannot otherwise account for her disappearance. Didn't you lose your Physical Training mistress at about the same time that Miss Murchan gave in her resignation?'

'Yes, she decided to go. She said that although the coroner's court attached no blame to her in the matter, she felt she could not stay. I was sorry, as I am sure she was not to blame in the slightest for what had happened. The child was very naughty and disobedient to have been at school at all at such an hour. It is true we were having a gymnastic competition during the following week, as I think I told you before, but that hardly excuses her, does it?'

'I don't know. I remember the point about the competition, though. Where do the grandparents live? – Or have they moved?'

'I have the address in my Admissions. I'll give it to you as soon as we get back to my room. I don't think they've moved. The poor wretched grandfather went into a mental hospital immediately after his outburst at the inquest, you remember.'

'Yes. Now the Physical Training mistress – her name was Paynter-Tree, I believe? – '

The headmistress smiled.

'Yes; Paynter-Tree. Although I happen to know that she was nicknamed Flak – Royal Air Force slang, I believe.'

'Could you describe her to me?'

'She was of medium height, wide-shouldered, slim, dark.'

'She was not the only Physical Training mistress, I believe? I think you told me last time I was here...'

'Well, she was the only one specially trained for the work. Three of the other mistresses used to help with the games; one helped with the hockey; she had captained her College for two years; one helped with the swimming (she was reserve for one of the Olympic Games' teams) and Miss Murchan helped with the tennis; although what her qualifications were, beyond a keen interest in the game, I do not know. I believe she had learned fencing, but that is hardly the same thing.'

'The accident itself,' said Mrs Bradley, when they were seated in the headmistress's room and she had been supplied with the address she had asked for, 'was rather remarkable. I did not think sufficient was made of that point at the inquest. What are the rules about the apparatus?'

'Well, the girls are forbidden to touch the booms unless the mistress is there. But I don't agree with what you say. The school was sadly called over the coals at the inquest. It was pointed out – rightly, too, and I think that is what decided Miss Tree to send in her resignation – that the ropes and pulleys of the gymnasium apparatus should be tested and inspected frequently. The rope must somewhere have worn through, although I cannot think how or why, and neither could Miss Tree. Still, I think she acted hastily in resigning over a thing like that, particularly as, in the end, we were completely exonerated.'

'I never met the child's grandparents. Was the grandfather a widower?' Mrs Bradley inquired.

'A widower? Oh, dear, no! There is a very puritanical, tight-lipped grandmother. We had lots of trouble with her, as a matter of fact, whilst the child was here. She did not approve of the physical training being taken in shorts and blouses; she wanted the girl to wear stockings; she did not want her to be included in games teams, in case she became hoydenish, and a lot of old-fashioned nonsense of that sort.'

'And the grandfather? Was he equally prudish?'

'I don't know much about the grandfather, poor man. He went mad, as you know, after the inquest.'

'He is recovered, I believe?'

'Happily, yes. He's been at home now for about six months.'

'Which hospital did he go to?'

'I've really no idea. I know his wife refused to visit him, wherever it was. That was an open scandal all over the town, where, of course, everybody knows everybody else's business.'

'That seems to have been unkind in the wife, does it not? Well, Miss Paldred, I must thank you again for your help, and for answering my questions. I'd like to ask just one more. Have you any idea where Miss Paynter-Tree went when she left here?'

'Yes; to Northern Ireland. She wrote to me once from Belfast – a letter-card from the post office to say that she had arrived, and promising to send me an address as soon as she was fixed up permanently.'

'Did you know which school she was going to?'

'No; and I did not hear from her again. After all, we had not known one another for very long, you know. She was in her fifth term here when the accident happened. I suppose she really saw no reason . . .'

'No,' said Mrs Bradley thoughtfully. 'There was not, I suppose, any scandal connected with her in any way here? Before the child's death, of course, I mean.'

'None that I ever heard. What makes you ask such a thing?'

'I am still trying to account for the child's death. It wasn't accident. Gymnasium ropes don't "wear through" in the manner suggested at the inquest. Besides, some odd things have happened since I went to Cartaret College, and if they are not connected, through Miss Murchan, with what happened here, I do not know how to account for them.'

She proceeded to give Miss Paldred details.

'And you are sure the cook was murdered?' asked Miss Paldred. 'It doesn't seem to me there was much to go on.'

'Enough,' said Mrs Bradley. 'She really would not have thrown her own corsets into the river and then thrown herself after them over the bridge, you know. She wouldn't like to think of people finding her uncorseted body.'

'Do people really consider such things at such a time, I wonder?'

'Emphatically they do. Besides, to drown her in the Athelstan basement bathroom would have been so easy, under cover of the sound of the bath-water running out. If people thought anything of it, they would only think it was Miss Cartwright.'

'What do you make of the ghost-noises, then?'

'Two things. First, I think someone wanted to stampede the Athelstan students into panic, and secondly, I think they were made to bring to our notice the fact that some unauthorized person was on the premises. They were altogether interesting.'

'But what could the cook have known, which made her dangerous, do you suppose?'

'Beyond the feeling that it must have been something about Miss Murchan's disappearance, one cannot tell at present. Ah, well, we shall live and learn, I hope. Oh, one more question. You said that Miss Paynter-Tree had been with you only five terms. How long had Miss Murchan been with you?'

'Three years. Another reason I was sorry I felt obliged to make her Senior Assistant, of course.'

*

The child's name had been Muriel Princep, and the maid who opened the door to Mrs Bradley said that Mrs Princep was at home.

Mrs Bradley, left in the hall whilst the girl went to speak to her mistress, gazed about her with polite curiosity. The house gave evidence that there was no lack of money on the part of the owners. It was handsomely furnished, warm, clean, polished and smelt unobtrusively of roast meat and furniture cream nicely intermingled.

Mrs Princep was a bony woman with haggard eyes. She looked sixty, but might have been younger. She greeted Mrs Bradley with a nervous smile.

'I don't think . . . ?' she said.

'Quite so,' Mrs Bradley replied. 'It was thought that you would prefer me to call rather than a policeman.'

'Norah!' called Mrs Princep.

'It's of no use to order me out of your house,' said Mrs Bradley, who had formed her plan of campaign. 'I am sorry if I was abrupt, but I have very little time. It's like this, Mrs Princep. You may or may not have heard of the strange and, so far, unaccountable disappearance of Miss Murchan, who used to teach at the school here. In association with the police, I am investigating the causes of that disappearance. Will you hear what I have to say?'

'You'd better come into the drawing-room,' said Mrs Princep. 'Miss Murchan,' she added, when they were seated and she had switched on an electric heater, 'was suffering from a guilty conscience, I suppose. Some of those people didn't tell the truth at the inquest.'

'Not a guilty conscience; an overburdened one.'

'You know about our trouble?'

'Yes. I know your granddaughter died as the result of an accident in the school gymnasium. That is why I have come to you.'

'I can tell you nothing about Miss Murchan. I had no idea she had disappeared, and I don't care, anyway.'

'No, but you can tell me something about your husband, if you will,' said Mrs Bradley. 'Is he better now?'

'I won't have my husband reminded of the affair.'

'I don't want to have him reminded of it, any more than you do, but I would like to know the address of the hospital to which he was sent.'

'It was at a place in Berkshire called Millstones. I don't know the exact address. I never went there.'

'You didn't go to visit him?'

'No.' She looked so uncompromisingly fierce, with her thin, pursed lips and large eyes lidded like those of an eagle or even (thought Mrs Bradley) a giant vulture, that it was not easy to know exactly how to continue the conversation.

'I am glad to obtain that address,' said Mrs Bradley. 'I want to confirm the impression of the police that your husband could have had nothing to do with Miss Murchan's disappearance.'

'I don't see why the police should have any impression about it one way or the other, but, as a matter of fact, and to save you trouble, I can tell you that my husband came out of the mental hospital last June, on the tenth of the month. I don't know when Miss Murchan disappeared, so I don't know whether, if he'd wanted to have a hand in her disappearance, he could have done so.'

'I see,' said Mrs Bradley. 'You blame the school, Mrs Princep, I know, for what happened. Do you happen to know whether your husband particularly blamed Miss Murchan?'

'I don't think he did, but I do know Miss Murchan promised to tell us a piece of news about it. She said she knew, and she supposed we knew, who was responsible.'

'But she didn't give any name?'

'We asked her – pressed her – but she declared it wasn't necessary. She said we must know whom she meant, and that, if we agreed, she'd take her story to the police. She said they'd know what to do.'

'Does that mean you refused to allow her to go to the police?'

'Oh, no. And I think she did go. What we couldn't understand was why she suddenly left the school.'

'And Miss Paynter-Tree, too. Still, I suppose there was felt to be some responsibility there.'

'Responsibility!' said the woman, with extreme bitterness. 'Well, you can use that word by all means. Anyhow, I know what I think.'

'We are coming to something,' thought Mrs Bradley. 'What *do* you think, Mrs Princep?' she inquired.

'Why, that those responsible for bringing the poor child into the world took the liberty of putting her out of it.'

'Oh?' said Mrs Bradley. 'And that means . . . ?'

But Mrs Princep was not prepared to amplify her opinion. She closed her thin lips, and then suddenly opened them again to add, apparently irrelevantly, 'I've been married three times, you know.'

'What I don't understand at all,' said Mrs Bradley, perceiving that Mrs Princep was not prepared to volunteer any explanation of this last remark, 'is how the child came to be in school so late. It was surely very unusual.'

'Thinking as I do,' said the grandmother, 'I'm sure the poor mite was decoyed.'

'By the murderer, you mean, if one accepts your opinion. An opinion, I may add, which I share and which the police are beginning to investigate.'

'Are they? Are they really?'

'So, you see, you can speak freely to me on the subject.'

'Yes,' said the woman, 'I see that. My husband was very fond of the child,' she added. 'Of course, he never realized who she was.'

'Are you sure of that? You mean she was the child of one of your sons or daughters, don't you?'

'Illegitimate,' said Mrs Princep, tightening her lips more than ever. 'I had a daughter by each of my previous marriages. The younger girl went wrong, and the other would have done, too, given half a chance. Of course I couldn't have them in the house. My husband doesn't even know I've got two daughters. I never told him. I'd been widowed for nearly ten years when he married me, and the girls had left home long before.'

'I wouldn't be too sure he doesn't know you have two daughters,' thought Mrs Bradley. Aloud she asked: 'Wasn't the mother fond of the child? Was she willing for you to take it?'

'It would have ruined her career. I had to have it. I told my husband it was an orphan I'd adopted. It was only five when we married. Of course, he may have found out about it later. The elder girl may have let him know. They couldn't stand one another. Yet they took posts together to be able to see the child, and watched one another like cats. The father of the child was by way of being engaged to the elder one, Blanche, you see, and then, when Doris bore the child – !'

'Yes,' said Mrs Bradley. 'An old story, isn't it? But now, if you'll forgive me for asking, can you tell me whether your husband had had any of his attacks previous to the inquest?'

'Oh, yes. He had spent two years in a mental home before I married him. I knew that. I liked him none the worse for it.'

With this oddly-worded statement she seemed to have finished all that she had to say on the subject.

'One more question, and then I'll go,' said Mrs Bradley gently. 'Did the child's mother believe that the child had been murdered?'

'She had the best reason of anybody to believe it, as I told you,' Mrs Princep replied. Mrs Bradley, digesting all the implications of Mrs Princep's illuminating remarks, and also this one, which seemed a trifle obscure, she felt, went off on her third errand.

*

'Mental hospital?' said the local reporter. 'Yes, he did. But if you want my candid opinion, he was as sane as I am. Eyewash, to get public sympathy. Been some scandal about him at some time, I should imagine. The wife hushed it up, but, hang it, there was the kid. What were people to think? She said she had adopted it, and, of course, they've only lived in the town about four years. But you know how people gossip, and some of it followed them here. It's certain the child was illegitimate.'

'That wouldn't necessarily prove that it was his,' Mrs Bradley retorted.

'No. But why did he throw that fit at the inquest, then? Gave things away, people thought. Of course, people love a bit of scandal, but, after all, no smoke without fire. Anyway, into the bin he went, and was discharged last June. I interviewed him on the subject of his experiences. No good. Merely got a flea in my ear. Couldn't stand the fellow, anyway. Unwholesome old devil, I thought him.'

'Have you seen him since?'

'Oh, yes, but not to speak to. He's always about.'

'When did you see him last? Can you remember?'

'Not to swear to it. Mayor's Banquet, last November – let's see – November 3rd, I think. But what are you getting at – murder? I thought so at the time.'

'Oh, the police have nothing to go on in the case of the child's death,' said Mrs Bradley. 'They are looking for the missing schoolmistress, Miss Murchan. As she lived here, and testified at the inquest on the child, they felt bound to begin their work from this end. That's all. By the way, the fact that she is missing is not to be emphasized. There may be no connexion between the two cases.'

'More in that woman than met the eye,' said the reporter, solemnly accepting the decree. 'Definitely a queer stick. Odd, worried sort of creature. Ought to have seen a nerve specialist, I would have said. Even school concerts used to upset her for days beforehand. Had nightmares, too, I believe. Thought the doctor could cure her of it, she told me once, at one of the school do's. Useless to tell her he couldn't, so he made her up some harmless dope – an iron tonic, I expect – and she took it and said it improved things. Couldn't do any harm, at all events.'

'Did she come to you after the child was killed and offer you information?'

'No. She left the town soon after. Seemed to think people felt it was her responsibility. Got some crack-brained idea that the child must have pinched her keys to get into the gym., and that therefore she had some moral share in the accident, or some such guff as that. All boloney, of course. The kid hadn't touched her keys. Climbed in through a window, I expect, or else somebody else forgot to lock up that night. Miss Murchan wasn't the only person who had a key to the gym. That came out at the inquest, but nobody else seemed worried, except the mistress who took the gym., of course. But, then, it was right up her street. Anyone could sympathize with her deciding to leave. But t'other – well, it was just her nature to brood, and magnify every little trifle, I expect. Suicide type, I shouldn't wonder. If she's disappeared, you'll find her in the river or somewhere.'

*

For her own amusement, and by way of a minor psychological experiment, Mrs Bradley spent the night at the Grand Hotel, which was built almost on the edge of the cliff and commanded, therefore, extensive views seawards.

Next morning she walked on the promenade for an hour, so that anybody who happened to be interested in her movements had ample opportunity of discovering that she had not returned to the College. She lunched at the hotel, promenaded again in the afternoon, and at a quarter to four had tea at the hotel before sending for the car, and going back to Cartaret.

She found Miss du Mugne enjoying her after-dinner coffee. She accepted an invitation from the Principal to join her.

'You have enjoyed your jaunt?' Miss du Mugne inquired, as a graceful way of approaching the topic she hoped and expected that they were going to discuss.

'Very much,' Mrs Bradley replied. 'But I doubt whether I have acquired any valuable information from Miss Paldred except the address of the dead child's grandparents.'

'No?' The Principal looked disappointed. 'But you hoped great things of your second visit to the Secondary School.'

'Well, I had some hope, I think, of being able to trace the other person who left just about when Miss Murchan did – the Physical Training mistress, you know. It was odd, if both were innocent of negligence, to go off like that, don't you think?'

'I don't know, I am sure. You see, except for what you have told me from time to time, I know very little of the circumstances under which Miss Murchan left the Secondary School.'

'Well, there I did make progress. It appears that Miss Murchan was the holder of a guilty secret.'

'Miss Murchan with a guilty secret?' The Principal laughed. 'I don't believe it.'

'Well, from what I can deduce, it seems possible that she was there when the child was killed.'

'Then why didn't she say so at the inquest?'

'I don't know. She seems to have been of a nervous, retiring, vacillating disposition. She probably decided to say nothing, discovered that these were wrong tactics, and then was afraid of becoming entangled with the law. She does seem to have made some attempt to communicate her knowledge to others, but she was not successful. She was here two years, was she not?'

'Exactly two years. She came at the beginning of the Christmas Term, and her disappearance, as you know, dates from last summer's End of Term dance.'

'Of course, yes. Now, how was it that Miss Murchan became Warden of Athelstan as soon as she arrived? Is it usual to make new lecturers Wardens in their first term? – I except myself, of course!'

'Oh, but Miss Murchan had a year here before she was given Athelstan, you know.'

'What was the reason for promoting her?'

'It was not so much a promotion, in her case, as the fact that she was really not such a very good lecturer, I am afraid. She was altogether too timid and deprecating. I cannot think how she was able to stand the life at a Secondary School. I should have thought it much too boisterous for her. She seemed to go in fear and trembling of everything and everybody.'

'It seems that she had good reason,' said Mrs Bradley dryly, 'if what I suspect is true.' The Principal started, and spilled a little coffee.

'I beg your pardon? Oh, yes, I see. But I understand that it was her general manner.'

'I understand so, too. That emerged clearly during my interview today with Miss Paldred. Interesting. So when she was a Warden, Miss Murchan gave fewer lectures?'

'And no Demonstration lessons. These seemed to be her particular terror, and so I arranged that the junior lecturer should do them.'

'There was never any question of dismissing Miss Murchan for incompetence, I suppose?'

'Oh, no, nothing of the kind. I don't choose lecturers who have to be dismissed for incompetence the next moment. Miss Murchan was learned and talented. She had an Arts degree as well as her Science qualifications, you know. She lectured here in English.'

'Having taught Biology at the school. Very interesting. Thank you,' said Mrs Bradley.

'There is that very close affinity of dates between the release of that child's grandfather from a mental hospital and Miss Murchan's disappearance. It seems to me that a fruitful field of investigation lies there, but that is a task for the police, I suppose,' went on the Principal. 'And, of course, she did change her occupation, there is no doubt, because of the death of the child. I think we are justified in making the connexion. But, dear me! It is rather a terrifying discovery that the College has been visited by a madman!'

Mrs Bradley ignored this remark, and asked casually:

'How much do you know about the students before they come up for interview?'

Miss du Mugne seemed surprised at this abrupt change of subject, but answered briskly: 'A good deal. We need to be careful in our choice. Most of the students come up with a school record, of course, and that simplifies matters considerably. Then we have to consider the financial circumstances of the parents a little, although we keep that side of our inquiries from the students as far as we can. But some of these girls' families are very poor, and even if the girls borrow the money for their fees from their

County Authority, they can't manage at all comfortably up here. Were you thinking of anybody in particular?'

'Yes. I was thinking of the One-Year Students.'

'Ah, well, there, of course, the financial difficulty is different. Sometimes it does not exist. The One-Year Students, for the most part, are self-supporting, and pay their fees out of their savings. Some are given grants by the local education authority, and some . . .'

'I was not thinking about their finances, but of their characters,' Mrs Bradley observed. 'The young students who come straight from school bring records with them, you said. How do you select the One-Years?'

'Quite frankly, we don't. We accept the first forty who apply.'

'Oh? You make no choice at all?'

'Often we don't have the full forty apply.'

'I see. So that if I wanted to know something of the antecedents of any particular One-Year Student, you could not help me?'

'Well, actually, yes, a good deal. We correspond with such students before they present themselves for interview.'

'Well, I want to know everything you can tell me about Miss Cornflake of Columba.'

The Principal smiled and rang the bell for the secretary. But Miss Cornflake's dossier was of the briefest.

'Except that she came here from a Church of England Senior Girls' School in Betchdale, and proposes to return there when she has obtained her Certificate, there seems to be nothing about her in our records,' said Miss Rosewell, tidying the file, 'except for her home address, which is Two, Elm Villas, Betchdale.'

'I am sorry it is so unsatisfactory for you,' said Miss du Mugne, looking, however, rather pleased, Mrs Bradley thought.

'On the contrary, it is just what I wanted,' she replied. She looked at her watch. 'Very many thanks for your patience, and a happy Christmas if I do not see you again before next term.'

*

Betchdale was only thirty miles by car from the College, and George made the distance in an hour over a bumpy moorland road and through the long, tram-lined streets of the outer town.

Arrived at the market-place, Mrs Bradley went into a small café, ordered coffee (whilst George had some beer at the public house next door but three) and, upon leaving, inquired for Elm Villas. She was interested but not surprised to learn that they had been pulled down some eight years previous to her visit, and the space used for a garage.

'I expect you knew old Mrs Banham,' went on the proprietress of the café. 'A dear soul, she was. Gone to live on the Madderdale Road now, with her nephew's family. I don't know the number, but it's about ten houses past Roote's, the little general shop on the Turlfield Corner. Anybody would show you, and everybody knows Mrs Banham.'

Resolved to pursue the mirage of Miss Cornflake's private address, Mrs Bradley was driven out to the Madderdale Road, and by inquiring at the little general shop on the Turlfield Corner, she soon found the house that she sought.

All inquiry for anyone named Cornflake, Paynter-Tree, Tree, or even Flack, proved useless, however, as she had guessed it would. The slender chance remained that the people who kept the garage might be able to supply some information.

The garage seemed at first to be in sole possession of a youth of about seventeen who was cleaning a car. George made the inquiries this time.

'Don't know. Boss in the office,' said the youth. The boss was searching a ledger. George waited patiently for nearly ten minutes.

'Name of Cornflake?' he said, when George was able to state his business. 'Sure!' He began to laugh. 'Fellow as worked for me for a week or two about five or six months ago. I still get his sister's letters sent here sometimes, although not so many lately.'

'And I suppose you have to re-direct them,' said George.

'Re-direct 'em? Ah. But what's it to do with you?'

'Cousin of mine,' George replied. 'Family trying to find him. Come in for a bit of money when his Grandpa died, but he cut his stick along with quarrelling with 'em back home, and they don't know where to catch up with him, that's all. We heard he'd worked in this town, so I thought I'd ask, on the off-chance, and it seems as if I've struck oil. Mind if I have that address, mate? The sister's address, I mean.'

'Well, I can't see it can hurt to give it to you, like,' said the proprietor of the garage.

He tore a piece of paper from the bottom of an invoice slip, looked up in a small, shiny note-book the reference he required, and wrote out the address in a neat and business-like hand.

'Shouldn't like the young fellow to miss what's coming to him,' he observed as he handed George the paper, 'although he served me not so good. Told me he'd got a job near Bradford, and hopped it, all in a morning.'

' 'T'ain't a lot, between you and me,' said George. 'Matter of sixty-five quid. Still, it means a lot to a young fellow starting out in life, I reckon, and he'd ought to have it. It's his. There's five of 'em, and they all share alike – three girls and the two young chaps. Well, thanks for the help. So long, mate.'

'You're welcome,' replied the garage proprietor, opening the ledger again. George walked round the corner and into the street where he had left the car and Mrs Bradley in it.

'I fancy the address may interest you, madam,' he said. 'I haven't looked at the paper since he gave it to me, but I couldn't help seeing what he was writing down.'

The address was that of the local post office of the College.

'Webbed like a fish, and his fins like arms,' said Mrs Bradley, with a grimace and a satisfied chuckle. 'This grows interesting, George. What was one of Cartaret's young ladies doing as a garage hand, I wonder?'

'The old chap certainly hadn't rumbled he was employing a young woman, madam, anyhow.'

'No. That's interesting, too. Probably confused the unusual with the impossible, a practice against which we are continually being warned by classic writers. Well, George, there is nothing more now, once I have been to the school. We shall have to ask the way again, I'm afraid.'

*

Saint Faith's Senior Girls' School lay in a little clearing amid some riverside slums. It was not on the telephone, and Mrs Bradley took it by surprise.

The headmistress was taking a class, and had to be brought out of it to answer Mrs Bradley's questions. Fortunately Mrs Bradley did not need to keep her very long.

'A Miss Cornflake?' she said, looking puzzled. 'No, we have never had an assistant of that name, I'm sure.'

'This girl I am trying to trace went to Cartaret Training College last September,' said Mrs Bradley. 'She may have called herself Flack, or even Paynter-Tree or Tree.'

But this suggestion met with no response from the headmistress.

'I have only three assistants,' she said. 'Their names are Smith, Wakefield and Cotts. They have been with me a number of years now. They are all certificated teachers.'

Mrs Bradley thanked her, apologized for taking up her time, and departed, well satisfied. The darker the horse, she concluded, thinking of Miss Cornflake and her apparently mysterious antecedents, the better. The problem now seemed to be to choose the best time at which to show her hand, confront Miss Cornflake with the evidence, such as it was, and ask her to explain herself.

The holiday, at any rate, was not the right time. She drove back to Athelstan. The motives for the death of the child and of Miss Murchan's disappearance seemed to be coming to light. The means used to accomplish the child's death had never been in question. The means used to kill Miss Murchan, if she had been killed, were still obscure, and were likely to remain so until, for one thing, the time, place and fact of the death had been established. Opportunity in both cases was also difficult to show. The child had been killed at the (in the circumstances) extraordinary hour of seven in the evening, or later. Miss Murchan had disappeared during or after the College dance. Had both been decoyed? And by what agency?

Mrs Bradley sat at her desk and unlocked the top long drawer. She drew out her notebook and shook her head at it. There was much to do, much to discover, before this curiously baffling task she had undertaken could come to an end.

She opened the notebook. There was also Cook's death to be investigated. The police had been persuaded that it was murder. She glanced out over the Cartaret grounds, now becoming misty in the dusk. The College was a pleasant place, on the whole. She wished she could have come there on some more savoury errand. She sighed, affected to make another entry in the notebook and closed the drawer. A curious sixth sense, which she trusted, was informing her that all was not as it should be.

'Reach for it,' said a voice.

'I beg your pardon?' said Mrs Bradley, blessing the sixth sense, not for the first time in her life.

'You heard! Stick 'em up,' said the voice. Mrs Bradley turned her head as she put up her hands. There was still that bulge behind one of the long dark curtains.

'Now pick up that notebook with your right hand and chuck it this way,' the voice went on. 'I know you can aim accurately if you want to. Flip it across, and no funny business. You're covered, and I shan't miss, mind.'

'I'm sure you won't,' said Mrs Bradley courteously. She was not unaccustomed to homicidal maniacs. 'But may I suggest, first, that you are mixing up two entirely different American accents, to wit, that of the Bronx with that of Chicago; secondly, that you are superimposing upon the mixture a kind of stage Cockney which – forgive me – you don't do terribly well, and, thirdly, that even if . . .'

'Stow the gab and shoot the loot!' said the voice. The curtains quivered slightly.

'Even if, I was about to remark,' Mrs Bradley continued, in her deep, agreeable voice, 'I do toss you my notebook, I can't see that it will benefit you at all, since I am prepared to declare that you will not be able to read a word of my writing.'

'That's my funeral,' said the voice, 'and I'm getting impatient. Don't you know who it is that you're keeping waiting?'

'Can you really see me through that curtain?' asked Mrs Bradley. 'I should scarcely have thought . . .'

'Near enough to plug you if you don't stow the gab and up with the . . .'

Mrs Bradley suddenly moved faster than could possibly have been expected of an elderly lady. She seized, not her notebook, but a beautiful little bronze which she used as a paper-weight. It represented the shepherd boy David.

'Down with Goliath,' she said with an unearthly cackle, as the heavy missile found its mark and she, like a tigress, leapt after it towards the bulge. The bulge fell forward with a crash which shook the room.

'My own revolver, too. I knew there was something wrong with the look of that drawer,' she said to the police when they arrived. Her victim, who was seated in an easy chair with bandaged head and an expression of extreme misery due to the most oppressive headache he had ever had in his life, looked dully at her.

'You will be Mr Princep, no doubt,' said Mrs Bradley. 'How did your wife know where you would find me?'

Mr Princep refused to answer this question. His head fell back, and he began to moan. Foam appeared at the corner of his mouth.

'Looks like a loony,' said the sergeant.

'His looks, poor man, do not belie him,' said Mrs Bradley.

CHAPTER 13

HARLEQUINADE AND YULE LOG

'You're going to charge him, ma'am, I suppose?' said the inspector. They were out of earshot of the patient, who was, at the moment, lying on the settee, with a sergeant and a constable in close attendance, whilst Mrs Bradley had carried off the inspector to Deborah's sitting-room whilst they had their little chat. 'Of course, he's loco, as you know, especially if it turns out he's the man you think he is.'

'Well, his wife will be here tomorrow,' said Mrs Bradley. 'She will identify him fast enough, I should think.'

'But if she gave him the dope where he would find you, she may be in league with him, and refuse to say she recognizes him. It wouldn't hold us up for long, but it's a possibility.'

'I don't think it is,' said Mrs Bradley, 'for the very simple reason that his wife could not possibly have told him that I was here. She has no reason to connect me with Cartaret College, and I doubt, as a matter of fact, whether she knows of such a place. I certainly did not mention it in my conversation with her.'

'That's funny, then,' said the inspector. 'What could have brought him along?'

'Not what, but who,' said Mrs Bradley.

'Now think carefully, ma'am. Who could have known you were going to stay here tonight?'

'The whole College, if they were interested. My own students all know, because some of them asked me, and I answered them.'

'Risking rather a lot, ma'am, wasn't it?'

'Yes. I'm glad I did risk it, too. What I anticipated would happen has happened much sooner than I expected it would, that's all. Tomorrow, therefore, I send my nephew a telegram informing him that I am able to spend Christmas in Oxfordshire, after all, instead of by myself, up here.'

'Do you mean to say you were going to hang on here alone,

and wait for that fellow to turn up?' demanded the inspector.

'Well, I wanted to see what he was like, and I wanted to know whether he was mad.'

'Oh, he's mad all right. Went right off the handle in the coroner's court, and spent two years in the bin,' replied the inspector.

'Yes,' said Mrs Bradley, 'so I seem to have heard, but I'd rather make my own tests. He can't be moved tonight. You'll have to leave somebody with him. In the morning he may feel a little better. I shan't worry him or hurt him, but his mental condition interests me very much indeed.'

'It'll interest the judge,' said the inspector.

*

'And now,' said Mrs Bradley, 'to the affair of your grandmother's aunt, and your own relationship to the duck-billed platypus.' The inspector cocked a wary eye.

'You've got your opinion ready, ma'am?'

'Yes, I have. The man is undoubtedly mad.'

'Then . . .?'

'We now have to make certain where he went and what he was doing during the two years which went by between the inquest on the child and the disappearance of Miss Murchan. I've no doubt that he went to a mental hospital, as you say. If he was discharged as cured, something has upset him again. He'll have to be taken care of. He's dangerous, of course, poor fellow. I should say he's been an unbalanced person from boyhood.'

'But, by your own showing, ma'am, there's something fishy about him coming to the College like this.'

'Not if he had heard from an interested party that I was going to be here alone. It's possible, you know, that the party in question had told him I murdered the child.'

'Miss Cornflake, ma'am, that you mentioned to me this morning?'

'And thereby hangs a tale, and a rather queer one,' said Mrs Bradley to herself, when the inspector had gone, taking the unfortunate lunatic with him. She waited until the house was empty and all the servants were gone, then she walked over to the Chief Engineer's house where she had arranged to leave her keys.

'Then, if I want to come back early, for any reason, I can get into Athelstan without trouble,' she had announced.

George drove her to the station, and she remained there for an hour, studying the local time-table and talking to the station-master and the booking clerk. The results of these conversations were negligible, as she had expected that they would be, for it had been in the highest degree unlikely that one student among so many should have been especially remarked at the station. If it became necessary to trace Miss Cornflake's movements in order to discover her real address, the police would be the people to do it; and as to connecting her movements with those of the insane Mr Princep, well, that was a task which could wait.

Mrs Bradley returned to Athelstan, superintended the locking up of the house, and ordered George to drive to Lincoln, where she proposed to spend the night, and from where she would telephone her nephew.

Once at Stanton St John, it seemed permissible and even desirable to relate her adventures, and the family, including Ditch, Mrs Ditch and Our Walt, her nephew Carey's servants, were encouragingly enthralled by the recital.

'And now,' said Carey, on the third morning of her stay, 'for news of the other Christmas visitors.'

He had letters, two of which he passed across to Jenny. 'Ferdinand and Caroline are coming, with Derek; Sally says she's coming on the day after Boxing Day, bringing her dog, and Denis has broken up at school, so he'll be here today. Good thing we knew beforehand, because this letter wouldn't have helped much! And – oh, he's bringing another kid with him.'

'They'll have to pig in together,' said Jenny. 'Then, let's see: Ferdinand and Caroline can have the room next to Aunt Adela's, and Sally and the dog can have that little room next to the bathroom. I don't know what to do with Derek. Do you think – no, it would spoil it for Denis and his friend. Oh, well, we'll just poke him in somewhere. He won't mind. If nothing else offers, he'll have to have a camp bed in the kitchen. It'll be warm there, any-how. Aunt Adela, more coffee?'

Breakfast over, everybody went through the morning ritual of 'seeing the pigs'. After that, George, who was sharing a room with Our Walt, drove Mrs Bradley into Oxford so that she could purchase Christmas presents. She had been half-expecting to hear that Jonathan was coming for Christmas to his cousin's house, as had been his custom for the past year or two, but concluded that he was remaining at Deborah's home.

To her surprise, she met him in the High Street, and saw him before he saw her.

'Hullo! What are you doing? I thought you were in Edin-burgh,' she said. Jonathan seemed pleased to see her.

'We were coming on to Carey's as soon as we'd finished shop-ping,' he answered. 'Matter of fact, we called at the College yes-terday, thinking you might still be there chasing your lunatic. Deb. was horribly worried about you.'

'My lunatic chased me,' Mrs Bradley responded, 'so I came on, after all. I'm sorry you bothered.'

At this point Deborah appeared, bearing several parcels. Mrs Bradley, rather touched by the warmth of her greeting and her obvious relief at finding her safe and sound, told her to put the parcels into the car and directed George to drive on.

'Could George drive me to the post office? I want to send a wire home,' said Deborah, when they were settled.

'And I'll telephone Jenny,' said Mrs Bradley, 'and let her know you are coming.'

They lunched at the Mitre, and, after some argument from the engaged couple, who declared that they were staying two nights in Oxford, and then were going to London for three or four days, George drove the whole party to Stanton St John. Mrs Bradley had noticed that the burden of the protestations had been borne by Deborah; Jonathan had joined in perfunctorily, but seemed pleased when objections were all overruled and the car was *en route* for Old Farm.

'I love this country-side,' said Deborah suddenly. The car, which had come up Headington Hill, had turned left by New Headington, and was following the Roman Road. It was cold on the return drive. They had not hurried over lunch and the sun was low and dusk at hand, even by the time they had covered the short distance from the city.

They went in and stood before the huge fire which Mrs Ditch was even then making up as they came in. Jenny kissed Deborah and welcomed Jonathan. 'But, really, Jenny, I'm not going to stay here, and put you all about. It's a real family time,' began Deborah.

'You're part of the real family,' said Jenny firmly. 'Besides, the babies want you to stay, and they always have their own way. Carey gives it to them, and it's too much to expect that I can cope with them and him, so I don't attempt to do it. Jonathan will have to share the kitchen with Derek and the turkey, but it's easy enough to fix in another female, so don't do any more arguing, there's a lamb.'

*

'Did you have a nice term, dear?' asked Kitty's mother anxiously.

'So, so,' replied Kitty. 'I couldn't bear it if it weren't for old Dog; but still, so long as she's around, I can make out.'

'Any adventures?' inquired Kitty's eleven-year-old brother.

'Stacks! Ghosts, murder, old Dog nearly getting pneumonia, somebody slashing up coats and breaking open trunks and tins of disinfectant, School Prac., all sorts of rumours that the last Warden disappeared at the end of last term, although some only say she was ill, and . . .'

'What was that about Laura getting pneumonia, dear,' asked her mother, detaching from this welter of rhetoric the one accessible and assimilable fact.

*

'I'll sing seconds,' said Alice.

'We thought perhaps when you came home from that there College, you'd be too grand to come out carol-singing with the Church,' said one of the sopranos.

'Oh, no, of course not,' said Alice, distressed at the idea. 'Of *course* I shouldn't be too grand. I'm not grand at all. I'm going to work for my living, like everybody else, when I've passed my examinations. Who plays the harmonium now?'

'Mr Twillett. Mr Ross has got his rheumatism bad again. It's cold work, that harmonium is.'

'Brother and Sister Tupper have kindly invited the choir to stop at their house for refreshments tonight,' announced the choirmaster, 'so we shall do Percy Street, Braddock Street and Towcester Street going, and Willmott Street, Upper Swan Lane and Bootin's Corner coming back. Would those with electric torches light the harmony, please? I think the air can manage.'

*

'Laugh,' said Laura, 'I thought I should have died! In fact, I believe, I *should* have died if the other two hadn't dried me and helped me dress. All the same, it's great to be in the thick of a murder, and my belief is that Mrs Croc. has got it all taped out, and is only waiting for the last clue, or something, to make her grab. Oh, the ghost! You really ought to have heard the ghost. It was great. We were all scared out of our lives. I say, if you're going to cut that slice in halves, bags the top half if nobody else wants it. I need fattening, and almond paste is just the stuff, I should imagine. Oh, and Aunt Alison sent her love when I was up there for half-term. I forgot to put it in my letter. She told me I'd lost my guid Scots tongue. Are we all going up there for the New Year?'

*

'I beg your pardon, madam,' said George, 'but if convenient, could I take Christmas Day?'

'Of course, George. Take what you like. Do you want to borrow the car? I shan't want it down here. Mr Carey has his, and Mr Ferdinand will come in his, and we can always hire one in Oxford, if it comes to the point. But it won't.'

She waited in some curiosity to learn the explanation of this request. George had not taken Christmas leave for several years. He was not bound to furnish an explanation, but she felt sure he would.

'The fact is, madam,' he went on, 'the Chief Engineer at the College has been kind enough to invite me to spend the Christmas with them. I shouldn't require a week, madam, but if I could get down on Christmas Eve, say, and be back the day after

Boxing Day – his brother's coming home on leave, and turns out to be my old sergeant-major, madam. It's only an ordinary name, so I never thought anything of it until we were having a yarn one day, so he asked me over.'

'By all means, George. And don't hurry back. I really don't need the car until, anyway, the New Year.'

*

'Have you brought a boar's head, Aunt Bradley?' was Denis's greeting as he descended from his motor-cycle and told his friend (riding pillion) to get off. He propped the motor-cycle against the stone wall which marked off the kitchen garden from the surrounding fields and introduced the stranger. 'This is Carter. I thought we could get up an eleven to play the village. Carter plays hockey, so he'll be quite useful, as it's only Soccer.'

'Hullo, Scab,' said Carey, coming out of one of the pig-houses. 'Hullo, Carter. Glad it's you. Scab didn't say who.'

'Hullo, Carey,' said Carter, demonstrating that his voice was breaking.

'I don't suppose Scab bothered to introduce you,' went on Carey, 'but this is my aunt, Mrs Lestrange-Bradley.'

'Oh, really?' said Carter, blushing. 'I say ... awfully glad, you know. Lestrange said you'd tell us about your murderers. I say, I wish you would.'

'Well, she will,' said Denis reassuringly. 'Come on and meet the others. I say, Carey, where shall I park the crate?'

'Your motor-bike? Oh, there's plenty of room in the garage. Come on up to the house.'

'I was thinking,' said Denis, 'that we could get up an eleven. There's me, and you, old Carter, who plays hockey, Ditch, Walt, Ferdinand, Jonathan, Derek – how many's that? – one, two, three, four, five, six, seven, that's eight. We could play three forwards, two halves, two backs and a goal, reduce the pitch by, say, a fifth, and ...'

'Oh, dry up,' said Carey. 'I don't know why I asked you to come. We never get any peace. And, by the way, what about luggage?'

'Oh, coming. We didn't pack much. It'll be here some time. Are we going to have Derek in our room? Because that's all right by us. You don't mind, Carter, do you? Oh, and bags I play the organ for Christmas morning service. I've been practising, haven't I, Carter?'

'He's rather good,' said Carter. 'He generally plays at school now, instead of Doctor Flaskett.'

As Denis's musical gifts were known and appreciated, this statement was received calmly. Mrs Bradley watched the boys go up to the house with Carey, and then decided to walk as far as Stanton Great Wood, call on her acquaintances at the next farm, a place called Roman Ending, and come back across the fields.

By the time she returned it was dusk, and a deep blue winter twilight lay upon fields and trees. From the large, warm, brightly lighted dining-room of Old Farm came the sound of carols and the thin music of Denis's flute. Mingled with all this was the sound of an approaching car.

'Ah, here you are, mother,' said Ferdinand, getting out and helping Caroline down. Derek also appeared, struggling with some of the parcels with which the interior of the car appeared to be packed. Ferdinand's sedate chauffeur began to open the boot and take out luggage.

'The gathering of the clan appears to be complete,' said Mrs Bradley, permitting Derek to load her with parcels. As they walked up to the front door of the old, stone-built house, she enumerated the guests.

'And you've actually managed to take a rest, away from the College *and* the case?' said Ferdinand, shifting the heavy baggage he was carrying from one hand to the other. 'By the way, I'm sending Bigger and the car into the village. We've managed to fix him up a room, so Jenny won't have to be bothered. What have you done about George?'

Mrs Bradley explained. The next two or three days passed pleasantly; the boys escorted Mrs Bradley into Oxford, selected their presents and bought hers; Ferdinand and Caroline spent most of their time driving into adjacent counties and calling on their acquaintances; the pigs also came in for a good deal of visiting and admiration, and the engaged couple walked over the winter footpaths and came home to tea each day tired, muddy, trailing ivy and holly, clouds of glory and bestowing on all and sundry, said Carey, grinning, the usual nods and becks and wreathed smiles germane to their estate and disability. Jenny's babies were everywhere – in among the pigs, under the feet of the adults, being perilously swung and tossed by the boys, or hanging on to Mrs Bradley's skirt and accompanying her wherever she might chance to go about the house.

Added to the noise made by the company, was the bustle of Christmas preparation. Christmas Eve came at last, with its usual last-minute rush of present-buying, sampling the food, carol-singing, decorations and anxieties. Then came Christmas Day and the ritual of early rising.

Denis did play the organ, and Mrs Bradley attended church. In fact, the Lestrange pew was the wonder and admiration of the village and so was its annexe, a second pew to contain those who could not be accommodated in the first one.

Christmas dinner was over, Christmas crackers had been pulled, mottoes read, and, the boys having been coerced into taking a walk with two of the dogs, Jenny was saying that she thought the babies ought to have their afternoon sleep, when the telephone rang.

'It's for you, mum,' said Mrs Ditch. 'Long distance.'

Mrs Bradley went into the hall.

'Speaking from Cartaret College, madam,' said George. 'We thought you might like to know we've been having a busy morning, putting out the fire in the basement.'

'Oh, so she got in, George?'

'Well, the Chief Engineer reckons she's been there all the time, madam, waiting her opportunity.'

'What damage?'

'Very little, madam. Please don't trouble to come along. Barring a bit of a mess in the bakehouse which took on from the petrol drips in the basement, there's nothing can't be set to rights, we think, before the young ladies come back. There's nothing really amiss.'

'Athelstan Hall?'

'Not touched. Not so much as a scorch-mark, madam, anywere except in the boxroom and a bit in the passage.'

'Oh, good. You didn't catch her, I suppose?'

'I think when she had dispersed the petrol about the place, she made her getaway, madam. There wasn't the slightest trace. We didn't see anybody, although we searched very careful.'

'Are either of you burnt at all?'

'No, madam.'

'Is that the truth, George?'

'Yes, madam, not a blister. Only I thought you'd be interested to know, or I wouldn't have rung you.'

'I see. Well, thank you very much, George.'

'A merry Christmas, madam.'

CHAPTER 14

FIELD-WORK

'I DON'T care what you say,' said Alice, 'although I think it's coarse to talk like that, but I shall get married myself, later on.'

'Why not?' inquired Laura, flinging clothing out of a suitcase in the manner of a terrier flinging up earth from a hole where it thinks it has buried a bone. 'Where the *hell* are my bedroom slippers? Oh, Kitty, you lout, you've got them on!'

'Well, teachers generally don't,' resumed Alice. 'But I come from the lower classes where marriage is the rule, not the exception, and I'm not ashamed of it. What I mean ...'

'The glories of our blood and state, are shadows, not substantial things,' remonstrated Laura, assuming the slippers lately snatched from Kitty. 'I do not recognize class-consciousness, young Alice, so pipe down. Don't be a snob.'

'Anyway, I hope the Deb. stays until the end of our first year,' said the denuded one, sitting on Laura's bed with her feet up. 'I don't suppose I shall be able to go down to tea, Dog,' she continued, surveying the ends of her stockinged feet. 'I can't find a thing of my own except the shoes I came in, and they're all mud, from that foul path out of the station.'

'Have mine. They were new for Christmas,' said Alice, putting both hands into her hat-box. 'Here you are.'

'And don't scuffle about in 'em,' added Laura. 'Incidentally, I suppose bedroom slippers at first tea are *de rigueur*?'

'Mrs Croc. won't be there, and anyway, it's a free country,' said Kitty, trying on Alice's slippers and holding out one foot the better to admire it. 'These from the boy friend, young Alice?'

'I haven't a boy friend,' said Alice, blushing. 'I was only stating my views in a general way about marriage. You needn't laugh.'

'You know, there's something a bit Little Lord Fauntleroy

about our Alice,' said Laura. 'I used to notice it last term. A kind of *je ne sais quoi*.' She began to comb her hair.

'Little Lord Fauntleroy?' said Alice.

'Yes. You know ... she means where they stick a placard on his back to say he bites,' said Kitty earnestly. Her friends gazed at her with fascinated admiration.

'What she owes to her spiritual pastors and masters will never be known,' said Laura. 'She goes from strength to strength. When we were at school she thought Dickens wrote *Under Two Flags*.'

'Well, I don't see why he shouldn't have,' said Kitty sturdily. 'Where's my calendar? I want to mark off the days. I think I'll mark today off straight away. It's practically over. When's half-term, Dog?'

The date was January 23rd. The Lent term had its own interests, did not include School Practice, and part of it would be devoted (as soon as the weather improved) to the various rambles and excursions which formed part of the First Year Course.

The scope and nature of the rambles depended largely upon the Advanced Subjects chosen; thus Laura, ignoring her gift for English, had elected to take Advanced Geography, and Kitty, having no particular preferences, had put her name down for the same group. Alice was down for Advanced Biology, and spent most of her time cutting sections and putting them under the microscope when she was not engaged upon Field Work.

For about the first five weeks of the term the weather was so bad that even some of the fixtures in hockey had to be abandoned. When March came, however, the wet and the heavy mists had cleared away, the sun shone, and the snappy, invigorating air seemed to invite the students out upon the moors.

One bright, cold, gusty afternoon, the Advanced Geography group, having been advised previously of the arrangements by the senior lecturer in the subject, collected after lunch in the Senior Common Room of the College with notebooks, pencils, cameras, geological hammers and Ordnance maps, 'ready for fairies at the bottom of the garden or a full-scale invasion, or anything in between the two,' as Laura put it, and prepared to set out upon an excursion.

'What have we here, Dog?' asked Kitty, as her friend

consulted a business-like little notebook completely filled with writing, maps and sketches.

'A pearl of great price,' said Laura, lowering her voice. 'My spies inform me that these bally outings or expeditions always follow the same course, year after year. Now this,' she tapped the notebook, 'was compiled, doubtless with much sweat, by one Tweetman of Athelstan, some five years ago. She left it to her junior, one Plumstead. Plumstead bequeathed it to a crony in the first year, y-clept Mason. Mason left it in her will to friend Cartwright (who informs me upon oath that the only reason she wasn't sent down last term was because her First Year Advanced Geography (Excursion Section) notebook was so impressive). Cartwright, having crossed the Rubicon and having no further use for the treasure, has passed it on to me. You shall share, on condition you'll edit your stuff so that it isn't word for word like mine.'

'What a godsend!' said Kitty, eyeing the notebook reverently.

'Not a word to young Alice, by the way,' said Laura, warningly. 'Her morals are not as sound as one would wish. She might think we oughtn't to use the beastly thing.'

'Good Lord! Why not?' said Kitty. 'A thing like that ought to go down to posterity.'

'Well, it probably will,' said Laura.

Kitty and Laura enjoyed their walk. Avoiding company, they strolled together, well in the rear of the party, conversing amiably and from time to time checking the geography of the landscape with the assistance of Miss Tweetman.

'Points of interest,' read Laura, standing still. 'Two morainic mounds, one to the right of the road between the canal and the railway, and one between the road and the river on the left-hand side. Got that, duckie? Swing bridges over the canal. Well, we know all about bridges over the river! At least, I do. I'll tell you what! Has it ever struck you to wonder where the deed was done?'

'What deed, Dog?' inquired Kitty, producing a paper bag and abstracting parkin, which she divided and the two of them shared.

'Why, the murder of Miss Murchan. You heard about the Great Fire during the Christmas Vac., didn't you?'

'No. Where?'

'Here in Athelstan, so far as I can make out. I searched for traces of it, but can't find any. Mrs Bradley's man was almost burnt to death.'

'Doesn't exactly show signs of it,' said Kitty. 'I saw him yesterday, turning Miss Hollis's car for her. He looked all right to me.'

'I am only repeating what I've heard. And another curious thing. You know that blighter Cornflake, who was at your school for School Prac.?'

'Yes?'

'Hasn't turned up this term.'

'Oh, I knew that. She's got measles.'

'Measles?'

'Yes. Can be jolly dangerous when you're grown-up, I believe. Somebody in Rule Britannia's told me. I forget who it was. I say, keep your eyes skinned for a pub. They'll still be open. We could get some beer.'

'A scheme,' said Laura, embracing it with some eagerness. 'Don't suppose the late Tweetman had the forethought to bung down anything useful like that in her notes.'

Kitty gazed at the landscape, and then sniffed the air.

'I can give you the next bit without any notes,' she said. 'Gas works and a sewage farm, both on the left.'

'You're telling me,' said Laura, wrinkling her nose. 'I suppose if we get gaol fever or typhus or anything, we can claim on the College. I shall tell my people to, anyway.'

'Change in the landscape. Shoot,' said Kitty, who had taken down in shorthand (to the never-failing amazement of her acquaintances she could put down a hundred and twenty to a hundred and fifty words a minute) the winged words dictated by her friend from Miss Tweetman's invaluable script.

'Eh? Oh, sorry. Yes. New housing estate. See it? Local building material used.'

'What's that? Red sandstone?'

'No, mutt. Limestone blocks, I think, but don't worry. Tweetman's sure to have a footnote about it somewhere. Just bung down what I say. Criticism unwelcome and unnecessary. River crossed – Yes, and here's the bridge ... and here's a pub. All clear? Bung in, then. This is today's great thought.'

Having drunk their beer they came on to the bridge and looked at the shallow swirling water.

'... and wool mills seen,' continued Laura, balancing Miss Tweetman's notes on the coping. 'Now the moor. Flat-topped. Canal. Railway embankment. Railway embankment? ... Oh, yes. Over there. See it? To the left was noticed an old quarry – Come on. We'd better get along and identify that. There's pretty sure to be a discussion on the outing, so we'd better have something ready at first-hand.'

'There's somebody down there,' said Kitty, when they had discovered the old quarry. 'I say, it's Mrs Croc. She's on her own, too. Wonder what she's doing?'

'Snooping for – Here, come on,' said Laura. 'I know what she's doing, and we could help.'

She began to scramble down the side of the quarry. After hesitating for a second, Kitty said:

'Dog, do you know what?'

'No. What?' inquired Laura, balancing on two tufts of the coarse rank grass with which the quarry was clothed.

'I believe she's looking for the body. I'd hate to help her find it.'

Mrs Bradley was surprised and not particularly pleased to see Laura, and gave her no encouragement to make herself useful.

'Are you exploring *all* the quarries?' asked Laura, pointedly.

'Yes,' replied the Warden. 'And you, Miss Menzies, are attached to a party for which your lecturer in Advanced Geography is responsible.'

'She won't miss me. I seem to have left old Kitty in the swim,' Laura replied, glancing upwards to see the last of her friend, who, with an apologetic wave of the hand, was disappearing over the skyline. 'Do let me help snoop. I know what you're looking for, and I bet I can find it if you can.'

'I doubt whether you *do* know what I'm looking for,' said Mrs Bradley, amused.

'Oh? Not Miss Murchan?'

'Of course not, child. Go away.'

'Well, if you're serious,' said Laura, looking extremely disappointed. 'Personally, I shouldn't think you ought to be out on the moors alone, especially in these quarries. Anything might happen to you, especially if there is something funny about Miss Murchan. And, further to that, Warden, what price Miss Cornflake, and the measles? You'd be in a lot better position with me here to heave a couple of half-bricks at that baby, than laid out with all the College looking for you with lanterns and St Bernard dogs and things.'

At this picturesque image Mrs Bradley laughed, and scribbling a message on a page of her notebook gave the leaf to the petitioner and bade her hurry up and give it to the lecturer.

'And bring Miss Trevelyan back with you. I'm not looking for a corpse. I want to find a large receptacle of stone, earthenware or metal, and the remains of a large bonfire,' said Mrs Bradley.

She was up and out of the quarry by the time her henchman returned.

'O.K. by Miss Catterick, Warden,' she said, breathing slightly faster than usual, 'and Kitty is following me up as quickly as – Oh, here she is. Where next?'

'To the next quarry wherever it is,' said Mrs Bradley, unfolding an Ordnance map.

'You don't want to bother with that, Warden,' said Kitty, joining them. 'Where's the book of words, Dog?'

'Please let me see your map, Warden,' said Laura, suddenly. Mrs Bradley handed it over. It was the ordinary one-inch map of the district. Laura folded it, handed it back with a word of thanks, and then observed: 'This is more the sort of thing you want, I should imagine. Six inches to the mile. Issued to Advanced Geography students on presentation of voucher supplied by Miss Catterick. Any good, Warden?'

But Mrs Bradley was already poring over the six-inch map. She then smacked Laura on the back.

'We're off the track, child,' she said. 'Those old quarries marked on the opposite side of the river are much more to our purpose.'

'What about the limestone boulder pits?' asked Laura, pointing to the map.

'Rather close to those large houses, don't you think? How deep are the pits? Have you seen them?'

'Yes. Pretty deep. Steep-sided, too. But that wouldn't worry Cornflake. She's quite the mountaineer, I should think, Warden, and she could tumble the corpse down. She wouldn't need to carry it.'

The limestone boulder pits were about a mile and a quarter from the College and about two from where the trio were standing. The footpaths were miry, but were so much the best and quickest way that, without hesitation, Mrs Bradley led the way by one which ran in a straight line to the railway, across by a footbridge and beyond to woods and the canal.

'Keep to the towing path here for a bit,' said Laura, 'and cross by the swing bridge. Then we shall have to follow the main road, and cross the river just below the weir.'

Once they had crossed the river, another footpath led by the flank of a wood, across parkland and then through trees to a round, wooded hill. On the south side of the hill lay the pits they sought, but exploration of them proved to be vain. Except for the limestone from which they took their name, they were bare and empty, and a further consultation of the map caused Mrs Bradley to decide upon some old quarries further west, beside a lane which crossed arable fields.

'Only the one farm near,' said Laura, when her opinion of the objective was canvassed, 'and a little stream to wash in if she got herself mucked up during the surgical operations. I shouldn't be surprised if we've hit on the right place, Warden. What say you, Kitty, old thing?'

'Nothing,' replied Kitty.

'Right. Keep your eyes skinned for enemy snipers, then, whilst Mrs Croc. and I do our bloodhound act,' said Laura under her breath. 'If you see the whites of old Cornflake's eyes, don't let her shoot first. Got it?'

'All right, as long as I don't have to look at corpses or anything,' agreed Kitty. The walk this time was a very charming one and completely rural. A very narrow footpath from the pits crossed a lane by two stiles, and then joined a wider path which crossed two fields of pasture. It then entered a wood and became a broad woodland ride for about a quarter of a mile before branching in four or five different directions.

Guided by the map, the party selected the most south-westerly of these divergent tracks, and came up upon a narrow road, which led to the solitary farm-house. They crossed the road, still kept within the confines of the wood, and so came upon the quarry.

'Of course, there are these two quarries, as well,' said Laura, pointing them out on the map, 'but they are nearer the village and further away from the stream. I should think she'd have to wash herself, shouldn't you?'

'If she did what I think she did, she'd need water for another purpose,' responded Mrs Bradley. 'Mind how you come. The bank seems a bit crumbly.'

'You'd better stay at the top and keep *cave*, Kitty,' said Laura. 'Unless we both do. What do you say, Warden?'

'Please yourselves, child. This is the right place, anyhow, I think.'

The remains of the bonfire were immense. Not only that, but the fact that the fire had been made up on a carefully-built hearth of bricks indicated no casual wayfaring but somebody with a set purpose who had imported into the quarry the means for resolving that purpose into action.

Mrs Bradley sketched and scribbled, took out a lens and made a detailed inspection of the hearth, and then sent the students back to College, for it was ten minutes to four, and she was afraid they would miss their tea. Reluctant but obedient, off went Laura. Kitty showed more alacrity. Mrs Bradley, left alone, explored the quarry indefatigably for footprints, and for traces of ingress and egress. The crumbling banks assisting her, she discovered, besides the traces left by herself and the two girls, tracks in several places, but these might have been made at any time and by anybody, for the frequent winter rains had washed out all individuality, and no actual footprints could be detected. She did, however, mark on her sketches the new landslide which marked that part of the bank which she and the students had used. Then she scrambled up it again and went off to the farm to ask permission to use the telephone.

She had other inquiries to make.

'Where,' she asked, 'was it possible to purchase bricks like those she had found in the quarry?'

The answer to this question was a broad stare from the woman who had answered the door, and a request to wait a minute.

Standing in the stone-flagged hall beside the grandfather clock, Mrs Bradley waited. In less than two minutes the woman came back, accompanied by a boy of about fifteen.

'Tell the lady about Mr Tegg's bricks,' said the woman. 'Her wants to know where to buy some like those her've seen in the quarry.'

'I suppose the police have sent you?' said the boy.

'The lady's just been on phone to 'em, any road,' said the woman. 'I told thee, and so did Father, there'd be more to say about they bricks. Now perhaps thee'll believe us as is older than thyself.'

'Leave me alone with him,' said Mrs Bradley. The woman hesitated, and then added, still speaking to the boy, but this time in a tone between apology and anger:

'Thee's brought this on thyself, and mun face it out best thee can.'

'I can take it,' muttered the boy, shifting his feet, lowering his eyes and giving all the other signs of obstinacy in wrong-doing common to boys in trouble.

'What's your name?' asked Mrs Bradley, taking out her notebook. The boy was silent. 'Afraid to give his name,' she added as though saying the words she was writing. The boy looked up.

'I'm not afraid to give my name. My name's William Turley, if you want to know. And I did steal the rotten bricks, but it was to oblige a lady. Yes, and I did build a fireplace for her, and I fetched water for her from the beck, and I helped her down with it so that it shouldn't all get spilt. Let the police get a load of that, if it means anything to them!'

'Dear me!' said Mrs Bradley. 'Can you describe the lady?'

'No. And I wouldn't, anyway. I don't get other people into trouble.'

'Good. So if I told you she was fairly young, dark, active as a cat, sharp-voiced and had a car, you would contradict me, I suppose?'

The boy did not answer, but put his hands in his pockets.

'And now,' went on Mrs Bradley, after she had scribbled a few more hieroglyphics, 'what did Mr Tegg have to say about the bricks?'

'Nothing, except that they'd been stolen.'

'How did he trace them to you?'

'Dad saw them in the quarry. I got mud on my Sunday clothes, and they wanted to know how. I didn't say, because I ought to have been in church, and I hadn't been, and Dad recognized the kind of mud, I suppose, and he told Mr Tegg he needn't look for his missing bricks, and asked him to let the police know I'd had them. That's all.'

'Very interesting, too,' said Mrs Bradley. 'What did Mr Tegg say to that?'

'I went to him privately and asked for time to pay, but he said he'd promised my father to let the police lay me by the heels.'

'And now you think they have, do you? My view is that your father paid Mr Tegg long ago. What makes your parents want to frighten you?'

'No business of yours.'

'You don't speak like the boys about here.'

'I've been to a decent school, that's why. I got sacked.'

'For thieving?'

'Yes, if you want to know.'

'Well, William, thank you very much for your information. I suppose you can't remember the date when you built the fireplace for the lady?'

'I might, but not for you.'

'Oh, that means last summer, then.' She wrote again. 'Where were you at school?'

'London.'

'Really? That seems a good way to go.'

'Lived with my aunt and uncle.'

'And liked it, I know. Pity you messed up your chances, wasn't it?'

'I don't want that from you.'

'No, I can tell that. How did it happen, William?'

'Foreign stamps.'

'Oh, yes. Wouldn't they have kept you if you'd made restitution? Or did you sell the stamps?'

'No, I didn't sell them.'

'I see. There were others in it.'

'I didn't say so, any more than I said you were right about the lady.'

'You have said so now. Well, good-bye William. I'm afraid the police *will* come, but not about the bricks as such. I should answer their questions, if I were you. Where is your stamp collection now?'

'Burnt it.'

'*You* did?'

'Dad did. I don't blame him for that.'

A curious and interesting household, thought Mrs Bradley, returning to the College, not by the footpaths and fields, but by the motor roads which a murderer burdened with a corpse would have had to take in order to arrive at the quarry. She reached the lane which ran past the wall of the College grounds at a quarter past five, stopped to speak to the Chief Engineer as she passed his house and met him coming out of it, and then encountered Kitty and Laura.

'Did you get any tea?' she inquired.

'We only scraped in at the death, but managed to grab a couple of cups and some rolls. Oh, and Kitty spotted an old zinc bath in another quarry, but we didn't stop,' responded Laura. 'Did you have any luck at the farm, Warden?'

'Yes. More than I expected. The son, a boy of fifteen, helped build the brick fireplace. Of course, it is most likely that the person he assisted is not the person we are after, but some investigation is called for, and I have asked the police to undertake it.'

'And the receptacle thing you wanted to find?'

'No sign of anything of the sort, but it may have been your bath. If it can be found, the police will find it, but not yet, because I haven't mentioned it.'

'What *is* this receptacle thing you both talk about? Not really that bath?' inquired Kitty, as the two students walked over to College for a late lecture in English.

'No; the pot thing, whatever it was, that the murderer used to boil the flesh off the bones, I think,' answered Laura. Fortunately for her own peace of mind, Kitty, who had never heard of the unsavoury details of the behaviour of certain murderers confronted by the bodies of their victims, did not believe what she said, and merely murmured reproachfully: 'Oh, Dog, don't say such beastly things.'

It was just as they reached the steps that Laura, lingering a moment to tie up her shoe-lace, spotted an unfamiliar car coming slowly along the back drive. But for their recent activities in the quarries, she would have thought nothing of it.

Alice, who was in their group for English, was already in her place in the lecture room, and had kept two front row seats.

'Why front row, chump?' grumbled Kitty, seating herself, and looking round for Laura.

'Because it's the Deb.,' replied Alice.

'And Alice can't bear anybody else's fat head to come between them,' jeered Laura, joining them. There was a fair amount of noise in the room, into which, looking, as usual, thoroughly frightened (in Mrs Bradley's view) or 'damned superior' (in the words and view of Miss Cartwright, who, however, approved of this attitude), came Deborah, carrying her lecture notes, a large Shakespeare with dozens of little bits of paper marking her references, the Group Roll (which she called, on principle, at late lectures because people, she thought, were disposed to cut them), and an 'acting copy' of *Richard of Bordeaux*, a play which she was going to suggest to the First-Years that they should produce in the summer.

'Good evening,' said Deborah, laying her books on the desk and dropping the copy of the play. 'Oh, thank you, Miss Boorman.' For Alice, from the middle of the front row and with a nippiness which was the product of the gymnasium and the netball court, had leapt upon the small, paper-backed volume and returned it.

'What was it?' whispered Laura. Alice wrote on the top of her English notebook the title.

'Glory!' commented Laura, rudely, and rose with languid grace. 'Am I in order in asking a question which probably does not have a direct bearing on the lecture, Miss Cloud?' she inquired.

'Yes ... yes, certainly, Miss Menzies,' replied Deborah, who dreaded Laura's end-of-the-day flights of fancy when she herself was tired and the indefatigable student apparently as fresh as paint.

'Thank you. Then what, please, is your opinion of Gordon Daviot as a dramatist?'

'Oh, well, rather good, I thought,' said Deborah. 'That is ...'

'And do you base that opinion on *Richard of Bordeaux*, or on any other of the dramatist's works?' pursued Laura with relentless courtesy.

'I was thinking only of *Richard of Bordeaux*,' said Deborah, eyeing her interlocutor with a good deal of dislike. 'And now sit down. I'm going to begin my lecture.'

Laura, with an audible remark about 'the ship full fraught', seated herself with easy grace. Deborah flushed, bit her lip, and then said sharply, in a 'classroom' voice:

'Don't make remarks, please, Miss Menzies. It is, to say the least, ill-mannered.'

'I beg your pardon, Miss Cloud. I was making a quotation from Michael Drayton. I withdraw it,' said Laura sweetly.

'Keep your quotations for your essays,' said Deborah, unwisely. 'Oh, God!' she thought, discerning an expression of rapturous amazement on Laura's countenance. 'Now what have I let myself in for?'

She shrugged, smiled at the rest of the group, and began to read her lecture. Laura sat, chin on hand, gazing at her for about five minutes. This steady, unwinking regard made Deborah nervous. She stumbled over a sentence, became involved in a – she discovered too late – slightly under-punctuated paragraph, and was roused to excessive irritation at hearing Laura's voice murmuring delicately: 'How men would love if they might, and how they would have women be.'

She stopped short, flushed angrily, scowled at the interruption and then said:

'Miss Menzies?'

'Eh? Oh, pardon, Miss Cloud. Am I in order if I ask a question at this point of your lecture?'

'I suppose so,' said Deborah hopelessly.

'What is your opinion of Arthur Symon's introduction to his collection of Elizabethan poetry?'

'That question, unfortunately, has nothing to do with my lecture,' replied Deborah, 'and therefore I must decline to answer it.'

'Thank you, Miss Cloud,' replied Laura.

'Thank *you*, Miss Menzies,' said Deborah belligerently. Laura waved a languid hand for the lecture to proceed, but before Deborah had completed another paragraph she was on her feet again.

'Miss Cloud!'

'Oh, dear, Miss Menzies!'

'Miss Cloud, do I understand you to say that Sidney was the greatest love-poet of the Elizabethan age?'

'No, Miss Menzies, you do not. What I said was...'

'I was afraid you'd forgotten Drayton, not to speak of Donne,' said Laura. 'I see I was mistaken.'

She sat down again. Deborah went on, slightly shaken, to her next paragraph. There was no interruption. The lecture went placidly on, the clock moved its hands towards the hour. There was no sound except Deborah's quiet voice and the methodical noise of students scratching down notes. Suddenly this blessed peace was shattered once again.

'Or, of course, Campion,' said Laura.

'Go *out*, Miss Menzies!' said Deborah. 'I shall report you to the Principal.'

'Good for you,' said Laura cheerfully. She edged out, and at the same instant the highly indignant Alice hooked her skilfully round the ankle so that she measured her length on the floor. There was some slight confusion whilst Laura picked herself up and dusted herself down, then, with a bow to Deborah and an apologetic smile, she withdrew and ran lightly down the stone staircase.

The English room was on the second floor. Laura ran on, descending from one landing to the next, and left the College building by darting past the large lecture theatre and the senior student's room.

On the main drive opposite the front entrance stood the small dark-green saloon car she had noticed before the beginning of Deborah's lecture. She stepped back so that the angle of the building screened her from view, and watched, automatically registering in her brain the number of the car.

A woman, neatly dressed in green mixture tweeds, got out and approached the front entrance.

'Gotcher!' observed Laura, *sotto voce*, and began very cautiously to stalk her. In spite of a greatly changed appearance, there was no doubt in her mind that the woman was Miss Cornflake.

Up the staircase she went, followed by Laura. On the first floor she halted, and, to Laura's intense interest, took out of her handbag a small revolver. She then glanced furtively about her, through a heavy, old-fashioned veil.

The College was silent. Through the well-fitting doors came no sound of the quiet voices of lecturers intoning their information. Students in the building were either in attendance at lectures or working in the library, the laboratory or the small handwork room at that hour of the day. There seemed to be no casual going or coming. Miss Cornflake, if she was bent on mischief, had selected an excellent time.

Laura had no doubt about what to do. The only difficulty was to decide exactly when to do it. Temperamentally she was almost without physical fear, but common sense informed her that if Miss Cornflake were a murderess it would be madness to tackle her at an ineffectual moment, especially when she was armed.

She had little time in which to make a plan. If Miss Cornflake's attitude and weapon meant anything, they meant that she was in search of somebody with intent to put that person out of action. Laura's first conception was that Mrs Bradley could not be the intended victim, since they had left her over at Athelstan. A second horrified thought informed her that there was no reason whatever why the head of the house should not have left it and come over to College.

It soon became apparent that Mrs Bradley was the quarry, for

Miss Cornflake turned to the right at the top of the first flight of stairs and went towards the First-Year's Education Room.

Laura crept nearer. Miss Cornflake listened at the door, then turned the handle with her left hand, keeping the revolver in her right. The corridor was almost pitch-dark, and by the time Miss Cornflake had proved that the room was empty, Laura had slipped into the Students' Common Room opposite to seek assistance, but nobody was there.

The other Education Room was on the ground floor. If Mrs Bradley were lecturing, that was the only other place in which she was likely to be found. It was next-door to a passage which opened on to the grounds, and had large windows slightly open at the top.

Miss Cornflake halted at the door and listened. Laura, drawing as close as ever she dared, listened, too. Her hearing was remarkably acute, more so, it seemed, than Miss Cornflake's, for she detected Mrs Bradley's dulcet tones almost on the instant.

'Probably know the voice better,' thought Laura, referring to herself. A plan presented itself. She withdrew, or, rather, passed on, as Miss Cornflake laid a hand on the door, until she was at the entrance to the Staff Cloakroom. Then she suddenly gave vent to a loud, successful imitation of Mrs Bradley's already famous cackle, and switched on the cloakroom lights. Like a flash, Miss Cornflake leapt away from the door and began to stalk Laura down the corridor.

Laura, now on unfamiliar ground, seized a towel from one of the hooks, and then put it down and picked up a good-sized cake of soap. Then she got behind the door and listened.

Miss Cornflake made not a sound, but the end, when it came, came quickly. Laura had switched on the light to obtain warning of the approaching shadow. As soon as she saw it, out she leapt, knocked up the revolver, which went off with a noise like a bomb, dashed the soap as hard as she could in Miss Cornflake's face, and then dived at her legs to bring her down.

Unfortunately, as she did this, and Miss Cornflake fell heavily forward, Laura hit her own head against the edge of the door. Half-stunned, she scrambled up again, however, and, with a last effort, leapt upon Miss Cornflake and proceeded to choke her with the towel.

*

'Warden wants to know if you feel equal to speaking to the Principal, Dog,' said Kitty in sepulchral tones. 'Says don't say yes if you mean no. What shall I tell her?'

'Oh, Lord! I suppose that means the Deb. did report me. I wouldn't have believed she was such a tick,' groaned Laura, whose head ached almost unendurably, in spite of Mrs Bradley's ministrations. To the amazement of both lecturers and students, Mrs Bradley, leaving Miss Cornflake, who was completely *hors de combat*, to be apprehended by others, had picked up the hefty Laura in her arms and had carried her over to Athelstan (a feat, observed Laura, to make strong men quail), and had put her to bed as though she had been a small child.

'No, the Deb. didn't report you. She just grinned at us when you'd gone and said she was sorry for the interruptions, but she thought you liked to show off what you knew. What shall I say about the Prin.?'

'What does the Lord High Everything Else want, anyway? Dope about Cornflake?'

'Yes, I expect so.'

'Righto. Bung her in. We will give her five minutes,' said Laura, contriving to return to her usual manner. The Principal came in 'as one approaching a deathbed', said Laura, recounting the incident later, and seated herself on the hat-box.

'Now don't disturb yourself, Miss Menzies,' she said. 'I shall stay not more than one minute. Miss Cornflake is in the College Infirmary, well guarded, and the police are going to question her as soon as possible. Now, that's a weight off our minds, isn't it?'

'Yes, Miss du Mugne,' replied the patient.

'That's all I've come to say, then, except...' She looked almost wistfully at the girl... 'except that I feel we owe you a very great debt, Miss Menzies, which we shall do our best to repay. It would never have done to have a – revolver accident actually on the College premises, would it?'

'No, Miss du Mugne,' replied Laura. The Principal gave her a smile of acid sweetness, told her to 'hurry up and get well', and left, much to Laura's relief.

'And now, Kitty,' she said, when her friend came in again, 'what am I having for dinner?'

'Good Lord! Are you *hungry*, Dog?' said Kitty, amazed. 'We never thought to save you anything.'

'Quite right, too,' said Mrs Bradley's voice outside the door. 'The heroine and I are going to have dinner together. Now, patient, what shall we have?'

'I suppose you can't manage a cocktail, to start with, Warden?' said the sufferer. 'It would just about save my life.'

CHAPTER 15

RAG

'I SAY,' said Laura with surprising diffidence, 'sorry I chipped in and all that, you know, but the fact is, I was expecting her.'

'Whom do you mean? Not Miss Cornflake?' asked Deborah, accepting the apology in the spirit in which it was rendered.

'Yes. I saw a strange car and deduced things. I knew you'd sling me out if I kept on long enough, and it seemed the best way to manage. I didn't want a lot of sympathetic goats offering to accompany me if I'd said I felt ill or anything, and one puts away childish things like asking to go to the what's it when one leaves school. So I thought I'd better rag. No evil intentions.'

'All right,' said Deborah.

'Many thanks. And now, Polly, to your affairs, for matters must not be left as they are. How safe are you as a confidante, I wonder?'

'About Miss Cornflake?' asked Deborah, who realized that it was her status and sense of responsibility and not her ability to keep a secret which Laura was questioning.

'Well, that's the trouble. If I said yes to that, you'd be absolved officially from having to blow the gaff, I suppose, wouldn't you?' said Laura. 'Oh, heck, it makes my head ache, trying to think. On the other hand, I don't like lying unless it's absolutely necessary, and it *might* not concern Cornflake at all. Have the police checked up on her yet?'

'Oh, yes. She's the Miss Paynter-Tree of the Secondary School,' said Deborah, who had been told this by Mrs Bradley.

'Has she come clean?'

'She hasn't confessed anything, and she insists that she was carrying the revolver in self-defence, a thin story which no-body believes. Still, she's wriggling pretty hard, and she hadn't actually attacked anybody when you tackled her, you see, so she claims she's being wrongfully detained. Still, she'd have to be kept in the Infirmary for a time, in any case, as Mrs Bradley told her.'

'I say, they won't let her go?' demanded Laura, sitting up in bed with a jerk which caused her to wince.

'Not a chance. Don't worry. Mrs Bradley is perfectly safe,' Deborah replied. 'We are all much obliged to you,' she added, assisting the patient to lie down again.

'We spent part of the afternoon with her, you know,' said Laura. 'With Mrs Bradley, I mean. And I had the feeling we were being watched all the time. Kitty and I kept our eyes skinned, but couldn't spot anyone, but then, that isn't surprising. And I never believed that yarn about Cornflake having the measles. We found the quarry where she did some of the fell work. I wish we could prove it on her, and have done with it. And that brings me full circle, by the way. Made up your mind yet?'

'What about?' inquired Deborah, who had forgotten the opening of the conversation.

'Whether I'm to trust you to keep your mouth shut,' said Laura bluntly.

'Oh, that! Well, I can't promise. How can I?'

'How can you? No, it's awkward. However, between friends, here goes! Cartwright has received a rummy communication from the lads, and has asked my advice. She went just before you came. They want to swap College skeletons with us. I'd tell Mrs Croc. – Mrs Bradley – only I'm afraid she'd have to go all official. I thought perhaps you needn't.'

'What lads?' asked Deborah. 'Do you mean the students over at Wattsdown? If so, I should tell Mrs Bradley. That's my advice. Where is the letter now?'

'Cartwright's still got it, I hope. But don't you see, darling, that if I break these tidings to Mrs Bradley, she'll immediately jump to the conclusion that old Cartwright was mixed up in the Great Receptable Rag which took place, if you remember, at the beginning of last term.'

'Well, but would that matter? If Miss Cartwright was not involved, she'd only have to say so.'

'Trouble is,' said Laura, 'she was in the thick, you see.'

'Oh? That does seem awkward. Was she in collusion with Miss Cornflake, then?'

'Oh, no. She merely saw that the going was good, and charged in with her quota of the devilment, that was all. Sorry I can't spill details.'

'I don't believe Mrs Bradley would care twopence about the rag as such,' said Deborah. 'After all, it's all over and done with, as far as that goes, and Mrs Bradley always thought there were two lots of ragging going on. But is Miss Cartwright certain who sent the letter? It couldn't be a hoax, or – or something unpleasant again, could it?'

'As a matter of fact, her brother sent it. He's her twin, and in his second year there, the same as she is here. She swears it came from him.'

'Writing genuine?'

'Oh, yes. And what's more – I went into all this, I might tell you, from this bed of sickness just now, Cartwright having cut a couple of lectures in order to seek me out and obtain my invaluable advice – he addresses her in the letter by a name which no one outside the family, she declares, would ever be likely to get hold of.'

'Well, really, Dog, my advice still is for you and Miss Cartwright to see Mrs Bradley, put the whole thing to her in confidence, as you have to me, and abide by what she says. I do think we must let her have all the facts we can.'

'What did you call me?' asked Laura.

'Dog. A revenge epithet,' replied Deborah. 'And it's not what I'd like to call you sometimes,' she added. She rose to go.

'Must you go?' inquired Laura. 'You're rather soothing, you know, after some of the bull-nosed idiots with great big feet who've been bursting in here to condole with me. I wonder how much longer,' she added, snuggling down, 'I can fool the general public that I'm ill? It's not a bad way of spending one's time, and Mrs Croc.'s invalid diet is to be commended. No messes. All good nourishing food. Well, if you must go – but come again soon, there's a love.'

*

'Well, as a matter of fact, Warden,' said Miss Cartwright, 'it's their annual theatre rag, and my brother complains that the skeleton they've got isn't properly articulated, and they want to borrow ours.'

'Very sensible,' said Mrs Bradley, 'particularly as I believe the skeleton at present in the Science Room cupboard is not College property. Now, Miss Cartwright, I wonder whether you can tell me how often the College skeleton has been used at lectures since you became a student here a year and a half ago?'

'Once, Warden. First-Year physiology.'

'Ah. And how often is the skeleton brought out at Wattsdown College, I wonder?'

'Well, they had a mock funeral last term, when a man was sent down for – was sent down,' observed Miss Cartwright.

'Sent down for bribing a cat's-meat man to call on Professor Mule and say that he'd heard the College had horse flesh for sale. I heard about that,' said Mrs Bradley. 'Well, Miss Cartwright, I want you to arrange with your brother for this exchange of skeletons to take place. You will not, of course, involve me in any way whatsoever, but I will undertake to see that the exchange is completed without official interference. I have my own reasons for interesting myself in the affair. When did your brother propose to effect the exchange?'

'He said that would have to depend upon us, Warden,' replied the completely puzzled Miss Cartwright.

'Very well, I will let you know later when it will be convenient for you to transport the College specimen to the *rendez-vous*, and where you will find it,' said Mrs Bradley, making a note. 'When is the theatre rag to take place?'

'I don't know, Warden. Next week, I imagine. Teddie would have to give us time to switch – to obtain possession of the skeleton, and exchange it.'

'Very well. Assure your brother of Cartaret's willingness to cooperate. I suppose they have a new lecturer in hygiene this year?'

'Yes,' said Miss Cartwright, surprised. 'Warden,' she added, 'there's something I ought to tell you. You know that rag with the j – with the – the –'

'The promiscuous vessels. Yes, child.'

'Well, I was mixed up in that a good bit more than was thought. I had a challenge, sent me during the holidays – typewritten – I don't know who it was from – daring me to change the skeletons over, and promising that ours would be ready, all boxed up, in the basement, and that certain of the lads would be along to collect it. As they were.'

'Ah,' said Mrs Bradley. 'Have a chocolate, child, I never eat them myself. I have known for some time that you were mixed up in the affair.'

Observing that half the top layer was gone, Miss Cartwright assumed, rightly, that the Sub-Warden probably had a better-educated palate than the Warden, and took a chocolate whilst she wondered how to reply. As her brain refused to assist her, she mumbled thanks, and immediately sought out Laura.

'I say,' she said, sitting down heavily upon the bed.

'Oh, gosh, Cartwright! Have a heart,' said the sufferer reproachfully. 'Not the whole ton at once!'

'Sorry,' said Miss Cartwright. 'No, but listen, Dog. First, the Warden is wise to our scheme for swopping Twister Marshmallow with their Dirty Dick – or, as I suppose you'd have to say, vice-versa – '

'Granted. I told her,' said Laura.

'But, dash it, Dog . . .'

'Cease foaming. What's that in your mouth?'

'Chocolate. She gave me one to terminate the interview.'

'And you selected the only hard one left, I bet. All right. Well, that doesn't sound as though she bit you in the neck exactly.'

'Well, that's the odd part. She didn't. She's all in favour of the scheme, and is offering to help us do the swopping when the lads turn up with Twister.'

'All to the good. Did you accept the offer?'

'Look here, Dog, quit stalling. There's something behind all this. Either Mrs Croc. is off her onion, which wouldn't surprise me in the slightest, or else there's something fishy going on, and I want to know where I stand.'

'You don't stand. You're sitting pretty,' replied Laura. 'Have faith, old goggle-eyes. Trust your Auntie Laura, who's never let her pals down yet, and you can't go wrong. What did she tell you to tell your *frère*?'

'Well, just that – just to carry on, and we'd do our part. Honestly, I can't make head or tail of the woman. And what on earth made you tell her anything about it?'

'Well, I put it up to the Deb. first. *She* said tell the Warden, so in an interview specially sought, I told her all.'

'I suppose she knows you saved her life,' said Miss Cartwright gloomily, 'and thinks you're allowed some fun on the strength of it. But you might think of me! I can't afford to have my name sent up to Miss du Mugne again this term. I'm still only hanging on by my eyebrows, you know. And, like a fool, I've gone and confessed that I worked that All Hallows festival at the beginning of last term, and helped in the original swop-over of the skeletons.'

'Fear nothing,' said Laura, 'and do exactly as the Warden tells you. I had to blow the gaff, dearie, for a reason which you'd be the first to appreciate if you knew it.'

'But what is her game, Dog?'

'Murder,' responded Laura. 'I might tell you that you pulled more of a bone than you know when you swopped those skeletons last time.'

*

'I must say that I am sorry to part with Dirty Dick,' said Mrs Bradley, leering regretfully upon the cadaver before packing straw on top of him as he lay in his coffin-like box. 'Now the rest I shall leave to you, Miss Menzies, and to your myrmidons. At what hour do you expect the young men?'

'At eleven, Warden. They said they'd have to wait until after Lights.'

'Well, you have your Lates, so you should be all right as long as they turn up to time. If they do not, you may give three sharp taps on my sitting-room window, and I'll let you in by the front door. The box is heavy. Can you manage to get it as far as the sports pavilion? I've squared Miss Pettinsalt and the groundsman. It is supposed, as far as he is concerned, to be a case of croquet mallets which my son is going to call for and remove some time this week, and he has Miss Pettinsalt's permission to leave the shed unlocked. There's nothing in it except some tennis nets, anyway.'

The students, six of them acting as pall-bearers, carried the box away and down the stairs. The hour was seven-thirty, that magic period at Cartaret when everybody was at dinner and disturbance and interruption were less likely than at almost any other hour of the twenty-four. This was fortunate, since the games pavilion was in full view of the front windows of all the Halls and also could be seen from the College building.

The bearers put down their burden gratefully. They consisted of Laura, Kitty, Alice and Miss Cartwright and also the twin sisters Carroway, who were staunch and trustworthy and had received with a meek look of astonishment the Warden's pronouncement that they were to hear, see and remember nothing of what passed between the hours of seven and midnight. They did not even ask, as Miss Cartwright had done, what the Warden's game was. Beyond a vague and hopeful expectation of a moderate amount of entertainment, they seemed to require nothing from this odd business of carrying the College skeleton about the College grounds and presenting it, in due course, to another College.

'There we are, then,' said Laura, rubbing her forearms and wrists and looking down at the long box. 'I told the Warden I thought we ought to mount guard, but she says it'll be safe enough where it is. Oh, and she's given me an electric torch, but we're not to use it unnecessarily. Anybody got another?'

No one had, but Annet Carroway thought she knew where she could borrow one.

'Better not,' said Laura. 'Secrecy is of the essence. We shall have to manage with the one.'

The conspirators separated when they reached the Athelstan dining-hall, and filled in the odd places which were left. Nobody questioned them, since neither Deborah nor Mrs Bradley was dining in Hall that evening, and therefore the fact that they were a few minutes late for the meal was of no account.

After dinner they pursued various occupations. The Carroway twins and Alice Boorman worked, Kitty sketched out a few new hairdressing styles she had thought of and wanted to try at some time, Laura wrote an article for the College magazine entitled

'The Vote Against Women', and Miss Cartwright wrote a letter to her young man in Canada.

At half-past ten, after a supper of bread and butter, biscuits and cocoa, it was the custom for students to be in their own rooms with the lights out. This custom was interpreted firmly by Deborah as a rule, and she went the rounds at twenty minutes to eleven each night with persistence and a sharp reminder to law-breakers. She smiled at the six pall-bearers, however, as, fully clothed and carrying their outdoor shoes in their hands, they slipped past her down the front staircase.

'All correct?' whispered Laura, when they had changed their shoes and were upon the doormat. She received a giggling reply from the twins, a solemn one from Alice, who was looking rather pale, a grunt from Miss Cartwright and an earnest 'O.K., Dog,' from Kitty.

'Out lights, then,' whispered Laura. Miss Cartwright switched them off, and the students stood a moment outside the Athelstan front door to accustom their eyes to the darkness before they set out across the grounds. The night was intensely dark. There was no moon and the stars were hidden by low, black clouds.

'Cheery sort of evening,' muttered Laura, feeling her way cautiously down the steps. 'For heaven's sake, come carefully. Don't break your necks.'

She led the way to the left for a few yards along the main drive which ran in front of all the Halls, and then shone the torch on to the steps leading down beside the rockery to the lawns and tennis courts. She switched it off as soon as the others had negotiated the steps, and they followed a path which led towards the College building. As soon as they reached the angle of the wall, which looked strange, a darker darkness against the black night, they turned off the path on to the games field, and, after stumbling on the edge of the bank, came to the pavilion.

Here it was safe to switch on the torch, for the bulk of the pavilion would hide the light from anybody who might happen to be looking out of any of the Hall windows.

'Forward, the body-snatchers!' observed Laura. 'When it's up and steady I'll shove the torch in my pocket and take the front right. Ready?'

It had not been easy to make their way to the pavilion in the darkness with no responsibility but the elementary one of remaining on their feet, but the walk, bearing the skeleton in its box over grass, stumbling into borders, on to unsuspected gravel paths which seemed to have lost their bearings in the blackness and to be meandering over parts of the grounds where no path had existed previously, was a nightmare journey relieved from horror by the fact that its object was, to everybody except Laura, who thought she could guess the origin of the bones which they were to receive in exchange for Dirty Dick, sharply humorous.

After what seemed at least three-quarters of a mile of anguished walking, they stumbled on to the main drive in its south-eastern slant to the lane which bordered the College grounds on the south. There were four gates in the wall which formed the actual boundary of the College demesne, and the arrangement to meet the men at the main entrance had been the subject of much argument before it was agreed upon.

'Suppose the Prin. happens to be out a bit late, and spots us?' suggested Miss Cartwright.

'She'd much better spot us at the main entrance than by the gate from the footpath,' Laura reasoned. 'Besides, the men will have a car, and they won't want to carry the thing along the road, and neither do we. The main gates are never locked. They can bring the car to the bend and drive out with nothing showing.'

A cautious caterwauling – the signal agreed upon – directed the girls to where the young men were waiting.

'Is that you, Teddie?' asked his sister.

'In person,' replied Mr Cartwright. 'What a row you made carting the thing! Here, Jeffries, lend a hand.'

The skeleton changed hands, and Dirty Dick was propped up against the seat beside that of the driver.

'Where's Twister?' inquired Miss Cartwright.

'Behind the bushes. Got a torch? Here you are.' He switched on his torch and disclosed a box similar to that which had just been placed in the car. 'Help you up with him, shall we?'

The two young men lifted the box and the girls formed up and took it from them.

'When's the rag?' asked Laura.

'Saturday week, but we wanted a rehearsal of some of the effects, so thought we'd have Dirty as soon as possible. Thanks for looking after him so nicely. Toodle-pip.'

'Bye-bye,' said Miss Cartwright. 'Oh, Lord, my shoulder's cracking in two. Nighty-night, ducks,' she added to her brother.

'Don't miss your step,' said he. As the six students began the long and awkward journey back to the sports pavilion they heard the car drive off.

'Can't see that it was much of a rag to change them in the first place, really,' said Miss Cartwright, after a pause, 'although I lent the affair some slight assistance. But what does puzzle me is how the lads got into that Science Room cupboard. The door's always locked, and yet they got Twister out and put Dick in.'

The twins, stoutly bearing the hinder end of the box, merely giggled, as usual. Kitty grunted. Only Laura was silent. But then only Laura was suspicious of the *bona fides* of Twister Marshmallow. She feared that that hero lay elsewhere, and that the occupant of his box was 'no less a Yorick', in her own phrase, than poor Miss Murchan.

*

'Gentlemen on my right,' said the president of the Students' Common Room at Wattsdown, 'will act as Guard of Honour to the skeleton, who will be referred to during this meeting, by his full and correct title of Richard Cœur de Lion, and *not* by his more usual sobriquet of Dirty Dick. Agreed, gentlemen?'

There was a chorus of approval.

'Messires Abbot, Paldock, Rees and F. J. Smith will be responsible for nobbling, disconcerting and generally putting out of action any Robert or Roberts on horseback,' pursued the chairman, 'and Mr D. R. Smith will look out for yokels throwing stones. Step out here, gentlemen, please.'

Five rubicund and large-limbed youths, forwards in the College Rugby fifteen and one of them also the College heavyweight boxer, stepped out and bowed to the Chair.

'And, lastly, gentlemen, two words of warning. If arrested, do not resist. That's the first and greatest commandment. We don't want anyone to land up in the jug. Secondly, nothing whatsoever is to be thrown on to the stage. After all, those poor blighters of actors have got their living to earn, the same as we have, and...'

On this note of chivalry the meeting ended.

*

Cartaret students were not invited to the theatre rag by mutual arrangement between the Principals of the two colleges, for it was thought better that the disorderly proceedings should not be complicated by the presence of girls. The men themselves subscribed so heartily to this view that it was a law of the Wattsdown Common Room that no attempt was ever to be made by the members to 'smuggle, inveigle, entice, invite or deploy' the members of Cartaret into the theatre on Rag Night.

In spite of this, however, Cartaret students had been known to attend. There was no embargo, authoritative or brotherly, on their turning up for the Meet, which was held half a mile from Wattsdown at the bus stop. There was no reason, either, if they could get on the public bus – the men hired private buses to take their large party to the theatre – why the Cartaret students should not accompany the procession through the streets of the town. Bold spirits, defying the Cartaret law of late leave, which had to be signed for, and was never granted on Rag Night except in case of family illness or on some such compassionate grounds, had even been known to penetrate the fastnesses and book seats in the theatre, but since the men's college invariably booked the whole of the circle, whether they could fill it or not, there was not as much excitement in going as the bold spirits would have liked to pretend.

Laura and Kitty, well within the law and proposing to remain so, went into the town on the bus to see the procession form up and move off towards the theatre. The four gentlemen to whom had been delegated the task of occupying the attention of the mounted police found their solitary victim round the second turning. Dressed as fairies in ridiculous ballet frocks which the College housekeeper and maids had been wheedled into 'making over' to fit the bulging torsos of the football-playing sprites, and wearing flaxen wigs, fairy crowns with long antennae, gauze and silver wings and carrying fairy wands tipped with lop-sided, outsize stars, the four skipped solemnly round and round the embarrassed officer, giving him no chance to do anything except manage his horse. When he stopped they joined hands in a straight line in front of him and began to sing. When he rode on again, they broke the hold and re-formed their circle.

Following the mounted policeman came a large horse, removed from the College playing-fields, on which a horse-mower was still used. On his back, sitting sideways with both legs over the left side of an embroidered table-cover which served as saddle and saddle-cloth, and held in position by iron supports specially forged in the College workshop and carried by the attendants who were dressed as devils, was the magnificent skeleton of Dirty Dick, until recently an inmate of the Science cupboard at Cartaret. He was conspicuously labelled, to the delight of the local populace, *Lady Godiva*.

The Theatre Rag itself passed off in traditional style and without unexpected incident.

CHAPTER 16

BONE

GEORGE and the Chief Engineer went down to the sports pavilion to collect the skeleton left there by the six students. They went during the students' dinner time, and no one except Mrs Bradley and the two men themselves knew when the box was transported to the College. Except that the Science Room was closed to all students for a couple of hours next day (greatly to the annoyance of Second-Years of the Advanced Group), there was no intimation that anything extraordinary was going on, except for the presence in the drive of three large saloon cars. One belonged to the police, one to a famous surgeon and the third to Miss Murchan's dentist.

The police had come 'in case there was anything for them' as the elliptical phrase goes, the surgeon and Mrs Bradley, in consultation, were going to determine, if they could, the age of the bones in question, and the dentist had been invited because upon his evidence would depend the important question of whether the bones were all that remained of Miss Murchan.

The dentist was given the first innings. Twister Marshmallow (or his deputy) was taken carefully out of his box. Mrs Bradley had sealed up the box in the presence of the Principal, the Assistant Principal, Miss Rosewell and Miss Crossley, and, those four ladies having sworn to the fact that the seals had not been tampered with, they were politely but firmly shown out, the door was locked behind them, and the fun began.

The dentist did not take very long.

'This isn't Miss Murchan's skull,' he pronounced. 'At least, they're not her teeth.'

He produced chapter and verse in support of this last statement, and Mrs Bradley cackled.

'Murderers have limited minds,' she said. 'There's always something they don't know, or forget or can't be bothered with.'

When the dentist had gone, she and the surgeon got down enjoyably to their own part of the job. Shorn of technicalities and rendered, therefore, into English, the sum total of their conclusions came to the facts that the skeleton was female, therefore it was not Twister Marshmallow, that the body of which the skeleton had formed part had been alive not more than a year previously, that the bones had been boiled to get rid of the flesh upon them, that the right arm had sustained a fairly serious fracture at one time, that death had probably followed concussion, that the fracture had been suffered previous to the damage suffered by the skull, and, finally, that the way in which the skeleton had been put together and articulated was clumsy and amateurish.

'And very nice, too,' said Mrs Bradley, taking the surgeon off to have a wash. 'If the police can't find out where that skeleton came from, I shall be greatly surprised.'

'But where do we begin, madam?' the stolid inspector inquired.

'Locally. The body can't possibly have come in from far away.'

'But nobody's been reported missing, madam.'

'No. The graves give up their dead, but they don't advertise the fact by radio,' said Mrs Bradley, with unusual tartness. The inspector's face, however, cleared.

'Robbed a grave, did they?' he said.

'She,' corrected Mrs Bradley. 'And what you want is news of a woman of about sixty, who had broken her right arm, and who died from concussion following a very nasty fall. Looks as though she fell off the top of a house, as a matter of fact.'

'Fell off the top of a house?' said the inspector. 'Well, Maggie Dalton might fit the bill. I don't know about breaking her arm, but it's true she fell off a window-sill four storeys up. Would sit on the sill to clean the outside. They begged her to have a window cleaner, but not she. Preferred to do it herself, she always said, and one day she overbalanced and down she came. Accidental death, of course.'

'And when did this happen?' Mrs Bradley inquired.

'Last June twelve-month.'

'Providential,' said Mrs Bradley. 'And who *was* Maggie Dalton?'

'Nobody knew. She was brought up in the Orphanage at Betchdale, so I heard.'

'No relatives?'

'Not as far as anybody knew. That all came out at the inquest.'

'And where was poor Maggie Dalton buried?'

'The local cemetery here. The one you see over on the right
when you get to Collard Swing Bridge.'

'You'll have to get permission to exhume her,' said Mrs Bradley.

'You don't mean – she couldn't have been murdered, madam,'
said the inspector confusedly.

'No, I know she wasn't. She died accidentally, just as you have
described. I meant that you will have to get permission to open
the grave.'

'Ah, now you're talking,' said the inspector. 'That's no Home
Office job. Ted Parker, at the Cemetery, is my wife's second
cousin. If I can't do a bit of digging in the cemetery with no
questions asked, one night when we get a decent moon, call me a
South Sea Islander.'

'I should like to be present,' Mrs Bradley observed.

'And welcome,' said the inspector heartily. 'I'll just have a word
with Ted, and let you know.'

*

The moon was in its third quarter. Digging a grave, Mrs Bradley reflected, was a grisly kind of business, but un-digging it, as
her grandson Derek might have said, was weird and ghostly indeed.

The inspector and his wife's second cousin were the only gar-
deners. Mrs Bradley, half-hidden in the shade of a yew tree,
brooded upon their employment whilst damp clay transferred its
clammy coldness to the soles of her shoes, and its chill communi-
cated itself to her bones.

At last the diggers struck upon the coffin and lifted it out. It
lay, strange husk, upon the heap of upturned soil.

'Nought in it. Too light,' said the wife's second cousin. He
prised off the lid with a crowbar he had brought with him. The
coffin stank, but was empty.

Reverently, to Mrs Bradley's sardonic amusement, the men re-
buried it. Mrs Bradley left them to their task – the reward to the

wife's second cousin for his kindly cooperation had been agreed upon beforehand – and went back to Athelstan.

She walked quickly through the College grounds, especially the part near the main gate, and, by a shrubbery, ran as fast as she could, and zigzagged from side to side of the drive. The ambush came just by the rockery, as she was about to ascend the steps which led from the grounds to the gravel.

Mrs Bradley dropped to earth, sheltered in the shadow of the rockery, and, very cautiously, began to stalk her antagonist. The quarry, however, either knew the grounds much better than Mrs Bradley did, or could see in the dark, for Mrs Bradley did not find him or her, and the moonlight was of no assistance whatever. She crawled back to the point at which she had been attacked, picked up the missiles which had been thrown – they were easy enough to see, for they lay far out in the moonlight on the soaking grass of the lawn – and took them into Athelstan with her, two half-bricks, which had been hurled with considerable force.

As she entered the house, stepping quietly and having used her latch-key to get in, she was aware of faint stirrings down in the basement.

She tested the door at the top of the basement stairs, found it locked, as usual, smiled contentedly and then stopped short as a thought struck her, not a pleasant thought, either.

'Goodness me,' she said to herself, 'it's Lulu's job to see that that door is locked. I suppose the maids forgot it in the half-term week-end, and that's how she managed to get up here and cut that poor girl's hair!'

CHAPTER 17

NYMPHS AND SATYRS

'You know, there's a lot of fetishism in the preparation of vegetables – in fact, in all cooking,' said Laura, roaming about the Athelstan kitchen (against all College regulations, needless to say) in quest of what she might devour.

'That there isn't!' said Bella, promoted to cook. 'And I wonder at you, Miss Menzies, using language like that!'

'But – well, take brussels sprouts,' for example,' pursued the educationist, discovering a jar of raspberry jam and helping herself to it by spreading it on a biscuit she had previously purloined. 'Now I bet you anything you like that when you do brussels sprouts you cut up each little stalk in the shape of a cross. Don't you?'

'Yes, so does everybody else, miss, and I hope you know that these here provisions have got to last the month. There's been trouble already, the way they've disappeared. I don't know what the Warden would think if she was to come in here now this minute and find you eating biscuits and jam and sultanas, the way you are.'

'Being a sensible woman, duck, she'd suppose, correctly, that I was putting to the proof the College memo. on the subject.'

'What's that, miss?'

'Well,' said Laura, poking interestedly underneath the top layer of a large tin, 'don't they call this stuff consumable stock?'

'Now, look, Miss Menzies,' said Bella, removing the Bovril bottle out of reach, and firmly handing Laura a clean damp swab on which to wipe sticky fingers, 'if you'll promise to leave the things alone and go back and get on with whatever you're supposed to be doing, and stop hindering me and getting in Lulu's way with that tray for the Warden's elevenses, I'll tell you a secret, so be you won't let it get round.'

'I'm on,' said Laura, wiping busily and finishing off on a clean handkerchief. She seated herself on a corner of the table. 'Spill. Half a minute, though. Can't I tell anybody at all?'

'Well,' said Bella, 'I suppose you could tell Miss Boorman. She's a quiet little thing. But don't you go telling Miss Trevelyan. I know her. It'll be all over College before you can say Jack Robinson.'

'Not if I swear her to silence, Bella. Come on. Just those two and no more.'

'Well, if you think . . .'

'I do think. Go on. You know you want to tell someone. Is it about your boy friend?'

'Go on with you!' said Bella, delighted. 'And me been married these thirteen years, going on!'

'Go on, you've not. I don't believe it! You wouldn't have a resident job if you were married! Who makes his evening cup of cocoa?'

'I'm sure I don't know, miss. He's a sailor.'

'Oh, I couldn't stick that! Well, go on. What's this yarn?'

'You'll never guess, so I'll tell you. You know the end-of-the-year summer dance, when the young gentlemen get invitations, and the young ladies' brothers and their other friends can come?'

'Yep. Though I haven't experienced it yet.'

'Well, you're going to, miss. The Warden has made a very special point with Miss du Mugne, and it's to be held at the Half-Term, or, rather, the Saturday night after, young gentlemen, cousins and all.'

'Well!' said Laura, jumping off the table. 'Well, what do you say! Hot dog, Bella! I'll have the Warden chaired from the bake-house to Rule Britannia's! Well, well, well! I never did! And they say the age of miracles is past! When's the good news to be spread?'

'That's for Miss du Mugne to say, miss. Now don't you go blurting it out and saying I told you, mind!'

'Trust your Auntie! And – Bella! Grub?'

'Ices and all, miss. Yes, the Warden said special as all the food was on her.'

'The Warden said that all the food was on her,' repeated Laura thoughtfully. 'Hm! Knowing the Warden's very sound attitude towards food, I am inclined, in no conservative spirit, to say Whoopee!'

*

Mrs Bradley had had some initial difficulty in convincing the Principal that the Half-Term Dance, as it was called as soon as tidings of it were broadcast to a surprised and enraptured College, was a necessity in helping to forward the ends of justice.

'I've got to know how Miss Murchan was decoyed,' she insisted, 'and as I can't imagine the circumstances I must attempt to reproduce them.'

'But it will turn College upside-down,' wailed the Principal. 'And, after all,' she added, with the first gleam of humour which Mrs Bradley had seen in her, 'you've already gone outside the scope which was to be allowed you. We asked you to investigate privately a College mystery – the disappearance of Miss Murchan. You would never have been asked, nor given any scope at all, if we had dreamed you were going to find a murderer, and let us in for all the horrible publicity of a trial.'

'It hasn't come to that yet,' said Mrs Bradley. 'But there it is,' she concluded. 'I want you to ask in the Staff Common Room for a volunteer to take the part of Miss Murchan. Please don't select Miss Topas. She's far too intelligent and enterprising. What I want is a good stupid horse that will eat his oats, as I feel that Miss Menzies would say. Miss Harbottle might do, and Miss Crossley would be excellent, so if either of them volunteers, please snap her up at once and ask her to come and see me.'

Miss du Mugne, although giving no impression that she was entering into the spirit of the thing, said she would do what she could, and next morning, the Wednesday before that Saturday on which the dance was to be held, a dignified but apprehensive victim, in the person of Miss Crossley, the Bursar, presented herself in Mrs Bradley's sitting-room at Athelstan and announced that she had come to be instructed.

'That's very nice indeed of you,' said Mrs Bradley. 'I hope you don't mind, but a particularly graceless nephew of mine is going to assist in the proceedings. I want someone very strong, so I had to get a young man, for I don't think we have another woman in College with the vigour and muscular control of Miss Cornflake.'

'Not the P.T. people?' inquired Miss Crossley.

'They might, but then, they've no imagination,' replied Mrs Bradley.

'I feel flattered!' exclaimed Miss Crossley. As it was kinder not to disabuse her of the notion that the same quality was required in the passive as in the active partner in the experiment, Mrs Bradley made no comment on this exclamation and invited the guest to have some sherry. Miss Crossley preferred coffee, she said, in the morning, so, with this and some biscuits to assist them, they got down to the plan of campaign.

'Don't bother about anything at all until ten o'clock,' said Mrs Bradley. 'Enjoy the dance, have supper with the students, and try to keep your mind off our little reconstruction of Miss Murchan's disappearance.

'At ten we shall have the twilight waltz. During it somebody will tweak your hair, and as soon as the lights go up a student will come up to you and ask you whether you know that your hair is coming down. That is your cue. Go at once to the hall door, as though you were going along to the Staff cloakroom.'

'Yes?' said Miss Crossley. 'And then?'

'Your part is over, except so far as you may be directed by my nephew, to whom, by the way, I will introduce you if you would care to come to dinner this evening. By the way, you will scarcely need to be told that you need fear no violence, either from my nephew or from anybody else. I say this, in case you thought there would be a struggle. There will be nothing unpleasant.'

'Oh, thank you for the assurance, but, really, I shouldn't have minded in the least,' replied the Bursar, surprisingly.

*

Jonathan presented himself before his aunt at a quarter past five, whilst the students were having tea. Deborah, who always had tea with the Warden unless they decided that one of them ought to be on duty, had not been informed that he was coming and nearly jumped out of her chair when he was announced.

Jonathan kissed his aunt between her brilliant black eyes, kissed the tip of Deborah's nose, took the lid off the teapot, sniffed, said: 'Lapsang? All right, I'll have some,' took the plate of cakes to the light and selected the largest, and generally behaved in the idiotic but attractive manner adopted by young men in front of affectionate women.

'But what are you doing here?' asked Deborah, when Mrs Bradley, by providing her nephew with the lowest chair in the room, had made it easier for him to remain seated in it than to attempt to get up and torment either of them.

'Come to take up my new appointment, please, ma'am,' replied her swain, stretching out his long legs and looking at them with great satisfaction. 'I've been given a job at this College.'

'I don't believe it! And, if you have, I shall resign. I can't bear the thought of having you all over the place all the time,' said Deborah decidedly.

'And to think we're going to be married in a couple of months! Still, never mind that now. How much of the terrain have I got to encompass this evening?' he demanded, turning to his aunt.

'None, dear child. Tomrrow morning you can walk round with George, who will show you the grounds and paths and the possible pitfalls you will encounter after dark, and then in the afternoon Deborah can show you all over the College buildings, including the best way to get to the Halls from College itself.'

'Including Columba?' inquired Jonathan. 'I *must* see Columba again. It represents the scene of my most ill-conceived and misdirected action. Deborah's hated me ever since she accepted me! Haven't you, Deb?'

'I'm not going to take him over College tomorrow,' said Deborah firmly. 'I refuse to be seen about with him. Until he knows how to behave, you can take him over College yourself.'

'I can't. I'm going to the mental hospital to visit Mr Princep,' said Mrs Bradley. 'And don't forget,' she smiled, favouring Deborah with a slight lowering of the left eyelid, 'that the Principal will expect to be introduced to him.'

'Good idea,' said Deborah, brightening up. 'Then he'll have to ask her for at least one dance on Saturday. That'll learn you, my lad,' she added triumphantly.

'I shall refer to you throughout as my girl friend,' said Jonathan, with a leer which vied in malevolence with the best efforts of his aunt. But when Mrs Bradley had gone, and Lulu had cleared, he got up out of his chair, stubbed out his cigarette, stood by the table a minute or two, and then, stooping over Deborah, picked her up with a grunt and carried her over to the settee.

'Don't!' said Deborah, who was still afraid of him.

'Mean it?' said Jonathan. Deborah, who realized that the question was rhetorical, did not answer.

*

The young gentlemen from Wattsdown, all washed behind the ears, as Kitty put it, arrived in private buses or in cars or on motor-cycles – the last-named carrying any number of passengers from two to five – at seven o'clock, to find the girls already in the College hall, for the proceedings had begun officially at half past six, following the usual Saturday high tea instead of dinner.

There was a programme of twenty-four dances, with space for extras, supper was to be at half past nine, and the party would be declared over at eleven.

There were banked flowers and evergreens on the front and sides of the dais, sitting-out corners had been devised with skill, taste and discretion, an orchestra, hired at Mrs Bradley's expense from Leeds, was looming behind the potted plants, and except for the one or two students who had asked for week-end leave, the whole of the College was prepared to be *en fête*.

Mrs Bradley had bought a new frock, not for herself but for Deborah. She had sworn Kitty to secrecy, and, to the mystification of the whole Hall, had sneaked her out of Miss Topas's lecture on Richard the Second with the full connivance and support of that enthusiast for Plantagenet kings, and had taken her, George driving, all the way to London, where they had spent the night at an hotel. Next morning they had gone out and chosen the frock, judging it for size and fit by one which Mrs Bradley had borrowed (on the excuse that she wanted to try it on?) and at nightfall on the Friday they made a triumphant return, pulled Deborah out of 'a mess of English essays', said Kitty, recounting the exciting story to an awe-stricken group, and put the frock on her.

Mrs Bradley had had no voice in the buying. Kitty knew exactly what she wanted, and dragged Mrs Bradley into and out of seven shops before discovering the object of her choice in the eighth.

'But what's all this *about*?' asked Deborah, pardonably bewildered.

'Birthday present,' said Mrs Bradley calmly.

'But – I can't – you can't give me a birthday present!'

'Oh, yes, I can. You're nearly a member of the family,' replied Mrs Bradley, sitting down and watching the kneeling Kitty.

Kitty got up.

'You'll have to put your evening shoes on,' she said. 'I can't see what *anything* looks like in those slippers. Where are they? I'll get them ... Ah, that's it. Now see how it goes when you walk ... Have a look at yourself in the long glass.'

She sat back on her heels, looked at Mrs Bradley and lifted her eyebrows.

'Thank you, child,' said Mrs Bradley.

Jonathan, meanwhile, had established himself solidly with both students and staff at the College. Athelstan, in fact, was the envy of every other Hall, not even excluding Columba, for having, as Miss Cartwright put it, an eligible male on the premises.

'But he isn't eligible. The Deb.'s hooked him,' observed Laura, with neither gracefulness nor truth. Alice pointed this out by contradicting her immediately.

'She *didn't* hook him! What a thing to say!'

'All right. All right. No offence. I merely intended to convey that his eligibility is all washed up and disconnected,' replied the heckled one, scrubbing dirt out of an abrasion on her left shin with her tooth brush. 'Some golfing fiend in the Second Eleven took a slap at me in a practice game this afternoon,' she explained, when the others expostulated with her on the score of her activity. 'I *must* get the dirt out. I might get blood-poisoning.'

'Not as likely as you'll get it from that germy object,' said Alice, trying to remove the tooth brush by main force from Laura's grasp.

'Look out, ass! You'll break the handle. Leave me alone. I'm nearly through,' said the surgeon, returning undeterred to her scrubbing. 'Wonder when old Kitty will be back? The old scout is losing all the fun of being in a Mixed Hall, isn't she?'

Jonathan enjoyed himself. He was not in the least bashful, took all his meals, including breakfast and tea, in public, under the eyes and on the tongues of forty interested girls who made inventories and laid bets respecting his likes and dislikes in the matter of food, was supplied with manly bottles of beer by Bella, to whom he made love in the kitchen, made idiotic and extremely well-camouflaged advances to Deborah, and was snubbed firmly, this to the indignation of Miss Cartwright, who had conceived a violent passion for the young man and talked openly in Hall of Deborah's coldness and of how he must be breaking his heart in secret, to which challenging gambit Laura unhesitatingly, unanswerably and very coarsely replied.

On the night of the dance there was much speculation as to how he would be dressed. Jonathan had received definite instructions from his aunt on this point, and appeared, 'white tie perfectly rendered' as Laura observed to her circle, in tails and with his hair brushed.

'All my own work,' said Kitty, pleased with the murmurs of admiration which greeted his appearance, first in Hall and then on the dance floor. 'I fluttered that butterfly tie of his with these two hands. But you wait till you see the Deb.'

'Girls,' she added, later, coming up to Laura and Alice just before the young gentlemen arrived from Wattsdown, 'he's asked me for my programme, and I'm having *two* with him, one in each half.'

'You *lucky* thing!' said Miss Cartwright. 'Never mind, I bet I get him at least twice in a Paul Jones.'

'I bet she does, too,' said Laura, grinning. The entrance of the Wattsdown contingent, fingering their ties and otherwise preparing themselves for the fray, ended the conversation and gave rise to other, although not dissimilar, interests.

Miss Crossley sat with Mrs Bradley during a waltz and the foxtrot that followed it, and confessed that she felt very nervous.

'Oh, you mustn't do that. Don't think about ten o'clock and after. I can scarcely recognize some of the students. Who is the dark girl in green, with gold shoes?'

'That is Miss Milper, of Edmund,' replied Miss Crossley. 'I don't suppose you would notice her in the ordinary way. She is what I call one of the two-year brigade.'

'And by that you mean ...?'

'Well, she's engaged now, and she will be married in two years' time, I imagine. Then good-bye to all the time and trouble spent on her training. Now your Miss Mathers is the type I like – honest, downright, capable – '

'Yes, a pleasant, sensible creature,' said Mrs Bradley, devoutly hoping that Miss Mathers was going to live up to that description later on in the evening.

'Who's the old girl like a lizard?' inquired a vacant-looking Wattsdown youth of Laura.

'Mrs Lestrange Bradley, the criminologist.'

'What? Been having a crime wave at Cartaret?'

'No, mutt. Psychology. Besides, she's our Warden at Athelstan.'

'Oh? I say, who is the girl over there? You might introduce me. Is she a Senior? – Third-Year, or something?'

'That, pet, is our Sub-Warden. She bites. And I won't introduce you. She wouldn't like you. You're not her type in the least.'

'Judging by the bloke she's talking to now – the Heathcliff specimen, I mean – I should say you might be right. Who's *he*?'

'Her fiancé.'

'Oh? Oh, really? Oh, I see.' He dropped the subject, but a good many enterprising young gentlemen insisted upon being introduced and Deborah danced every dance in the first half except for two which she sat out with Jonathan, sedately, in full view of one and all.

Jonathan, finding himself paired with Miss Cartwright in a foxtrot during a Paul Jones, had time to tell her that there was something he wanted to ask her.

'To settle a bet,' he began; but the music changed before he could put the point, and he was not surprised when she flagrantly grabbed him the next time and said:

'Go on. To settle a bet?'

'Those snakes in that Demonstration lesson. Did you ...?'

'Yes, of course. But I daren't confess to it because my record's so rocky. How did you . . . ?' But the music separated them again.

Jonathan, to the joy of Athelstan, had the next dance with his aunt.

'Listen,' he said. 'You were right about the snakes. She did it. She's just told me. Don't give me away for telling you, but I thought you'd like to be certain.'

'Thank you very much, child. That clears away all doubt. A pity the little silly didn't own up sooner.'

'Still, your argument that it couldn't have been part and parcel of the other works of art was perfectly sound. Who else ought I to dance with? I've done Miss du Mugne, Miss Butts, Miss Crossley, Miss Topas, Miss Harbottle and now you.'

Mrs Bradley took him off at the end of the dance to 'team him up' as Miss Cartwright disgustedly expressed it, with more of the staff, and half past nine seemed to come along very soon. Mrs Bradley, Miss du Mugne, Miss Topas, Miss Crossley, Jonathan and Deborah shared one of the small tables in the Demonstration Room, which had been turned into a refectory. The Science Room, the two Education Rooms, and the Students' Common Room had been similarly treated, and parties sitting out on the stairs were 'also a feature', as Kitty gracefully and tactfully remarked.

'Get rheumatism, silly little fatheads,' said Miss Topas. 'Most of 'em have got nothing on under those frocks except a pair of panties and a bust bodice.'

At ten the Twilight Waltz was announced, and Jonathan and Deborah danced it together. The lights were lowered gradually until only the two over the dais and the one over the door were left shining. By the time the hall was fully lighted again, Miss Crossley had begun to carry out her share of the arrangements by giving her partner, a student named Pettinger, the excuse that she must tidy her hair. She then hurried out. As soon as he saw her go, Jonathan went after her, and scarcely had he caught up with her outside the Education Room, which was next to the Staff Cloakroom, when Mrs Bradley joined them.

'Did you manage it?' she asked. The two stopped short.

'No, I didn't,' confessed Jonathan. 'I marked her position in the hall very carefully when the dance began, then, as the lights were lowered, I pushed along to where I supposed she would be, but by that time the hall was almost in darkness and I don't believe I could have found even Deborah to pull her hair, much less a lady whom I met for the first time on Wednesday.'

'Splendid,' said Mrs Bradley.

'I mean,' pursued her nephew, 'one can scarcely make the round of a dance floor pulling people's hair at random.'

'Quite,' said his aunt, who seemed subtly pleased about something. 'Well, carry on.'

Jonathan offered Miss Crossley his arm, and they proceeded to the outer door.

'Now,' he said, 'we've got to get to Athelstan without being spotted. I say, it's plaguey dark. And – er – hadn't you better have a coat?'

'I have my silk scarf. Poor Miss Murchan wouldn't have had more on a summer night, I imagine,' replied Miss Crossley.

'This way, I think.'

They followed, stumbling, the gravel path which led past the grass tennis court to the steps beside the rockery which fronted Bede Hall.

'Left now,' said Miss Crossley. She led the way at this point, and mounted to the front door of Athelstan, where she inserted Mrs Bradley's latch-key in the door. The door swung open. They closed it as quietly as they could and waited outside.

'We have to count forty,' said Miss Crossley. Long before forty was up, however, a quick step in the hall, and the gleam of a light informed them that one of the maids was at home.

'Who dar?' asked Lulu's voice, as she came to meet them.

'Mrs Bradley wants a clean handkerchief, please,' said Miss Crossley. 'Aren't you at the dance?'

'Oh, no, mam,' replied the maid, 'Ephraim don't like it.'

'Well, that's that,' said Jonathan. 'I don't see how we could have shut the door more quietly, but, you see, she heard us all right. Aunt Adela said her hearing was abnormal.'

'Well, if we couldn't sneak in by the front door, we certainly couldn't at the back,' said Miss Crossley, who seemed to have shed her nervousness, and was enjoying herself. Jonathan agreed.

'Now I'm to escort you back to the dance floor,' he said, 'and I do hope you're not booked for the next one, whatever it turns out to be, because I think we ought to dance it together.'

'I'm not booked up *really* after the Twilight Waltz at all,' Miss Crossley confessed, 'because I didn't know when I should be able to return, and I didn't want to disappoint anybody of their dance, *or*, of course, to excite suspicion by being noticeably ab-sent. Your aunt pointed out that it was essential to arouse no suspicion.'

'Quite,' Jonathan agreed; and they went back to the revels. He watched the clock, however, and at twenty-five minutes to eleven he went into the corridor, rather obviously displaying his cigar-ette-case and lighter. Scarcely had he reached the door of the room where the pottery oven was housed, when there was the sound of flying footsteps and Deborah came running up to him.

'You're to come back with me,' she said. 'I don't want you to do any more snooping about in the dark ! It's dangerous !'

Jonathan held both her hands and looked at her gravely.

'Listen, Deb. There's no danger. And you can't come out in that frock. But I've got a little job to do. It's nothing much. You go back, and in about ten minutes I'll be there. You *have* saved me the last dance, haven't you?'

'If you're going across the grounds again, I'm coming with you,' said Deborah.

'All right. But run and get a wrap, there's a good girl. It's cold. Bring my silk scarf if you can see it, as well, will you?'

He waited until she had reached the opposite end of the cor-ridor, then he went into the adjoining room and changed his coat for a lounge jacket which he buttoned closely, turning up the collar. Then he went noiselessly down the steps and walked briskly along the path towards Athelstan. But, instead of going up to the front door this time, he walked along until he came to the covered way connecting the Hall with the bakehouse next door to it on the west.

He crouched down and strained his ears. After a short time he heard an owl hoot twice. He gave a low whistle. The owl hooted again, but only once this time.

CHAPTER 18

IDDY UMPTY IDDY UMPTY IDDY

DEBORAH came back with a wrap and with Jonathan's scarf and looked out into the blackness of the grounds. She did not dare to call out, for she knew that the reason he had come was to assist his aunt in her machinations against murderers, and she supposed that he was in process of carrying out instructions.

She had no intention, however, of allowing him to get rid of her at what was, presumably, a moment of danger, and was about to step out into the inky pall which clothed the College demesne when Miss Topas, followed by Laura and Alice, came up.

'What's up, Deborah? Come out for a breath of air?' inquired Miss Topas.'

'No. I'm looking for Jonathan. The wretch sent me back for some wraps and now he's taken the chance to disappear.'

'Out there?'

'Yes, I think so. You didn't see him just now inside the hall, I suppose?'

'No. Well, come on in. It's cold out here, and the senior student is about to propose a vote of thanks to Mrs Bradley before the proceedings terminate. Where *is* Mrs Bradley, by the way?'

'I don't know. With Jonathan, I should think. At any rate, I'm going over to Athelstan. That's where he was going, I'm fairly certain,' said Deborah. Miss Topas laid a restraining hand on her arm.

'You can't go chasing about in the grounds while a vote of thanks is being passed,' she pointed out. 'Besides, you may queer the pitch. There's a peculiar do on tonight.'

'Well, when I do find him I'm going to tell him what I think of his manners,' said Deborah crossly.

'Plenty of time for that after you're wed,' observed Miss Topas reasonably. 'Come on in. You can't remain in this doorway, silhouetted against the light. It isn't healthy.'

Deborah observed that Laura, grinning, and Alice, looking faithful and determined, were closing in on her. She laughed, and went in with them.

Neither Jonathan nor Mrs Bradley came back, although, all the time she was dancing, she watched the door, and at five minutes to eleven came the announcement of the last waltz.

'Take young Alice, and make her happy for life,' muttered Laura in Deborah's ear. It seemed as well to make somebody happy, even though she was far from happy herself, so Deborah took Alice's hand, smiled at her, said 'Shall we?' and swung her into the dance.

The general opinion that it had been 'jolly decent of the Prin.' to consent to the inclusion of Wattsdown College in the festivities, together with the necessity for the young gentlemen themselves of returning to their own territory some time before dawn, precluded any attempt to get Miss du Mugne to extend the time for the dancing, and by half past eleven the good-byes had been said, a last kiss or two snatched by the more enterprising, and lights had begun to appear in the uncurtained windows of the various Halls to guide the Cartaret students to their beds. The Athelstan contingent remained behind, having received word that they were to wait for Mrs Bradley. They stood about the hall in little groups, surprised and, at first, amused by the order. Deborah was talking to Miss du Mugne and Miss Crossley, and the three of them were glancing continuously at the door.

In a minute or two Jonathan came in. He nodded, and Miss du Mugne, raising her voice a little, invited Athelstan to 'go home' and wished them good night. Mrs Bradley still had not appeared, and just as she was leaving the hall, Miss Mathers, the senior student of Athelstan, was called back.

'Not very pleasant for you, my dear,' said Miss du Mugne, 'but we want you to help us. Miss Cloud, you had better return to Athelstan, I think, with the students. Somebody ought to be over there. Perhaps, Mr Bradley, you would accompany Miss Cloud, and I will see that Miss Mathers returns as soon as possible.'

Miss Mathers, her sensible, homely countenance not even having an expression of surprise, went with the Principal and Miss Crossley to the Board Room, next door to the Secretary's office.

Miss Rosewell was in the Board Room, looking thoroughly ill-at-ease, and there also were Mrs Bradley and a faded-looking woman with fair hair going grey and an expression of intense malice lighting her grey-green eyes. It was the senior student who spoke first.

'Miss Murchan!' she exclaimed. Then she looked suddenly horrified, for Miss Murchan's wrists were tied together and her thin ankles were similarly confined.

'Yes, Miss Murchan,' said Mrs Bradley. 'At least . . .' she looked at Miss du Mugne, 'so I supposed. Do you, too, identify her?'

'Without a doubt,' the Principal replied, 'but I cannot believe my eyes.'

'That I can imagine,' said Mrs Bradley. 'My nephew and I had some difficulty in bringing her over here, but that is nothing compared with the difficulty I have had in accounting for her disappearance, locating her hiding-place, and bringing her back to the world. Miss Mathers, my dear, go back to Hall, and not a word of this to anyone. You understand?'

'But – but what made you do it, Miss Murchan? What were you afraid of?' inquired the Principal, gazing perplexedly at the one-time member of her staff, as soon as Miss Mathers had gone. 'Surely it was not like you to give us all so much anxiety!'

The greyish woman in the chair began to laugh. It was not the laughter of hysteria, but it had such an odd, unnatural sound that the Principal recoiled from it as she might have recoiled had someone spat at her. She recovered herself in an instant, and went up to Miss Murchan and laid a hand on her shoulder.

'Please tell me all about it,' she said steadily, with her air of authority.

'Tell you all about it?' said the prisoner. 'Yes, I'll tell you. I lectured in English, didn't I? Didn't I?'

'Yes, certainly, but . . .'

'Then I can tell you all about it.'

'Is she mad?' whispered the Principal. Mrs Bradley shrugged.

'In your view and in mine, certainly,' she replied. 'According to the law, poor soul, I strongly doubt it.'

'According to the law? But, surely, there's no question of that?'

It was impossible to proceed, for Miss Murchan, fixing her eyes on a cupboard in the corner of the room, an unused cupboard which had one door swinging open as though to display the emptiness within, was already declaiming, in a horrid monotone, some stanzas from Swinburne.

> 'Swallow, my sister, O sister swallow,
> How can thine heart be full of the spring?
> A thousand summers are over and dead.
> What hast thou found in the spring to follow?
> What hast thou found in thine heart to sing?
> What wilt thou do when the summer is fled?
>
> 'Swallow, my sister, O singing swallow,
> I know not how thou hast heart to sing.
> Hast thou the heart? Is it all past over?
> Thy lord the summer is good to follow,
> And fair the feet of thy lover the spring:
> But what wilt thou say to the spring thy lover?
>
> 'O swallow, sister, O rapid swallow,
> I pray thee sing not a little space.
> Are not the roofs and the lintels wet?
> The woven web that was plain to follow,
> The small slain body, the flower-like face,
> Can I remember if thou forget?
>
> 'O sister, sister, thy first-begotten!
> The hands that cling and the feet that follow,
> The voice of the child's blood crying yet,
> *Who hath remember'd me? Who hath forgotten?*
> Thou hast forgotten, O summer swallow,
> But the world shall end when I forget.'

The monotone moaned itself away, and the speaker appeared to have lulled herself asleep. Suddenly she straightened up, tried to make a gesture with her bound hands, managed to get them to her lips, swallowed, smiled, dropped her hands, gazed at them, it seemed perplexedly, and then dropped her head back against the padded head of the chair. Mrs Bradley went across to her and released her hands and ankles.

There was a sound of heavy footsteps outside.

'That will be the police,' she said. 'They will have to take charge of her now. She has given us the last clue, but it will, I think, mean nothing at all to them.'

'Oh, dear, I do hate this! I do hope they won't hurt her, poor thing,' said the Principal, becoming suddenly and demonstrably human. Mrs Bradley again walked over to the still figure. She straightened herself and shook her head.

'They won't hurt her,' she answered, 'for she has disappeared again.' Then, to the Principal's surprise, she crossed herself, muttering what sounded like a spell but which must have been a prayer.

CHAPTER 19

ITYLUS

'WELL, it seems,' said Laura, 'that although the skeleton not turning up trumps settled the thing more or less, Mrs Croc. had had her suspicions for some time previous to that that Miss Murchan wasn't dead. She thought Cook being murdered proved it. The only reason for murdering Cook seemed to be that she had recognized somebody she wasn't supposed to recognize, and that couldn't have been Cornflake because Cornflake could always pull that gag that old Cartwright produced among the Edgar Allans – say she was somebody else. That, being as how she was a student of the College, would more or less let her out. And, anyway, Cook couldn't have had anything on her about former doings, because she didn't know her.

'Then, the disposal of Cook's body, as discovered by the police, followed by us finding the corsets. The difficulty about bringing that home to Cornflake simply was – when could she have done it? I mean, I know, theoretically, we each have our own room, and all that, but it actually takes some doing to slide out at night from one of these Halls, even if you used the communal passage and hopped it on to the wide open spaces from a Hall not actually your own. And then you'd have the dickens of a job to slide back. Of course, it wasn't impossible, but it had all the earmarks of wild improbability, says Mrs Croc.

'In fact, if you go all through the rags and other things, you can pretty well deduce that only somebody very close at hand could have carried out most of the stunts. The snakes were one thing that didn't seem to fit, but Cartwright has come clean about those, so they can be disregarded in the final summing-up. I mean, you can say what you like, but actually, as I once pointed out, it isn't really feasible to suppose that Cornflake could have run the gauntlet of Hall after Hall like that, right along that passage. Much more likely to be somebody who had direct access to the bakehouse and could operate from there. And who so likely to have access as Miss Murchan herself? After all, she'd had all the keys in her possession when she was Warden.

'Of course, she "disappeared" after she'd spotted Cornflake, in the previous summer term, coming up for interview with the Prin. She knew her number was up once Cornflake got on her track. *She'd* killed that kid at that school, you see, and Cornflake, it appears, had seen her do it, and . . .'

The subsequent explanations, inadequate and, on the whole, ill-informed though they turned out to be, lasted the fascinated group for some time.

*

'You're perfectly right, Deb.,' said Jonathan. 'My manners are awful. But, you see, I do want to keep in with you until we're married – after which, I ought to point out, I intend to put it across you in no uncertain spirit, you carping cat! – and, in the circumstances, it didn't seem to me that you would view amiably a bloke of my size and weight scrapping practically all out with Miss Murchan, murderess though she may be. That's all. We've got her, and she took some getting. Not a pretty do, and I'm glad it's over.'

'Yes,' said Deborah, slipping her arm in his. 'All right. I withdraw what I said. Shall we go into my sitting-room or into Mrs Bradley's?'

'Hers. I bet your fire's gone out. Hers won't have done, if I know her.'

'I'll bet you . . .' said Deborah. Her fire was burning with a deep, red, comfortable glow. She put out her tongue at him.

'Whisky?' she said, going to the cupboard.

'You having some?'

'I loathe it. But you look as though you need something . . . Here you are. You can splash the soda in for yourself. You know, I'm all at sea about Miss Murchan. When did Mrs Bradley decide that she hadn't disappeared after all?'

'Why don't you call her Aunt Adela?'

'Well, she isn't.'

'Not yet, but it's only a question of time.'

'A good long time. I must stay on here until the end of the

summer term. I've got to get these girls through their examinations.'

'Oh, no, you haven't. We're being married some time within the next six weeks. It's simply up to you to say when.'

'But . . .'

'None of it. I know you're sorry you ever consented to the match, but as a woman of honour I don't see how you're going to get out of it now.'

'There's Mrs – there's Aunt Adela,' said Deborah. 'I'll let her know where we are.'

'No need, child. I saw the light,' said Mrs Bradley. 'In fact, I saw lots of lights, not only from this room, but from almost all the rooms.'

'Aren't the students in bed?' asked Deborah. 'I'd better go the rounds, I suppose.'

'Oh, the students, bless them, will sit up until all hours,' replied the head of the house comfortably. 'Leave them alone, and relax, child, or, better still, go to bed. I want to talk to Jonathan.'

'Can't I listen, then? I promise I won't interrupt.'

Mrs Bradley said nothing for a moment, but leaned forward and put coal on the fire. Her nephew watched her. Then, as she leaned back in her chair, an unusual relaxation in her, he caught her eye, and framed a question with his lips. Mrs Bradley nodded.

'Suicide,' she said. 'Cyanide of potassium. I thought perhaps she would, and it is much the best way out for the College.'

'How did you know we should get her tonight, if you'd never set eyes on her before?'

'I guessed she would take advantage of the fact that the house was empty to get into the kitchen to steal food. Most of the servants go over to the College entertainments, and the coast would be perfectly clear, once Lulu had gone to bed. I didn't want a public fuss if it could be avoided. On the other hand, I didn't want to lose her, by coming across here too late.'

'Has she really been living in the bakehouse?'

'Yes. It is used only twice a week for baking bread, cakes, and pastry for the whole College. Knowing the routine, she could always hide in the Hall when the bakehouse was in use. She then used the large cupboard on the top floor, the one built over Deborah's bathroom, I expect. From a point of vantage like that, she could annoy and disturb us as much as ever she liked.'

'But that's what beats me. Why did she want to disturb you? Why all that childish ragging?'

'Oh, that has been plain all along. She simply wanted to get rid of me. She did not want me following her trail. She was desperately afraid of being found. She did not care whether she frightened me away, or whether I was dismissed for mismanaging the discipline of the Hall. Having attempted to injure me by tying strings across doorways at the beginning of last term, she then got ideas from Miss Cartwright, who organized the bonfire rag. The most interesting thing about the other ragging has been the way her mind worked over it. I knew that couldn't be students.'

'No; malice all through. Wicked stuff, some of it, too; that girl's hair, for example.'

'Quite.'

'How do you know, by the way, that it wasn't Miss Cornflake who tied the string across our doors?' asked Deborah.

'Because I don't think Miss Cornflake was in College that night. She travelled from London the next morning, and could not have made the double journey in the time. The trains don't fit.'

'What about a car?'

'Yes, that would have been a possibility. But I don't see how Miss Cornflake could have gained admittance to the building at that time. She couldn't have had any keys. Besides, I don't see how she could have known that I was to be in residence that day. There are all sorts of reasons against its having been her doing. And then, how can one account for the first exchange of skeletons unless Miss Murchan worked it? She knew Miss Cartwright from the previous year, remember; knew her home address; knew what would be the effect on her of a challenge.'

'What about slashing the clothes and punching holes in the disinfectant?' asked Jonathan.

'That was Miss Murchan, I am sure, and it gave her state of mind away. As soon as those things happened, I knew that we had to look out for a person of a type familiar to all students of the morbid psychology of sex. I knew there was no one of the type among the students or servants, and as soon as I became acquainted with Miss Cornflake I knew that she was not the type either. From that point I deduced that Miss Murchan was not dead, but it was the murder of that poor, stupid, greedy cook that made my theories into certainty.'

'Greedy?'

'Certainly. She blackmailed Miss Murchan, having discovered her one evening in the storeroom. Food was Miss Murchan's chief difficulty, because, although she had plenty of ready money, she did not dare to shop for fear of being recognized. Well, the cook became a constant danger, so, knowing the ways of the house, and Miss Cartwright's ways, in particular, of having baths at ungodly hours, Miss Murchan sent Cook a message after I had dismissed her, brought her back by giving her the hope of obtaining more money, and drowned her in the servants' bathroom.'

'And the bones?'

'Miss Murchan provided those. She did not realize how easy it would be, with the help of that craftsman, the dentist, to prove that the skeleton was not hers.'

'And who did the 'orrid cookery down in the quarry?'

'Miss Murchan. The police, no doubt, will tackle the boy again, and obtain a complete account of what happened and a full description of the woman. Besides, it is unlikely that Miss Cornflake would have enlisted his help so openly. Miss Murchan, made up to resemble her half-sister, worked out that, if the description were given, Miss Cornflake would be involved and not herself. The police have found the old zinc bath she used. Some students found it first.'

'There's one other thing. Why did Miss Cornflake stalk you in College with that revolver?'

'Oh, but she didn't. She really did carry it in self-defence. That seems quite certain now. I've visited her several times since she's been in the Infirmary, and, as soon as I was sure of my ground, I told her that as Miss Murchan had undoubtedly killed Cook, that was sufficient to put her within reach of the law. I suggested that although there was no evidence beyond Miss Cornflake's unsupported word that the child's death had been anything other than accident, there was plenty of evidence to show that Cook had been murdered, and I said I was prepared to act on it. Of course, the one thing I did not foresee was that the plucky, idiotic Laura Menzies would lay her out.'

'And you call yourself a psychologist!' said Deborah.

'But what *is* all this about the Cornflake and Miss Murchan?' asked Jonathan. 'I know they were half-sisters, and I know Miss Murchan killed the child, but why should the two of them lay for one another?'

'Well, the thing began as a love story,' said Mrs Bradley. 'You see, the child happened to be Miss Cornflake's own ... That much I deduced from a conversation I had with old Mrs Princep, the grandmother. The half-sisters, Miss Murchan and Miss Cornflake – oh, yes, that made the bad blood between them, the fact that they were related through their mother – both loved the same man. What happened to him I don't know. I only know that although – whether by accident or design – he married neither of them, Miss Cornflake, or, as I suppose we ought to say, Miss Paynter-Tree, had the child and Miss Murchan envied her, and killed the child in spite, after years of bitter brooding. Miss Paynter-Tree saw it done, from the gymnasium gallery at the School. The mother told me they watched one another like cats, and the headmistress agreed that a person passing quietly along the gallery could see what was happening below.

'At first Miss Paynter-Tree thought that the verdict at the inquest was the truth. Her half-sister, by writing that anonymous letter to the police, showed her the truth, that the child had been killed deliberately. Half the beauty of the revenge would have been lost, you see, had Miss Paynter-Tree continued to believe that the death was accidental.

'Miss Murchan was not safe from her half-sister's vengeance once the truth was disclosed. She hid from her very successfully at Cartaret for a couple of years, but Miss Paynter-Tree found her at last, and she knew her number was up unless she could disappear.

'Together with the idea of the disappearance came the thought of how much safer she would be if Miss Paynter-Tree were dead. Then she saw *me* as an enemy. She didn't want to be found, and she was terribly afraid that I should find her, especially as we were living in the same house!

'Of course, this Athelstan building lends itself admirably to hide-and-seek, what with its communal passage with other Halls and its back and front staircases. I could have caught her, I expect, at the end-of-term dance last term, but I wasn't ready with my proofs. Hence our performance tonight.

'She quoted *Itylus* before she died.'

'Sure proof she wasn't really an English specialist,' said Deborah sleepily, 'or she'd have known that she'd got the story backwards.'

'No she was really a scientist,' Mrs Bradley agreed. 'That's how she was able to articulate the bones of poor Maggie Dalton. She was powerful, too. I suppose she and Miss Paynter-Tree inherited their physique from the mother.

'That's another interesting thing. A woman who marries three times is almost bound to be either super-normal, abnormal, or sub-normal . . .'

'Same like you!' said Jonathan. He picked up Deborah and carried her off to bed.

'Don't go over the threshold. It isn't lucky,' said his aunt.

'Always the gentleman,' he replied. He passed on, up the front staircase, on which the lights were still burning, to encounter, on the first-floor landing, the wide gaze of Laura Menzies. He had forgotten that the students were still about.

'Oh, lor!' said Miss Menzies, 'young Lochinvar in person.'

'No,' said Jonathan. 'Shove open that door for me, would you? And don't bellow, there's an angel. The baby appears to be asleep.'

'Bit of luck for me. She'd hate me for ever if she thought I'd seen you carrying her like this. When are you going to be married?' Laura inquired.

'Don't know exactly. Let you know in plenty of time. Meanwhile – I suppose she'll wake the minute I put her down –

> "For whilst our brows ambitious be,
>   And youth at hand awaits us,
> It is a pretty thing to see
>   How finely beauty cheats us;

And whilst with time we trifling stand
To practise antique graces,
Age with a pale and withered hand
Draws furrows in our faces." '

'You shall write it in my album,' said Laura, grinning.

2/01